WHISTLING WOMAN

CC TILLERY

SPRING CREEK PRESS

To our dad, Raymond Earl "John" Tillery, for entertaining us with stories from his childhood and for reminding us every time we talk to him how important family is. Also, for the beautiful painting that graces the cover of this book. We love you very much, Daddy. This book would never have existed if it weren't for you!

And to our great-aunt Bessie, the woman behind it all. Thank you for sitting at our shoulder while we wrote your story and for being a 'Whistling Woman" who lived a life that's fascinated us from the time we were small children.

Chapter One

Fall 1895

A whistling woman and a crowing hen never come to a very good end.

Death first touched my life on an early fall night in 1895 when Papa came home carrying a dead man in his arms. I had fourteen years behind me and a good many more to go, though I didn't know that at the time. Something else I didn't know, and in the long run this one affected my life as much as, if not more than, living to an advanced age: Death would take two of my loved ones not long after it first showed up in my life. According to my Cherokee great-grandmother Elisi, that was the way it usually happened. "Death always comes in threes," she claimed. I didn't think much about it at the time because Elisi was as stuffed full of adages and little bits of wisdom as a tick on a hound dog's back is filled with blood.

Mayhap if I'd been in the kitchen when Papa came in, I would have caught a glimpse of Death slipping in behind him, as if a member of the funeral procession. But then, probably not. The sight didn't come clearly to me until I was older and even then the visions were more of an ethereal knowledge, things I knew but couldn't see or touch. I could hear them on occasion but it was sometimes hard to put a picture with them.

This uninvited guest stayed with us for almost five years and finally went away in the summer of 1900, proving Elisi wrong. Death doesn't always come in threes. That time it came in fours and for all I know the number might have been higher if Death hadn't decided to go off in search of more fruitful killing fields. Perhaps It found them in China where the Boxer Rebellion was winding down or maybe It went off to Italy to help with the assassination of King Umberto. It might even have gone off to Texas to prepare for the bountiful harvest that was to come Its way in September when a hurricane and tidal wave struck in Galveston, killing 6,000 poor souls. No matter, it seemed like there was always a war or some natural disaster somewhere and Death wasn't hurting for business back then, just as It isn't now.

The oldest of five children, I often felt more like an adult than a child, but then, according to Mama, I'd been born old. Perhaps that was why she named me Vashti Lee—Vashti after Queen Vashti from the book of Esther in the Bible and Lee after Papa's mother. I didn't think either name suited me at all. Vashti, to me, being Biblical, implied a meekness of spirit or a good girl, one who follows all the rules. And Lee was just dull and ordinary. Women destined to live life on their own terms, as I felt I was, had light, carefree names like Bessie, which my little sister called me when she first learned to talk, or firm, no-nonsense ones like Bess, which Papa took to calling me when he tried to curtail my often inappropriate behavior. Bessie or Bess, both of them fit me like one of my proper Aunt Belle's kidskin gloves.

Of course, if I'd known the kind of woman the original Vashti had been, that she had defied a king and stood up for her rights as a woman, I might have kept the name and been happy with it. As it was, I didn't learn her full story until later in life and by then everyone, with the exception of Mama and Aunt Belle, called me Bessie.

In 1889, at the age of eight, I told everyone I knew to call me Bessie and refused to answer to Vashti by my friends or brother and sister. I even informed the teachers at school my name was now Bessie and signed all my papers that way. Once when my third grade teacher wrote *Vashti* on the chalkboard and told me to stand in the corner for sassing her, I calmly walked to the board, erased the offending name and replaced it with *Bessie* before I did as told. When I announced it at the supper table at home, Papa laughed but he listened and never called me that ill-fitting name again. But Mama, well, Mama, like me, had a mind of her own. She liked Vashti and, though that was how she usually referred to me, she did slip up sometimes and call me Bessie. When she did, I took this as a sign she might someday accept me for the person I was.

Because of Mama's delicate health, I was often left with the responsibility of looking after my younger brothers and sister. A daunting chore at times but Mama had never been very strong, and after the birth of my youngest brother, the spirit and fire which Papa said first drew him to her, a fire I'd seen plenty of before Thee's birth, seemed to dampen down and sputter out like a flame left unattended through a long, winter's night.

On that night when Death came for an extended visit, Papa stepped inside with the dead man in his arms, walked over to the large wooden table in our kitchen and laid the body out there, arranging his arms and legs just so. I stifled a nervous laugh. His actions put me in mind of Mama fussing over the arrangement of her good silver and china when the preacher came for Sunday dinner.

Tall and lanky, the man stretched from one end of the table to the other. His scuffed boots hung over the far edge, dangling in the air above Mama's chair, and his head, with the neat bullet-hole dead center of his forehead, rested at the other end where Papa sat when home at mealtime. As if we were all sitting there waiting to eat, Papa bowed his head and, his hand resting on the man's shoulder, mumbled something I couldn't catch—a quick prayer, an apology or admonition, I didn't know what. Papa wasn't the most religious of men but insisted on saying grace before each and every meal.

As Papa muttered over the man's body, I suppressed another laugh. The whole scene, while strange and unusual to me, seemed to mock our everyday life.

"John? Is that you?" Mama's voice, wispy and soft as the finest goose down, called from the parlor where she'd been giving my sister Loney a piano lesson.

I stood on the bottom step of the back stairway, peeking

3

around the door jamb. From the window of my bedroom, I'd tracked Papa as he walked down the street to the house. I'd been banished there earlier that afternoon for bloodying my brother's lip—a punch Roy richly deserved, though Mama didn't see it that way. Mama, as usual, didn't bother to listen to me and ordered me straight to my room. I'd spent the time in exile preparing my defense, hoping I could catch Papa before Mama did.

At Mama's voice, he sighed, taking off his hat and hooking it on the back of one of the chairs. I pressed back against the wall of the stairwell, hidden but stationed where I could hear and get a quick glimpse of the show if I wanted. This was bound to be good. Mama would probably succumb to a fit of the vapors at the very least. At the most, she'd pitch a hissy fit that would have all the neighbors within shouting distance whispering behind their hands for days.

William Fore—I found out his name later that night from Papa—rested on the table, hands crossed over his chest, eyes closed, face serene, appearing to be taking an afternoon nap. Papa squeezed Mr. Fore's shoulder as if in silent apology then turned his back on him, facing the door to the dining room. He leaned his hip against the table and crossed his arms over his chest, the Silver Star pinned to his coat glinting briefly in the light from the oil lamps as the material bunched up over his arms.

"It's me, Cindy." He sounded tired and I could tell he wasn't looking forward to Mama's reaction.

Mama bustled into the kitchen from the dining room. The baby rested against her shoulder and Green held one of her apron strings in his chubby toddler fist as he staggered behind her in that flat-footed walk all babies have when they first take to their feet.

"John, you need to talk to Vashti Lee. I don't know what I'm going to do with the girl, she—"

I hunched my shoulders but, other than that one defensive move, remained perfectly still. Papa hadn't been home two minutes and already Mama was launching into a conniption fit about my behavior that day. She would, I knew from

4

experience, lecture him for at least fifteen minutes about my actions, subtly suggesting it was his fault I acted the way I did, and then tell him he needed to punish me for hitting Roy.

Not that I minded her leaving the discipline to Papa because he would take the time to listen to me. He understood me far better than Mama ever would and we often ended up laughing about what I'd done to incur Mama's wrath. Papa, in my eyes, was the best part of my life. I cared much more about pleasing him than I ever would about minding my manners or acting like a proper lady as Mama always said I must.

Mama gasped as she came into the kitchen, her hand flying to her chest, and I edged back a little further on the step. She'd surely squeal like a stuck pig if she saw me standing there. As it was, Papa and the dead man on the table held her attention.

"John Daniels!"

"Now, Cindy..."

The baby, reacting to Mama's distress, opened his mouth, burbled and let out an ear-shattering cry. In an automatic maternal gesture, Mama jiggled him and swayed, something that usually ended the tantrum before it got started. Theodore Norton, or Thee as we called him, snuffled and quieted as Mama continued to bounce him up and down.

Green tottered over to Papa and held his arms in the air. Papa crouched a little and picked him up, tossing him over his shoulder and patting him on the bottom. Green giggled.

Mama stared at the dead man and inched her way back to the dining room doorway. Her mouth pursed and she shuddered before squaring her shoulders. She bounced Thee a couple more times and let her other hand fall from her breast. It came to rest on her hip, her right eyebrow arching as she looked at Papa and waited for an explanation.

I clamped my mouth shut over the giggle bubbling in my throat. Oh, good, it looked like the neighbors would have a lot to talk about in the next few days.

Or so I thought until Mama surprised me by saying in a low voice, "Come into the dining room, please, John. I can't talk in here with that...that." She pointed at the table.

Propping Green on his hip, Papa looked at him and shrugged before following Mama out of the kitchen.

"You can't leave a dead man on my kitchen table, John." Mama's voice, low and strained, held a touch of horrified disbelief that Papa would even consider doing such a thing.

In the parlor, Loney picked out the opening notes of some happy tune on the piano. I covered my mouth with my hand when I realized she was trying to play "Seven Drunken Nights." Mama would surely throw a dying duck fit if she recognized the song. It wasn't one she considered proper for a young lady since it was about a man coming home "as drunk as" he could be. It also didn't sit well with her because Papa had been known to spend a few drunken nights of his own at the local saloon. I sighed, knowing I would be the one to pay the price for teaching it to Loney. Leave it to my sister to play Papa's favorite song. She was forever trying to find a way to get Papa to pay attention to her.

I looked over at the dead man. I didn't know him but figured he might object to having that particular song as his funeral dirge. Or maybe not; for all I knew, it was a fitting sendoff for him.

"Aw, now, Cindy, I couldn't leave him at the jail. Norton's got Hankins and Shepherd in the cell and you know how those two are, they fight over which direction the wind's blowing. My deputy has enough on his hands without having to stand guard over a dead man. 'Sides, Fore there ain't hurtin' anything. He's dead." Papa, of course, didn't see the need for making a fuss over such a simple thing as using our kitchen table as a makeshift coroner's slab.

"I know he's dead, John Warren Daniels. That's precisely why you can't leave him there."

"It's only for tonight. Norton and I cleaned him up a bit before I brought him home and I have some canvas in the barn that Roy can help me spread under him. I'll take him to the courthouse in Marshall first thing tomorrow."

"The courthouse? You mean to tell me he's a...a...criminal?" The last word whispered as if Mama didn't want the dead man to hear her less-than-complimentary description.

"Why else would I shoot a man? It's my job to protect the citizens of the town, ain't it?"

I stepped off the bottom step, checking to see if the coast was clear. The voices came from the dining room, Papa's cajoling, Mama's higher and a little desperate. Hiking up my nightgown, I tiptoed on bare feet into the kitchen. The argument might keep them busy long enough to let me explore the curiosity of having a dead man in the house. A dead man! Shivering with excitement, or more than likely fear, I held my breath and approached the old, scarred wooden table. Coming to a stop beside it, I stared. My eyes moved slowly from the tips of the man's scuffed boots, up his legs and torso, and didn't stop until they encountered the neat, circular hole in his forehead.

Papa shot a man in the head and killed him. This was another curiosity to be taken out and explored later. As Constable of Hot Springs, it was his job to shoot people if they needed to be shot just like it was his job to collect taxes from the people who lived there. As far as I knew, he'd never shot anyone before and he sure hadn't ever brought a dead man home and stretched him out on our kitchen table like he was running a backroom funeral parlor.

I snickered then shook off the thought. Right now, I wanted to investigate the results of Papa's action, examine the gruesome reality of death.

Holding tight to the edge of the table with one hand, I reached out with the other and poked at his arm. It felt like any old arm, maybe a little colder than most, but since he wore a long-sleeved coat and it was a chilly night outside, I couldn't really tell. I trailed my fingers down to his hand but ran out of courage before I actually touched that dead flesh. I yanked my hand away and the breath I hadn't realized I was holding rushed out of my lungs with a whoosh. I stilled, took a cautious glance over my shoulder just in case Mama heard, then focused on the hole in his forehead again.

Round and small, the skin puckered around it as if the

man's brain had swallowed a sour lemon instead of a bullet. The hole looked to be about the same size around as my index finger and what little blood had leaked out had already dried to a rusty red-brown color. I leaned down, studying it closely. To me, that little hole didn't seem to be enough to kill anyone, but I guessed it was since this man was lying on Mama's kitchen table, his face pasty gray and most undeniably dead.

Still, just to be sure, I placed my hand on his chest, feeling for a heartbeat or the rise and fall of air going in and out of his lungs. I couldn't find any sign of life, nothing at all. As I stood there, I wondered if he'd felt the pain of the bullet and how long he'd continued breathing after that tiny piece of lead invaded his brain.

My eyes moved up to his forehead again and I stared in fascination at the little round hole. Had Papa aimed for that spot or just plugged him dead center of the forehead by accident? Leaning down, I studied the bullet hole closer and marveled at its perfect roundness. What would happen if I stuck my finger in there? I reached out but drew my hand back when I heard Roy clomping down the back stairs.

Perfect! Maybe I could get Roy to put his finger in there and tell me what it felt like. Two years younger than me, Roy liked to pretend he was all grown up, a man instead of a boy. I walked over to the stairs and grabbed his arm to keep him from jumping off the bottom step as was customary for him. With his big feet, there was no way Mama wouldn't hear that. I pulled him into the kitchen, clamping my hand over his mouth.

"Be quiet," I hissed.

His eyes widened but he nodded and I withdrew my hand. That was the best thing about Roy: he made a fine collaborator most of the time.

"What's going on?" he whispered.

I leaned in close to his ear. "Papa shot a man in the head and killed him and," I paused and lowered my voice even more, "he brought him home and put him over there on the table." I pulled Roy over so he could see. "Mama and Papa are in the dining room and Mama isn't very happy with Papa right now. She doesn't think it's proper to have a dead man on the table."

Loney hit a sour note in the parlor and stopped playing for a moment. Seconds later, she resumed, starting at the beginning of "Seven Drunken Nights" again. The giggles came back and I slapped my hand over my mouth.

Roy bent over the table and looked at the dead man, much as I had a few minutes before, taking him in from the toes of his scraped work boots all the way up to the hole in the center of his forehead. He swallowed hard, threw a glance over his shoulder, turned back and reached out a hand to the man's face. Also like me, he jerked back before he could touch that cold, dead flesh.

"Go ahead," I whispered. "Touch him."

"Uh-uh."

I ran my finger down his spine and brought it forward, studied it before wiping it on his sleeve. "Your yellow streak's showing. Go on, chicken, put your finger in there. I want to know what it feels like."

He shook his head. "Nope. You want to know, you do it." He looked me in the eye. "I dare you."

I hated to back down from a dare, especially when it came from my younger brother, so I shoved him aside and moved closer to the table. Wiping my damp hand on my nightgown, I balled it into a fist with only the index finger sticking out and touched the man's cheek. It was slightly rough, his whiskers stiff and bristly beneath my finger. I traced a path up the side of his face, across his forehead, skirting around the hole then moved my finger down the other side.

"Buk, buk, buk," Roy taunted. "Go on, Bessie, do it."

"Shh. I will."

Moving my finger back up to his forehead, I approached the hole, stopped and prodded the flesh around it.

"His skin's cold," I said.

Roy nudged me with his shoulder. "You're just stalling. Go on, chicken, stick your finger in there."

Suddenly, this didn't seem like such a good idea, but if I didn't do it, Roy would never let me forget and would tell all our friends I'd backed off from a dare. It would be years before I lived it down.

Raising my chin, I moved my finger closer and touched the puckered edges of the hole. Roy leaned down, crowding me, and I jabbed an elbow in his stomach to get him to move back. He giggled before slapping both hands over his mouth.

It was that slightly frightened giggle that did it. I lifted my hand and slowly lowered my finger to the hole. The skin, when I finally touched it, felt rubbery, and as I pressed down into the hole, it seemed to close around me as if greedy for live flesh. I almost lost my nerve until Roy gasped out another nervous giggle and I shoved in deeper. I could feel the bone now, rough with jagged edges where the bullet had torn through to the brain beneath. There was a slight resistance before my finger sank into something that felt like cool jelly.

"Oh my goodness, Vashti Lee Daniels, get away from there! John, get her away from there!" Mama's shocked voice rang out and I snatched my hand back. Without thinking, I wiped my bloody finger on my nightgown.

"Oh, Vashti." Mama sounded like she was going to swoon.

I looked down at the streak of red running along the white skirt of my nightgown. Darn, I was probably going to have to pay for that by doing a plentitude of boring chores around the house for the next month.

Standing beside Mama, Papa put his arm around her shoulders, keeping her upright as he peered at me. His handlebar moustache twitched before he firmed his lips in a straight line.

"Damn, Bess, you can't be playing around with a dead man." He tried to sound stern for Mama's benefit but I could see the amusement dancing in his eyes, even though he narrowed them in an attempt to hide it. Papa might pretend that some of the things I did annoyed and flummoxed him, as they usually did Mama, but I knew the truth. More often than not, he enjoyed my scandalous behavior. Not that he'd ever let Mama see it.

I ducked my head to hide the grin. One of my greatest

pleasures in life came whenever Papa looked at me like that and said, "Damn, Bess," in that exasperated tone of voice. It was his favorite saying when it came to me and my improper behavior. As a deterrent or reprimand, it didn't bother me at all. In fact, it sometimes goaded me on. I loved to hear those two words come out of Papa's mouth.

Every time I heard them, they reinforced my desire to be my own person though I didn't have the words to describe my independent nature until Elisi gave them to me a couple of years after that night. We were foraging in the woods for wild herbs and talking about the goings on of a particular woman in our small town. Elisi, who swore she didn't like gossip but was always willing to listen and offer the occasional comment, laughed and told me Miss Cordy was a whistling woman and didn't care who knew it. When I asked her what that meant, she said, "A whistling woman and a crowing hen never come to a very good end, or so they say. Now, Miss Cordy spends a great deal of her time whistling and I'd say she'll go on whistling until the day she dies, no matter what the outcome or what people think of her."

I thought about it as we grubbed in the dirt for 'sang, and by the time we headed back to the house, I knew a whistling woman was exactly what I wanted to be. A woman who lived her life the way she wanted no matter what other people said or thought about her. Lord knows, I'd already bucked so many of Mama's prim and proper rules of etiquette where a young lady was concerned, and though I didn't like doing so many extra chores to pay for my indiscretions, I dearly loved it when Papa looked at me with a twinkle in his eye and said, "Damn, Bess." I cared much more about pleasing Papa than I did Mama—or society in general.

Chapter Two

Fall 1895

She's enough to make a preacher cuss.

Early the next morning, Mr. Fore still rested on our kitchen table, swaddled in the paint-splattered canvas Papa and Roy brought in from the barn. Mama wouldn't go near him and, in fact, stayed in the dining room to nurse Thee instead of her usual place in the rocking chair which sat in one corner of the kitchen by the warm stove specifically for that purpose. When she did finally come into the kitchen, she skirted around the table as far away as she could get, as if death might be contagious. Or maybe she feared Mr. Fore would grab her hand and drag her along with him on his ascension into Heaven or his descent into Hell, whichever the case might be.

I packed a lunch for Papa and when he and Roy were ready to take Mr. Fore's body outside held the door open for them. Under its shroud, Mr. Fore's body didn't appear to bend at all and I wondered how he would feel if I poked at him then as I had the night before. Papa and Roy carried their stiff burden to the waiting wagon and eased him into the bed. When they finished, Roy hightailed it off to the barn to get started on his morning chores. I handed Papa his lunch and went up on my toes to kiss him goodbye.

"You be a good girl while I'm gone, Bess, mind your mama," he said as he climbed into the wagon.

I couldn't help myself. I begged one more time to go with him.

"No, Bessie, girl, not this time. Stay here with your mama." He looked up at the sky. "Probably get some rain later and that'll slow me down some, but I'll be back by nightfall if I can."

My shoulders slumped but I plastered a smile on my face. I wanted Papa to know someone would miss him while he was gone since Mama hadn't even come to the door to wave him off. I didn't know what they said to each other after I'd gone to bed the night before but I'd heard them arguing and it was all too apparent to me that Mama hadn't forgiven Papa after a night of sleep.

"Tell you what, Bess, the next time I have to go somewhere on business, I'll take you with me. That make you smile for me like you really mean it?"

Papa always knew when I was disappointed even when I tried my best to hide it.

"Oh, yes, Papa. When can we go?"

He laughed. "I'll let you know as soon as I do. Now, go on back inside and help your mama with breakfast. I'll see you when I get back." He clucked to the horses and slapped the reins to get them started. "Be good, Bessie."

I waved and called after him, "Safe trip, Papa."

He turned and grinned at me over his shoulder. I watched until the road curved and he disappeared from my sight.

When I went back into the kitchen, Mama stood over a pot of boiling water on the stove. Thee rested against her shoulder, smiling his foolish baby's grin. He raised a chubby fist and waved it at me. I tiptoed over, grabbed his hand and nibbled on his knuckles.

He burbled out a giggle and Mama jumped. Her hand flew to her heart as she dropped the long-handled spoon and whirled around. I sighed. I swear, sometimes Mama's skittishness irritated the fire out of me.

"My stars and garters, Vashti, you like to scared me into an early—never mind, we need to scrub that table down before we set it for breakfast. I won't have the children eating on the same table where a dead man spent the night."

I don't know if Mama resisted saying the word *grave* because she thought it would be bad luck or if she was already forming her opinion Papa had brought Death into the house and at least two of us would pay for his foolishness.

Probably the latter, although to be fair, she would defend Papa's unseemly behavior later that same day when her sister Elizabeth, or Belle as she was known in the family, came over for afternoon tea.

It was my job to watch the children during those meetings and keep them quiet so Mama and Aunt Belle wouldn't be disturbed. Mama said it was the only time during the day when she could catch her breath and just sit for a few minutes, though I knew that wasn't true. After all, she almost always put the bulk of the household chores on my shoulders, leaving her with plenty of time to sit in the front parlor doing needlework or gossiping with her lady friends.

That morning after we'd eaten breakfast, Mama said her nerves wouldn't settle so she decided to make jelly with the elderberries Roy and I had picked the day before. She said they were the last of the season and there was no need to let them go to waste. An hour or so after lunch, we were waiting for the last of the juice to drain when Aunt Belle popped her head in the kitchen door with her customary trill of "Yoo-hoo, Lucinda, you home?"

I bit my lip to keep from laughing. Aunt Belle liked to think of herself as the fashion-fly of Hot Springs and today she had outdone herself. Dressed as if she had an audience with the Queen of England, her skirt cascaded from the broad sash around her tightly corseted waist, flowing smoothly over her ample hips and flaring out at the bottom. She had recently given up wearing a bustle—one of the last ladies in Hot Springs to do so—but she must have had on six petticoats, all starched within an inch of their lives, to achieve that upside-down tulip effect. Her prim white blouse strained across her ample bosom, the leg of mutton sleeves almost touched the doorframe, and the brooch set dead-center of the collar sparkled in the sunlight when she swayed from side to side; her version of preening. She wore a hat with a brim so wide I swear she had to cock her head sideways until her cheek touched her shoulder just to get in the door. Flowers crowded around the crown and brilliant blue ribbons cascaded down behind, fluttering madly in the breeze. On her hands, she wore immaculate white gloves, something she said a "proper lady" never left home without.

Aunt Belle's nickname fit her like one of those gloves. She was the perfect southern Belle in my eyes.

Mama wiped her hands on her apron then ran them over her hair as she smiled at her sister. She reached for the tea kettle on the back of the stove and filled it with water from the jug. "Hello, Elizabeth. Bessie, you can finish this up, can't you, so your Aunt Belle and I can visit for a few minutes?"

Mama and Aunt Belle's "few minutes" would more than likely stretch into a couple of hours and I wondered what she would do if I said no. Maybe I would have if she hadn't called me by my right and proper name, so I only nodded and turned back to the elderberries slowly bleeding their dark purple blood from the muslin jelly bag suspended over a big bowl. Besides, I figured I was in enough trouble and didn't need to add disrespecting my elders to the mix.

"Yes, Mama," I said as meekly as I could and made the mistake of squeezing the jelly bag.

Mama slapped my hand. "Vashti, don't squeeze the berries. You know it turns the jelly cloudy."

Well, so much for being in Mama's good graces. I should have sassed her after all.

She bustled around the kitchen, chatting with Aunt Belle as she placed cups and a plate of the molasses cookies she'd made a day or two ago on a tray. When the water boiled, she poured it over the tea in her good china teapot, set the teapot on the tray and she and Aunt Belle left for the parlor, their delicate voices flowing behind them like the train of an elegant party dress.

As soon as I judged it safe, I reached out and gave the bag another squeeze. I might as well since I would be blamed when the jelly came out cloudy as it did every summer when Mama canned.

A couple of hours later, I placed the jars on a rack to cool. I washed and dried the dishes, put everything away in its proper place, and gave the counter a halfhearted swipe as I peeked out the window at Roy and the younger children.

Mama had declared this year that Roy was old enough to take care of our younger brothers and sister. I thought this a good thing at the time because it would free me up to pursue my own interests. It didn't work out that way, though. Mama still wanted me to watch over the watcher, so to speak, and so I ended up with the burden of three children and one half-grown man more often than not.

I watched them for a minute, noting Roy had remembered to settle the baby and Green before going off to play a game with Loney. He'd laid Thee on a blanket under the big elm tree and Green sat beside the blanket, happily digging in the dirt with a stick as Thee napped. Roy and Loney were nearby, tossing a baseball back and forth. Roy wound up like a pitcher and hurled the ball at Loney, almost hitting her in the head. She ducked then stood up and slammed her hands on her hips.

"I'm not playing with you no more!"

"Aw, come on, Loney, I didn't mean it. I won't do it again, I promise." Roy loved baseball and had visions of becoming a professional pitcher when he got older. But his failure to make the ball go where he aimed it most of the time would soon put that dream to rest.

Loney stomped over to the blanket and sat down beside Thee, rubbing her hand gently over his back. Thee stirred and Loney started singing softly to him. She dreamed of becoming a concert pianist on most days, of being a mother of a large brood of children on others—something I never understood the appeal of, but then I wasn't anywhere near ready to marry and have a family. Loney would, in time, attain one of those dreams on a limited scale, and in reaching it, she promptly forgot about the other one.

"Hey, Green," Roy called, "you wanna play some ball? Come on, buddy, I'll teach you how to catch." Green, his face covered with dirt, grinned at Roy and held out his hands. "Nah, I can't throw it to you over there. If you don't catch it and it hits sissy-pants in the head, she'll tell Mama on us." He squatted down and motioned for Green to come to him. "Come over here and we'll play." Green got up and tottered over to him.

Roy caught him and swung him around then set him on his feet. "You stay right there and I'll show you how it's done."

Green held up his arms. "More, more."

Roy shook his head. "We're gonna play ball, Greenie."

He tossed the ball gently to him. Green watched it drop to the ground at his feet then picked it up and took off in the other direction. Although he had not found his balance yet, he loved to try to run even though he usually ended up falling down. But that didn't seem to bother him. He'd just pick himself up and take off again.

Roy made a show of chasing after him, getting close, and when Green screamed, he'd drop back and let him go. Some days, it seemed they could keep that game up forever, Green screaming and laughing in delight, Roy pretending to be unable to catch him.

It always made me smile.

When Green was born, Papa said he was a gift from God. He'd thought Loney would be his last child, especially since it had been almost ten years since she'd been born.

And so Papa named Green after another gift he'd been given way back when he was a boy during the Civil War. When the Yankees came, bringing devastation with them, Papa's mama lost their farm. Her husband was off somewhere fighting the war and since she didn't have any family nearby she had to go to a women's home in Greenville, South Carolina, the biggest town near Cowden, where Papa was born. The shelter would only allow her to take her youngest child, my Aunt Beth Anne, with her. They wouldn't take Papa because they didn't allow men, not even boys who hadn't had time to reach their full growth yet. Granny Daniels hadn't had any choice but to apprentice Papa out to someone. Mr. Green, the local blacksmith, took him in as a striker, and by the time the war ended, Papa was well on his way to becoming an expert blacksmith. Mr. Green was also a builder and Papa learned that trade, too. After the war, he continued to work with Mr. Green until the old man died, after which, Papa packed up his bags and went off to explore the world. He barely made it over the border of North Carolina before he met

Mama in Brevard, fell in love, and got married. Papa continued blacksmithing and building, working at odd jobs here and there while Mama had three children in six years. When she miscarried for the second time after having Loney, Papa decided it was time for a new start. He packed us up and moved us to Hot Springs in 1887 when I was six years old.

Since we'd moved, we'd lived in four different places although our first wasn't really a house but a large building with a store-like front located in the middle of town where the bridge crossed Spring Creek. Mr. Newt Lance sold goods in the front and we occupied the upstairs and back. Our next house was a pretty cottage Papa built. It stood just behind Dorland School and had a porch all trimmed with jig-saw stars I'd watched Papa cut himself. There was a big apple tree in the front yard with a swing hanging from a sturdy branch. Lining one side of the garden was a row of gooseberry bushes from which Mama cut switches to use as a threat when we misbehaved. I don't recollect her ever using them on us but just seeing her holding one of those thin, supple branches in her hand was enough to make us behave.

After Papa sold that house, our next home was in front of the Baptist Church on Bridge Street, the main road through town. It, too, was a sweet little cottage all prettied up with scroll work, courtesy of Papa's skilled hands. Papa gave fifty dollars for the land, which was a good-sized lot with a barn in the back where he kept a wagon and two horses, one, a big red mare that for some unknown reason he called Bob. And of course, it wasn't long before we had other animals, a cat, a dog, and some chickens, sharing the barn with the horses.

Because teams of horses with big wagons sometimes ran away down the street, Mama was afraid one of us children would get run over, and when Papa had the house ready to be sold, she convinced him to swap with Newt Lance for a house over on Spring Street. It was a big two-story house with a well in the center of the front yard and a paling fence with a gate near the well. It also had a barn in back, so when we moved, we took the animals with us.

It wasn't long after that move that Papa was offered a job

as town constable of Hot Springs. He accepted the position, perhaps remembering Mr. Green who had also been in politics, but continued to build houses and blacksmith in his spare time.

Outside, Green shrieked, bringing my attention back to him. I watched Roy grab Green, pick him up and swing him around before he took him back and sat him down by the blanket again. Green picked up his stick and went back to playing in the dirt as Roy stretched out beside Loney and Thee on the blanket. He stacked his hands behind his head and gazed up at the sky.

Peace looked to be the order of the day, at least for now, so I turned and tiptoed out of the kitchen to go see what Mama and Aunt Belle were talking about. If I stood in just the right spot in the hall, the mirror on the coat rack beside the outside door gave me a clear picture of the two of them sitting on the small sofa in the parlor.

"Lucinda," Aunt Belle's voice rang with urgency, "you need to have Miss Cordy come in and cleanse this house."

Mama tittered, waving that away with a flutter of her hand. "Pish-posh, Belle. Why in the world would I want to do that?"

"Because John's brought death to this house and you know Elisi says death always works in threes."

"John's done no such—"

"Listen to me," Aunt Belle's voice lowered to a whisper. I moved forward a few inches so I could hear her better. "You should never have allowed John to come into this house with that dead man, because when he did, he brought death in with him."

"Don't be silly, Belle. Death isn't something that comes for a visit, and besides the man didn't die in this house, he died out on the street. John brought him here because he had nowhere else to take him."

"It doesn't matter in the least where he died. What matters is John brought him here and death walked right in the door behind him as if it was an invited guest."

Aunt Belle's words echoed my thoughts of the night before, and I shivered. Was it possible Death was a tangible being and Its spirit now haunted our house?

"Lucinda." Aunt Belle took Mama's hand. "I can feel it in this house. Death never takes one that it doesn't take two others. You know that. The only way you can get rid of it is to have this house cleansed before someone else dies. Miss Cordy can do that or tell you how to do it. We'll go see her right now."

Aunt Belle stood up and I took a few careful steps back. Mama would pitch a fit if she found me eavesdropping, something she'd chastised me for in the past. Young ladies didn't gossip and they didn't listen in on conversations not meant for them to hear. I didn't have time to make it back to the kitchen, so I painted a smile on my face and reversed direction, as if coming to join her and Aunt Belle.

"Mama, I was just coming to see if you and Aunt Belle needed more tea."

Aunt Belle pinned me with her evil eye and I knew she didn't believe me but I ignored her and kept talking to Mama. "More cookies, Mama? I'll be glad to fetch them for you."

"Oh, Vashti, no, no, we don't need anything, but would you watch the children for a few minutes while we take a walk?"

I folded my hands at my waist. "Of course I will, Mama. Would you like me to get your shawl?"

"Heavens, child," Aunt Belle said. "It's warm enough out there today to scald a pig, why would she need a shawl?"

I shrugged, something Mama would usually reprimand me for, but her eyes were all for Aunt Belle and she said nothing. Aunt Belle, however, with her rigid code of behavior for young ladies, didn't let me down.

"Don't shrug your shoulders like that. You look like a common ni—field worker. And stand up straight. I swan, girl, you're going to be carrying around a hump on your back before you even get out of school."

"Yes, ma'am." I straightened my shoulders, though I wanted to hunch them even more than they were already. I'd learned a long time ago, the best way to deal with Aunt Belle when she went off on one of her "prim and proper Southern lady" tirades was just to agree with her. If I bothered to protest or tried to defend myself, she'd keep talking until I suffocated from all the hot air flowing out of her impressive bosom.

Satisfied, she turned back to Mama. "Come with me, Lucinda. You need some air. We won't be gone long, Vashti. You make sure the children behave."

The old bat tugged on her gloves, grabbed Mama's hat from the hat rack and breezed out the door, dragging Mama with her.

I raced into the parlor and looked out the front window. Miss Cordy, a widow-woman and the town midwife, as well as a soothsayer—though some called her a witch—lived with her no-account son on the outskirts of town, halfway up a mountain, in a run-down, shabby house all the town children avoided like the plague. Her yard overflowed with weeds that grew high enough to hide a wildcat—or the Melungeon boogie-man Mama often warned me would take me from my bed one night if I didn't behave.

Mama and Aunt Belle turned to the left and I admit to feeling a tug of fear for Mama but not for Aunt Belle. I didn't believe in monsters, but why take chances by walking up that pitted walk to that crooked door and waking some unknown creature by knocking on it? I didn't want Mama to get hurt but Aunt Belle, well, that was another matter altogether. If the Melungeon boogie-man got her, it would at least put a stop to all her negativity where Papa was concerned and her lectures about being a proper young lady.

Of course, if the monster did get her, he'd probably bring her back after spending five minutes listening to her harangue him about how he should bathe more often, cut his hair, shave his beard, and dress in proper clothes.

Aunt Belle, as Papa said, was enough to make a preacher cuss at the best of times, and at her worst, she could depress the devil.

Too bad Mama balked at the last minute and refused to set one foot on the weed-strewn path leading up to Miss Cordy's front door. If she hadn't insisted on turning around and coming back home, the Melungeon boogie-man may have grabbed Aunt Belle and I wouldn't have had to suffer her presence in my life for the next seven years.

Chapter Three

Spring 1896

Chugged full.

Our lives quickly got back to normal after that. The winter that year was a mild one with hardly any snow to speak of, and on a bright, sunshine-filled Saturday the next spring, Papa made good on his promise to take me with him when he went out of town on business. He planned to go to Paint Rock to talk to a man about doing some repair work on a house and he told me I could accompany him. Needless to say, I was overjoyed at getting away from home and spending the entire day with him all to myself.

After I packed a picnic lunch with thick slices of ham and fresh biscuits, I put on the new red dress I pestered Loney into finishing the night before. Mama, her feathers ruffled about me going, spent the days leading up to our trip in a pout. That morning when I came downstairs, she frowned and muttered something about putting on airs. I pretty much ignored her. I was as happy as a dead pig in sunshine and refused to let her spoil my day.

Papa hitched up the horses while I tucked our lunch under the seat then waited impatiently to leave. When he was ready, I climbed in the wagon without his help. My eagerness to be gone had me practically leaping up and grabbing the reins. It wouldn't take us very long to get to Paint Rock since it wasn't that far away and I planned to savor every single minute of the trip. After we passed out of town and wouldn't be bothered anymore with greeting friends and neighbors as we went, we settled into an easy rhythm, talking about this, that and anything else that crossed our minds.

I could always talk to Papa, and when he started telling me stories about being a boy during the Civil War, the trip seemed to fly by. A natural-born storyteller, he could spin a yarn better than anyone I ever heard before or since.

We stopped outside the town to eat lunch in a pretty clearing by the French Broad River. I had to go into the woods and walking back to the wagon, I heard a rustling sound behind me. Since I'd overheard Mama threatening Green with the Melungeon boogie-man the night before, that was the first thing that came to mind. I lit out of there like a scalded cat and almost knocked Papa down when I got back to him.

"Law, girl, you look like you just saw a ghost. Something scare you?"

Of course, being close to Papa settled my nerves and I laughed to cover my embarrassment. I had turned 15 in January and was too old to be jumping at noises and running to the safety of my papa's arms. Still, I knew Papa would understand. "I heard a noise and the first thing that popped into my head was Mama's Melungeon boogie-man."

"Pshaw, Bess, ain't no such thing as a boogie-man, Melungeon or not. The Melungeons are people just like you and me. Hell, we probably even have some kinfolk in common. You shouldn't be scared of people just because they're different. There are plenty of scarier things in this world."

"What do you mean, Papa?"

We sat on the ground to eat and he told me about the Shelton Laurel Massacre that happened back in the Civil War. He began the telling in the same way he always did, "Well, if I recall rightly..."

To me, those words were better and more exciting than "Once upon a time."

"...this happened along about 1863, right in the middle of some of the fiercest fighting of the war. 'Twas January and some say the winter that year was the coldest ever known. All I know is it was as cold as a well digger's backside down in South Carolina, and if it was cold down there, you can bet it was colder here."

I laughed, delighted that Papa used a phrase I knew he'd never dream of uttering in the presence of a proper lady like Mama. Having no use for propriety or people who put on airs was just one more thing that made me feel closer to him than I ever could to Mama.

"Back then, Shelton Laurel was known to the Confederates as a Unionist hotbed. Suppose it would be more proper to say the whole of Madison County since a lot of deserters, both from the Confederacy and the Union, came over here when the war started, although most of the folks who already lived here didn't really care one way or the other which side won. Since the biggest part of the people in the county didn't have slaves, they figured they didn't have a dog in that particular fight and paid no nevermind to who was winning or losing. But quite a few of them leaned toward the Union side of things, probably because the soldiers around these parts were mostly Confederate and it seemed like they were always doing something to get the people in an uproar, whether it was rationing food or strutting around like they were the cock of the walk just because they wore a uniform.

"Anyhow, when food got scant, the bushwhackers and Tories started raiding both here and over in Tennessee. That's when the higher-ups over in Knoxville decided to put the North Carolina 64th in charge of keeping the peace here in the county. The man in charge of the 64th, a Colonel by the name of..." he stroked his handlebar moustache as he thought "...Keith. J. A. Keith, that was his name, and he was meaner than a striped-eyed snake, meaner than any Melungeon boogie-man could ever be. A body heard tell of torture, whippings, beatings, and Keith wasn't one to spare the womenfolk or the children, either, for that matter. Folks say he had a heavy hand with a whip and a partiality for stringing people up but not enough to kill them. He'd tie them by the neck to a tree and just leave them hanging there until they were more dead than alive." Papa shook his head. "Don't rightly understand what kind of man would do a thing like that to a woman or a child but Keith doesn't really qualify as a man, if you ask me."

Papa adjusted his gun belt, stretched his legs out, and leaned back on his elbows. "One of the things hardest to come by during the war was salt, and when it got scarce as hen's teeth, there was a particularly bad raid on some of the stores in Marshall. Keith got word that it had been a group of men from up Shelton Laurel way and he had his men comb the area up there, looking for the ones who'd done it. Problem was, the bushwhackers went into hiding and all Keith's men could find was old men and young boys, and most of 'em weren't strong enough to have done any sort of raiding. But that didn't matter to Keith. He had his men round 'em all up and locked them in the jail in Marshall, telling them they'd be held until they could be taken to Knoxville and turned over to the authorities there.

"Well, it seemed that trip was doomed from the start. First it got put off because of a spell of bad weather, and before it warmed up enough to travel, a couple of the prisoners escaped, which only made Colonel Keith madder and meaner.

"When the weather finally cleared, they set out early one morning in February, and only a few miles down the Knoxville road in a clearing beside the creek, Keith called his men and the prisoners to a halt. He picked five of the prisoners and told them to kneel beside the creek. I can't imagine what they were thinking, they must've been scared out of their wits, but I'm pretty sure I know what Keith was thinking."

"What, Papa?"

"Oh, it's a bad thing when a man gets to feeling like he's God and has the power to say who lives and dies. That's something that quite a few lawmen have fallen prey to and I think that's what Colonel Keith gave in to that day."

"What did he do?"

"Well, he ordered some of his men to form a firing squad. The prisoners begged for their lives but Keith wouldn't listen, even when the men he'd chosen to do the firing refused to shoot. He threatened them with the same fate if they didn't." Papa shook his head. "He didn't give them a choice, just like he didn't give the prisoners a choice. The soldiers did as ordered and shot those poor people, killing four of them outright and wounding another in the gut. In an act of mercy that probably went against Keith's grain, one of the soldiers on the firing squad shot that prisoner in the head to end his misery. Then Keith told five more to kneel and ordered his men to shoot them, too. One of those five was a young boy, only fifteen years old. Not even old enough to enlist but old enough to die and die he did. He pleaded with them not to shoot him in the face like they did his father and the men on the firing squad must've listened because he ended up gut-shot, too. Still alive, the poor boy begged to go home to his mother and sister, but they shot him again and killed him that time. Then Keith did the same thing with the last three. Thirteen people died that day, Bessie, all at the hand of one evil man. Keith may not have pulled the trigger on all those shots, but he ordered them and threatened more if his men didn't do as he wanted."

He sighed. "That's the kind of evil you should be scared of, the man who does vile things in the guise of doing good. The Melungeons, far as I know, aren't that way. They're kinda' like the Cherokee. They don't bother people for the most part and just want to live their lives in peace. Fact is, some of the Melungeon folk claim to be Cherokee just so they can have a better life, because while some people frown on the Indians, they frown even harder on the Melungeons."

"What happened to Colonel Keith and his men, Papa?"

"Well, Keith ordered the men to dig a grave, but with it being winter, they couldn't dig very deep. I've heard tell that they left more than one of the bodies lying on top of the ground, uncovered like. Their families waited till the next day then went to the creek where they'd been shot and gave them a proper burial, lined them all up right there where they'd died." He shook his head again and smoothed his moustache. "As for Keith and the rest of the 64th, I never heard tell of anything being done to them. I guess they lived out their lives at home with their families."

"But that's wrong, Papa."

"I know it is, Bess, but sometimes that's the way of the

world. Evil isn't always recognized as such, especially when it's dressed up in a uniform. What I'm trying to tell you is there are a lot worse things for you to worry about than the Melungeons and made-up boogie-men. Monsters walking around disguised as people, they're the ones you need to watch out for."

We packed up the rest of our lunch. It was awful what Colonel Keith had done that day, not just to those poor prisoners but to his own men as well. I climbed back in the wagon, wondering how it felt to be put in a situation like that, to have no choice but to do something you knew was wrong. It sent chills up my spine thinking about it, but like Mama's snit, I refused to let it dampen my spirits. We continued on our way, and when we got to Paint Rock, it was just after one o'clock. Papa drove the wagon directly to the saloon smack-dab in the middle of the main street that ran through the small town.

It was in an old two-story house with a wide front porch and double swinging doors leading into the saloon. Judging from the noise pouring out, it appeared to be the gathering place for every man who lived in or around Paint Rock. My eyes widened when I looked at the upstairs windows and saw a couple of women leaning out, dressed in frilly petticoats and not much more, from what I could see. With their painted faces and hair piled loosely on the top of their heads, they were a sight. One of them grinned at me and waved. I could feel the blush rising in my face but I smiled and waved back while Papa hitched the horses to the rail.

"This shouldn't take long, Bess. I need to talk to Mr. Danvers for a minute about some work he wants me to do on this place. You stay here with the wagon."

"Can't I come in with you, Papa?"

"Why, your mother would skin me alive if I took you inside a saloon."

I wanted to say, *That's more than a saloon and what Mama doesn't know won't hurt her*, but smiled at him instead. His insistence that I not go in made me as curious as a cat. I had to force myself to stay in the wagon and not jump down so I could follow him inside.

I watched as he walked up on the porch and through the swinging doors. He didn't see the women, didn't even glance up at them once. For some reason, that put a smile on my face.

When the doors swung shut behind him, I turned my attention to the town around me. It wasn't much, probably didn't even deserve to be called a town from what I could see. It certainly couldn't hold a candle to Hot Springs which always bustled with activity. Of course, even then, Hot Springs was known as a tourist town because of the springs, so it would naturally be busier. It seemed to me the town of Paint Rock existed only because of Mr. Danvers' saloon.

Bored and wishing Papa would hurry, I focused on the upstairs windows of the saloon. The women had vanished and I could hear a piano playing from downstairs. It wasn't long before I hopped down out of the wagon and went to stand by the horses. Then I strolled around, pretending to check their harnesses, patting Bob's neck and mumbling to her but really listening to the music and trying to get a peek inside.

The music cut off and I heard loud laughter, mostly male. I wanted to go inside so bad I could almost taste it. When the music started playing again, I walked right up to the door and stood there gawking over the tops of the swinging doors. That's when I noticed the player piano. I guess I could claim the piano enchanted me and drew me to go against Papa's directions but I think it was more a matter of curiosity than enchantment.

I'd never seen a player piano before but I'd heard of them and a thrill chased through me as I watched those keys press down without a person's fingers there to push them. The loud and lively music pulled me even further toward the door.

When I finally took my eyes off the fascinating piano, I saw the saloon itself was nothing but a few tables scattered about, a long bar running across the back of the room with stools and spittoons placed here and there in front. The customers were all men and I wondered if the women I'd seen in the upstairs windows weren't allowed downstairs. That got my back up and made me even more determined to go in. I looked around and, taking a deep breath for courage, sidled in the door, keeping to the shadows to get a better look at the place.

I'd always loved music and that piano sounded so gay and carefree that I couldn't help but tap my foot. When the song ended and an even livelier tune poured out, I started moving, just swaying at first, but before long, I was in the middle of the floor spinning like a top and having the time of my life. I didn't notice when all the customers stopped and watched me or when some of the men formed a circle around me and clapped their hands in time with the music. I just kept on dancing.

By the time the song wound down, I was out of breath and thirsty enough to walk up to the bar and order a beer myself, but the applause stopped me. My face turned as red as a pickled beet, but when I saw the woman who'd waved to me hanging over the banister upstairs and clapping, I curtsied to her as if she were the Queen of England, practically touching my forehead to the floor.

When I came back up, there stood Papa, shaking his head and trying not to grin.

"Damn, Bess, I thought I told you to stay outside. Your mama's going to have my hide if she hears about this."

I looked at the woman, and when she winked at me, I grinned back at Papa. "What Mama doesn't know won't hurt her—or me either, for that matter."

Papa threw his head back and laughed. "You just better hope she doesn't get wind of this or we'll both pay for it." He walked over to me and held out his arm like the finest gentleman escorting his lady fair.

I dropped a slight curtsy before I took it. "Did you get your business taken care of, Papa?"

"I did and I had planned to have me a drink before we started back home but reckon I ought to get you out of here before somebody we know comes along and carries the story back to your mama."

I patted his arm. "You get your drink, Papa. I'll go on out and wait for you in the wagon then we can start home."

"Damn, Bess, you're a good girl." He led me out the door,

helped me into the wagon, and patted my knee. "You stay put this time, you hear? I'll be right out after I finish my drink."

I smiled. "I won't go anywhere." I'd already had a day that left me chugged full with happiness and enough memories to last a lifetime.

Chapter Four

Fall 1896

Be like the old lady who fell out of the wagon.

On a warm fall day in 1896, as Roy, Loney and I walked home from school, a friend of Roy's came tearing down the road, yelling about a fight at the Mountain Park Hotel. Roy took off at a run, me close behind, towing Loney with me. We slowed down when we went by the jail, fearful Papa might be inside and would wonder why we weren't home, but once past, started running again. A bunch of men had already gathered by the time we got to the hotel. As I pushed my way into the crowd, I saw Papa's deputy, Theodore Norton, talking earnestly to some man I didn't recognize, though his fancy clothes marked him as one of the northerners who came to Hot Springs for the waters.

I stopped behind Mr. Gentry, the owner of the town's hardware store, cocking my head to the side, trying to hear Mr. Norton. Beside me, Roy watched for a few seconds before turning and whispering in my ear, "I'm going to go get Papa." I opened my mouth to tell him not to but he was already gone.

Loney grabbed my arm and tried to pull me out of the mass of men. "Come on, Bessie, we should go home."

I dug in my heels and swatted at her hand. "You go if you want. I'm staying right here."

The thrill of a fight between the man Thee was named for and some man who, more than likely, was a jealous husband fascinated me almost as much as that player piano had.

"Mama's going to be mad if you don't come home with me, Bessie."

"So? I don't answer to Mama."

A bald-faced lie, of course, and Loney knew it as well as I did. She huffed before turning around and stalking off but couldn't resist a parting shot. "Don't say I didn't tell you so. Mama will probably make you do extra chores for this."

Not willing to let her have the last word, I hissed, "Go on, be a good little girl and hightail it home to your mama."

She kept walking. I should have gone with her but I didn't want to miss the fight. Though I knew I'd pay the price when I got home, I wanted to stay. Mama and I had argued that morning over some silly bit of nothing and I figured her anger at me had only grown as the day wore on. I didn't look forward to facing her disapproval. Besides, Mr. Norton had a reputation as a ladies' man, especially with the tourists who came to sit in the waters of the springs in the hopes it would cure whatever ailed them, and his shenanigans never failed to offer some form of entertainment around our bustling little town.

More than that, I liked Mr. Norton and wanted to make sure he was all right. That's what I told myself anyway.

I edged closer but not close enough that Mr. Norton would see me and stop the fight. Standing on tiptoe to see over the hats of the men in front of me, I mentally urged Mr. Norton to throw a punch at his opponent. They were jawing more than anything else but I hoped they would get to the actual boxing before Papa arrived. I didn't like to fight myself, other than the occasional punch I threw at Roy, but I only did that because I knew he wouldn't hit back. Papa would skin him and serve him for breakfast if he ever hit a girl so I was safe from any retaliation on his part.

If truth be told, I stayed because there were few things I liked better than watching someone else engage in fisticuffs.

Mr. Norton, it seemed, didn't want to oblige me that day. He held up his hands in a peaceful gesture and my hopes fell. Thank goodness the other man wasn't in the mood to make friends. I could almost see the steam pouring out of his ears. He took his hat off and threw it on the ground before reaching out and knocking Mr. Norton's from his head. He practically had to jump a foot in the air to do it.

"You worthless son of a gun, I'll teach you not to mess around with another man's wife," he yelled.

I realized I'd guessed right when I heard the Yankee accent. Not from around these parts, as Papa would say. Mr. Norton must have gotten caught toying with the man's wife's affections and this one wasn't going to take it lying down.

When Mr. Norton continued to try to placate him with reassuring gestures and soft words, he swung. Mr. Norton, being quick and having lots of experience with jealous husbands, danced back and the Yankee's fist only glanced off his shoulder. Several men made sounds of approval and Mr. Norton turned his head, throwing a smile their way.

Determined to have his pound of flesh, the man backed up and ran toward Mr. Norton with his head down, butting him in the stomach. Mr. Norton grunted and doubled over, placing his hands on his knees as all the wind left his lungs with a loud whoosh.

I got my wish. The fight was on.

Mr. Norton was a big man with fists the size of hams and it wouldn't take more than one good punch to put the other man on the ground. An amiable person who didn't really like to fight, he wasn't afraid to put his fists to good use when needed. He considered it part of his duty to flirt with all the women, and though I can't say for sure, I don't think he ever took it beyond flirting. Or that's what I thought at the time. A few years later, Mr. Norton would be shot dead in the middle of Bridge Street by a jealous husband. That time, he must have taken his flirtations too far.

When he got his air back, Mr. Norton straightened up and tried once more to reason with the man. "Look, Sawyer, I didn't lay a hand on your wife, only kept her company while she was waiting for you."

Sawyer, however, wasn't in the mood to listen. A small man, he looked more like a feisty rooster than a charging bull, with a pointy chin sharp enough to draw blood if he was lucky enough to get a good poke in with it. He must have weighed at least sixty pounds less than Mr. Norton. It surprised me when he didn't back down but moved in with both fists flying. Mr. Norton held him off with his long arms for a while but Sawyer was quick and got in a few good punches.

By this time, the crowd was egging Mr. Norton on. Caught up in the spirit of the whole thing, I swung my own fists and yelled, "Go ahead and hit him, Mr. Norton. One punch ought to do it."

I should have kept my mouth shut because Mr. Norton's head snapped up at the sound of my voice. He turned and peered into the crowd. I ducked behind Mr. Gentry but not fast enough to keep Mr. Norton from spotting me.

He laughed as he continued to hold off the little runt. "You better get yourself home, Bessie girl. Your mama will have both our heads if she gets wind of this."

I peeked out from behind Mr. Gentry. "Go ahead and clout him, Mr. Norton. He's just a little thing. One good thump will put him on the ground and then I can go home."

"No need for that, sweetheart. We can straighten this out if Sawyer will just—"

I have to give him credit, the sneaky Yankee saw his chance and took it. He delivered a roundhouse blow to the stomach, knocking the wind out of Mr. Norton again. When he bent forward, gasping for air, Sawyer bunched his hands together and hit Mr. Norton on the head, sending him sprawling into the dusty street. I held my breath and waited but he didn't get up.

A few of the men, mainly tourists, cheered Sawyer on but the rest of them, the local ones, laughed. It was a rare thing to see Mr. Norton take a licking and several of the men standing around had firsthand knowledge of the pain those big fists could deliver.

I ran over and knelt beside him, shaking his shoulder and trying to get him to wake up. I tried to turn him over but he was too heavy. He just lay there but when I shook him again he moaned so I knew he was alive.

Mr. Sawyer, apparently feeling his oats because he'd bested a man bigger than himself, walked up and kicked Mr. Norton's leg.

"Maybe you'll think twice before messing with another man's wife," he said.

I saw red when he drew his leg back to deliver another kick. I scrambled up, fists clenched and ready to fight. Before I could swing, Papa was there, holding me by the shoulders.

"Damn, Bess, what do you think you're doing?"

"He's a dirty cheat, Papa. He kicked Mr. Norton when he was down. Even I know you're not supposed to do that." I glared at the man. "And I'm a girl."

Papa sighed as he turned me to face him. Looking me in the eye, he said, "Go home right now, Bessie. I'll handle this."

"But Papa, he—"

Papa might enjoy my scurrilous behavior at times but one thing he would not stand for was backtalk of any kind. His eyes narrowed as he squeezed my shoulders. "Home, Bessie. I said I'd handle it."

"Yes sir."

I didn't have any choice. When Papa's voice took on that hard tone, I knew better than to argue with him. I turned to go and ran smack into Roy, standing there grinning at me.

"Mama's gonna tan you for this," he whispered.

I pinched him. "You just keep your big mouth shut and she'll never even know."

"Bessie," Papa called, "you tell your mama I'll be home in a bit, as soon as I take care of Norton."

I turned back. "I will. Are you going to throw that dirty, lowdown cheat in jail?"

"Never you mind. Just go on home now...and Bess?"

"Yes, Papa?"

He took my arm and steered me away from the crowd. "I guess you know your mama doesn't need to know about what went on here. Don't you?"

I grinned. Trust Papa to remind me not to do anything to upset Mama. If she heard about this, I wouldn't be the only one to suffer.

"I won't but I can't say the same thing for this turncoat standing beside me."

Papa grinned back. "That's my girl." His eyes hardened

when he looked at Roy. "Reckon I don't have to remind you of your mama's delicate nature, now do I, boy?"

Roy shook his head. "No, Papa, I won't say anything but Loney might."

"Loney was here, too?"

"Yes, sir, but she left before anything happened."

"Well, that's something, I guess. You two scoot on home now. I'll see you in a little bit."

I walked home with my head floating up somewhere in the clouds. Papa had called me his girl. Those two words were almost better than him saying "Damn, Bess." They soothed my conscience better than anything he could have said or done. I was his girl and I always would be. There wasn't anything I couldn't tell him, any situation I wouldn't trust him to make better, or any problem he couldn't solve.

Roy chattered away, trying to get me to tell him what he'd missed when he left to fetch Papa, but I ignored him. I headed straight home, secure in the knowledge that Papa would soon follow, and between the two of us, there wasn't anything we couldn't handle together.

Chapter Five

Fall 1897

She looks like she was inside the outhouse when the lightning struck.

Fall, to my mind, is the best time of year to live in the mountains. Or just about anywhere else for that matter since I'm sure people the world over have some of the same traditions we have here or others that are just as fun. In western North Carolina in the late 1800s, fall was the time for sorghum molasses making, corn shucking, and hog killings. I can't say I was terribly fond of that last one but it was a part of fall, and if you could ignore the squeal of the dying pigs and the other gruesome goings on, there were good times to be had with friends and neighbors and family, too.

On a Saturday in early October, 1897, we went to our uncle's farm in nearby Walnut to help with the molasses making. With the sun barely peeking over the horizon, Papa hitched up the wagon. He helped Mama up into the seat first then boosted Loney and me into the bed where we nestled in the hay he'd had Roy spread on the wood floor. Roy passed Thee to Loney and hopped in himself while Papa corralled Green and handed him up to me.

Loney sang softly to Thee, who had just finished his breakfast, and he fell asleep before we were even outside of Hot Springs. I hung onto Green by the waist of his britches. If I hadn't, he would have jumped out every time he saw something he wanted to investigate closer than a wagon ride would allow. Life was a constant source of amazement for him, and by the time we got to Uncle Robert's farm on the outskirts of Walnut, it surprised me I hadn't wrenched the waistband right off of those trousers—or my arm out of its socket.

Fall in the mountains was full of wonder to me, too, so I can just imagine what it was like for Green. With his naturally curious nature, everything from a bright-red maple leaf to a rabbit hopping beside the trail was a marvel. He jumped up to try to grab one of the leaves, hung over the side of the wagon to watch the rabbit's nose twitch as we passed, and all but pulled my arm off as he craned to get a closer look.

When we got to Uncle Robert's farm, Papa pulled the wagon around to the barn, set the brake and hopped down. To distract Green while Papa helped Mama down and Roy jumped out to assist Loney and me, I pulled him onto my lap and tickled him. He giggled and squirmed, trying his best to get away, but I held tight. His laughter brought a smile to everybody's face, including Mama's as she walked around the side of the wagon to take Thee from Loney.

She hadn't been feeling well that morning and I knew the long wagon ride was a trial to her delicate constitution. But Green had a special way about him that could bring a smile to the hardest face or the saddest heart. The world was a happy place for him and he spread that happiness every place he went.

With Thee safely in Mama's arms, Papa helped Loney down. As soon as she was out of the way, I released Green and he catapulted out of the wagon right into Roy's arms, screaming with laughter the whole time. Quick as that, Mama's smile disappeared. When Roy swung Green around and his scream turned into a high-pitched screech, she rubbed her temple and said, "Don't do that Roy. He'll be sick."

"Hush now, Lucinda. That boy's got too much meanness in him to get sick," Papa said as he helped me down. Not that I needed it, but if I hopped down like I wanted to, Mama would turn her frown on me.

Uncle Robert came out of the barn, trailed by his three children. When I saw Caroline, I hitched up my skirts, ran to her and took her hand. Caroline was Uncle Robert's oldest daughter, fifteen years to my sixteen, but we'd been fast friends almost since the day she'd been born, although we only saw one another a few times a year. The best part of the visit for me was that Caroline and I would be together through it all.

Her smile was as bright as the sun and, though younger than me, she stood about the same height. Mama sometimes said we were like two coins cast from the same mold, so much alike we could have passed for sisters. We both had Elisi's Cherokee heritage to thank for that.

Caroline squeezed my hand and her twinkling eyes let me know she had something she wanted to share with me and no one else. She nodded toward the barn and I turned in that direction, but she pulled me the other way, toward the house.

"Let's go see if Mama needs any help with dinner, Bessie." She ducked her head and lowered her voice, "Wait till you see him."

"See who?" I whispered back.

She laughed and squeezed my hand again. "You'll see."

I couldn't imagine who had her so worked up. Like me, Caroline had never paid much attention to boys. Apparently that had changed since I last saw her.

"What are you two whispering about?" Loney wanted to know as she came up beside me.

"Shhh, your mama will hear," Caroline said.

"Mama will hear what?"

I grabbed Loney's hand. "Just keep quiet. Caroline will tell us as soon as she can."

Loney frowned but didn't say anything else.

To keep Mama from getting suspicious, I raised my voice and said, "Caroline, have you talked to your papa about coming to stay with us and going to Dorland Institute?"

We chatted on about the school and the possibility of both of us boarding there while we helped prepare dinner. I was dying to know what Caroline wanted to tell me but didn't dare ask while we worked side by side with our mothers. It was obvious she didn't want them to know.

When the food was prepared, Aunt Nell told Caroline to

call the men folk in and I stepped out on the back steps with her. She reached up to ring the bell hanging beside the door. After giving it a couple of swift tugs, she leaned over and whispered in my ear, "Now you'll see. He'll come in for dinner and you'll see."

"Who are you talking about?"

"His name's Fletcher Elliott. He's from over Old Fort way and he came into John Rumbough's place one day looking for work at the lumber mill."

"Why in the world was he in the saloon if he was looking for work at the lumber mill?"

"If you'll let me finish, I'll tell you why. He went in the Annex because the lumber mill can't take him on for a while yet and he thought the saloon was the best place to ask if anyone in town was hiring. Papa was picking up supplies in Hot Springs that day and offered him work through the harvest and he's been staying here with us, helping Papa around the farm." Her eyes sparkled in the sun. "I think he's handsome." She lowered her voice even more. "But he isn't for me."

Caroline had changed since I'd last seen her. She'd always been something of a tomboy like me and hadn't had any use for boys, but it seemed they were now a matter of some interest to her.

I shrugged. "What's so special about him?"

"You'll see. Here he comes."

I looked over toward the barn and had to grab Caroline's arm to keep from swooning. What in the world? I'd never had that reaction to a mere boy before but something about Fletcher Elliott had my heart beating fast and my vision going slightly blurry. He was taller than me which was saying something, and just on the right side of thin. His dark hair glistened in the sunshine until he shoved a hat on his head, hiding all that thick brilliance.

The only thing that would have improved his looks in my opinion would have been a handlebar moustache like Papa's.

Beside me, Caroline covered her mouth with her hand. "I knew it."

I didn't look at her but kept my eyes on Fletcher Elliott.

"You knew what?" I asked without bothering to hide my words behind my hands. After all, he was too far away from us to hear and couldn't know we were talking about him unless, of course, we gave ourselves away by trying to hide what we were saying.

Caroline dropped her hand. "That's the man for you. I knew it the minute I set eyes on him."

She bounced on her toes when I stared at her. I tried my best to give her a stern look but couldn't hold her gaze and darted a glance toward the cane field at the men.

"Don't be a silly goose, Caroline, I don't even know him."

"You may not yet but I can see it in your eyes."

I finally turned to her. "See what in my eyes?"

She took my hand. "They went all soft when you looked at him. When Papa brought him home, I had an immediate feeling about him, sort of like one of Elisi's feelings. It took me a few days to recognize it but then I had a dream."

I couldn't help but be skeptical since Caroline had never had *feelings* before. "What did you dream?"

"'Twasn't much, only that you and Mr. Fletcher Elliott would be married some day."

My stomach clenched and my mouth fell open. I shook my head. "No, we won't."

"Oh, yes, you will. I saw it just like Elisi sees things. I saw you marrying him." She sighed. "And both of you looked very happy."

I dropped her hand and turned to go back inside. My head spun as I reached blindly for the door. Caroline had given me a lot to think about and my reaction to seeing Fletcher Elliott gave me even more. Could it be possible that I'd recognized him on some instinctive level and that was why my heart raced and my vision blurred? Was it a physical reaction or did I, like so many of the women in Mama's family, have the gift?

Caroline followed me inside. "They're coming, Mama." She moved around me to take the bowl of green beans Aunt Nell had in her hands.

Aunt Nell laughed and patted her cheek. "I swan, child, have you ever known a man that didn't come running as soon as they hear that bell?" She moved over to the kitchen table and surveyed it. "Take those into the dining room, Caroline. We'll eat in there and the children can eat here in the kitchen. After you set those down, you and Bessie go make sure the little ones have washed up, please."

"Yes, ma'am. Come on, Bessie."

I started to follow her into the dining room without even thinking to ask Aunt Nell if there was anything I could carry in for her but Mama's voice stopped me.

"Vashti Lee, take these biscuits with you."

"Oh, I'm sorry, Mama, Aunt Nell. I don't know where my mind was." A lie, of course. My thoughts were on one Mr. Fletcher Elliott. I reached out to take the basket from Mama, hoping she wouldn't notice my distracted air or the blush I knew stained my cheeks.

She wiped her hands on her apron then brushed her fingers over my face. "Why, what in the world has your color up, girl?" The hand moved to my forehead. "You don't have a fever. Do you feel ill?"

"No, Mama, I'm fine. I must have stood out in the sun too long."

She looked into my eyes then smiled and shooed me away with her hands. "Next time you go out, remember your hat."

"Yes, ma'am." I took the biscuits to the dining room. Had Mama recognized the stunned look on my face as similar to what she'd seen in the mirror when she'd first met Papa?

I don't remember much about the rest of that weekend except it seemed every time I turned around there was Mr. Fletcher Elliott looking at me with his piercing blue eyes. He never said anything directly to me and never smiled, just watched me. Of course, I didn't say much to him, either. For the first time in memory, I was tongue-tied, and though I'd never had a shy moment in my life before, I suddenly found myself blushing every time I met those intense eyes.

By the time we started home the next day, I felt as if I'd been stuck in an outhouse that had been struck by lightning. And I probably looked it, too.

I spent most of the trip home tending to Green just as I had on the way over, making sure he didn't topple out of the wagon. He kept me busy but not enough to stop my mind from dwelling on Fletcher Elliott and the things Caroline said. I hadn't wanted to talk to her about him last night and instead pretended to fall asleep so she'd stop going on about him and me being destined to marry. But as we rode through the late afternoon back to Hot Springs, I wished I had talked to her about these strange feelings.

Loney started singing and Green snuggled in my lap, drifting off to sleep right on the outskirts of town. I wished I could go to sleep, too, since I hadn't slept much at all the night before but as I leaned back against the side of the wagon and closed my eyes I knew there was no hope of a quick nap for me. There was simply too much going through my head, all of it having to do with Fletcher Elliott.

I had to agree with Caroline that he was a fine specimen of a man, handsome and tall. He was also very strong judging by the way he'd stripped the cane and carried huge bunches of it to the mill to be crushed. Then when the time came to cook the juice, he'd taken off his shirt as he stood over the pots, running the skimmer over the top of the boiling syrup. I'd watched the muscles in his back as he moved and Caroline finally had to nudge me to get my attention back on the juice I was stirring as it went through the last step of the boiling. Keen eyes are important at that point; if you boil it too long, the end product is thick and has a strong taste.

I'd made it through the day without burning the molasses, thank goodness, and the next morning at church, Caroline had maneuvered it so I sat next to Fletcher Elliott. When the preacher called for the congregation to stand and sing, all I'd been able to manage was moving my lips even though I'd sung those hymns many times before and knew them all by heart. I hoped God would forgive me for my inattention that morning during the service but my mind had been taken up with thoughts of the man standing beside me.

As Papa drove us into town down Bridge Street, Roy poked me in the side. "What are you smiling about, Bessie?"

I opened my eyes and scowled at him. "I wasn't smiling, I was sleeping."

"You must have been having a really good dream then."

I frowned at him but kept my mouth shut. This weekend had brought changes and a glimmer of what the future might hold for me. The following weekend fanned the glimmer into a spark and at the same time threatened to blow it out. But it would be a good many years before I realized what it all meant and that little spark in my heart exploded into a full-fledged fire.

Chapter Six

Fall 1897

Trying fortunes.

Over the course of the next week, I tried every way I could to determine what Fletcher Elliott was to mean to my life. I'd never indulged in the act of trying fortunes before but had been to enough hog killings and quilting bees and other social gatherings where the young women engaged in different strategies to get clues about who they were going to marry. I'd seen them all so knew a bit about what I was doing but the season worked against me on some of them.

For instance, since the autumn wheat had all been harvested, I couldn't go out to a wheat field in the early morning and place a piece of paper on the dew-drenched plants to see if my true love's name would appear. Likewise, I couldn't drape a handkerchief on the wheat at night and then check it in the morning to see if the night moisture had etched his initials there.

The number nine was much on my mind as I had always heard it was very important in matters of love spells, but again, the time of year worked against me. I couldn't eat nine redbuds in nine days and then count the men I saw to see if Fletcher was the ninth one because the redbuds weren't in bloom. I wasn't too fond of eating flowers anyway, and besides, there wasn't much hope of him being the ninth man I met since he was living at Uncle Robert's. Still, there was a chance he might be in town on some errand.

Aunt Belle was having a quilting bee for Ellie Henson the next Saturday and I knew she'd include at least one way for the young ladies to try their fortunes. For the first time I would participate but hoped I would know something before then which meant I didn't have nine nights to go outside and count nine stars then on the last night put a mirror under my pillow so I would dream of the man I would marry. I figured I could do that after the quilting bee if my questions weren't answered there.

Tossing that strategy aside for the time being but keeping it in mind for possible use later, I indulged in the ones I could. I hid a mirror in the folds of my skirt and took it outside where I used it to cast a shadow into our well, watching eagerly for Fletcher Elliott's face to appear. The only image I saw was my own anxious face peering back at me. Each day, I went outside and listened to the birds, waiting to hear a dove coo to its mate. When I did, I sat right down and took off my shoe and checked inside. There was never a hair there to tell me the color of my true love's hair. I even walked along Spring Creek for a mile or more, looking for a branch flowing east so I could drop a pebble in and see my future husband's face as the ripples died down. The only east-running branch I found didn't have enough water in it to get the rock fully wet, much less ripple.

There were plenty of crabapples hanging on the trees so I ate some, nine to be exact, though I'd never heard a girl should eat that many but figured it wouldn't hurt since nine was the magic number where love charms are concerned. I didn't make a face while consuming any of them, a good sign I could get any man I wanted to marry me. I was very careful not to step in front of the broom when Loney was sweeping, which would mean forfeiting my chance to marry during the coming year. Of course, that one didn't concern me overly much since no matter how hard I tried I couldn't turn a hotcake without breaking it, and that meant I wasn't ready to marry yet. I wanted to finish my schooling before I married anyway so I had almost two years to wait at the very least.

Although I had time, my curiosity was up and I wanted to know something right then. Still, I couldn't bring myself to kill a red-winged blackbird even if doing so meant I could get any man I wanted and marry him immediately. Killing one of those regal birds just went against my grain and, besides, I didn't have anything to kill it with. I could ask Papa to let me borrow his gun but then I would have to explain why and I didn't want to do that.

Like the crabapple trees, our holly bush was full of berries but I didn't know if that one would work at any time other than Christmas. I would wait on that one but I had every intention of collecting nine holly berries during the twelve days of Christmas and naming each of them before I tossed them into the fire. Hopefully, the one named Fletcher Elliott would be the first to pop. But that seemed a little foolish to me. How would I know which one was named what after I tossed them all into the fire?

I made plans for the next time I saw him, vowing to slip the web of a gander's foot into his drink to ensure he would love me. That one was only supposed to work if a man did it with the web of a goose's foot in the shoe of the woman he wanted, but I figured what's good for the goose is good for the gander.

By the time Aunt Belle's quilting bee rolled around, I had wasted quite a bit of time attempting to "try my fortune" and even more time thinking about Fletcher Elliott and the strange feeling that came over me when I first saw him. I had never believed another man could be as important to me as Papa, but Fletcher was different somehow. I didn't know if it was simply that he was the first man I'd met that caught my interest or those intense looks he'd given me all weekend that had me thinking about him so much. I only knew he seemed to have some sort of power over my heart.

If I could have, I would have spent more time with him, hoping to be out one night on a walk and hear a mockingbird sing. That was the luckiest of signs, especially if I put his hat on during the song, for it meant we would be married within a year, and more important, I would be happy in my choice.

But that wasn't possible so I had to wait for Aunt Belle's quilting bee. I knew she would most likely go with the saucer method for trying fortunes and I went, determined to find out at least if I was meant to marry a young man, a widower, or remain single for the rest of my life.

Since I wasn't the most accomplished with a needle and thread, I'd never looked forward to a quilting bee before but found myself impatient for Saturday to arrive. With cold weather and Ellie Henson's wedding on the horizon, it was the perfect excuse for all the ladies of the town to get together, finish the quilt tops Ellie had made in anticipation of her wedding, and socialize. Of course, socializing was just another way of saying gossip, but that was fine with me. I enjoyed the gossip more than the quilting.

Aunt Belle didn't let me down. In her front parlor, she'd set up a table with three saucers on it. One saucer was empty, the next held clear water, and the last had sudsy water in it. Each unmarried woman would take a turn at the saucer table to try her fortune. She would be blindfolded first and spun around then led to the table where she was to stick a finger in one of the saucers. If the finger landed in the one with clear water, that meant a young husband in the girl's future. The one with soapy water promised a widower and the empty saucer meant she would never marry.

While I waited for the other guests to arrive, I stood in the parlor staring at the table, trying to memorize the positions of the saucers because I wanted my finger to land in the clear water. Fletcher was a young man, too young to have been married before, which meant he couldn't be a widower.

"Who are you dreaming about, Bessie?" Sally Gibson asked when she caught me standing there.

"No one in particular. I'm too young to marry anyway."

"Well, I'm not."

She spoke the truth. At 19, if Sally didn't catch a man's eye before long, she would officially be declared an old maid. Her hand hovered over the saucers and she made playful jabs at the one filled with clear water as if practicing for her turn.

Ignoring the fact that I'd been doing the same thing in my mind only minutes before, I laughed. "Memorizing where they are won't do you any good, Sally. You know they'll spin you once they have the blindfold on and they might even move the saucers around before they lead you over here."

She sighed. "I know, but wouldn't it be grand if I did choose the one with the clear water? Not that I would mind a widower. That Mr. Anderson would be a fine pick. He's not too old but I guess he's going to marry Eliza Dawson."

I smiled. "Have you got your eye on anybody else? I mean, beyond Mr. Anderson?"

"Well, there aren't that many widowers in town but maybe Mr. Goforth. As for bachelors, if I'm lucky enough to choose the saucer with clear water, there's always one of the Gentry boys or maybe Mr. Rumbough's son, John Jr., but I don't think I'd like being the wife of a saloon owner."

"Maybe John Jr. won't see fit to follow in his father's footsteps. A lot of the boys are looking for something more since Dr. Dorland opened his school here."

She clasped her hands under her chin. "If I had my druthers, I'd marry one of those rich tourists that come down here for the waters. Then off I'd go to Boston or New York, where I'd live in a fine, brick mansion and wear beautiful clothes. I'd have servants to do all the work for me and I'd never have to sew another quilt again." Her blue eyes sparkled as she giggled. "Wouldn't I be the envy of every girl in Hot Springs then?"

I laughed. "Well, I don't know about any of the other girls, but I wouldn't envy you. How could you stand to be so far away from your family and the ones you love?"

"Oh, I'd come back every summer and take the waters like all those fancy men and women do. I could see my family then. That would be enough for me."

"Not me. I'd miss Papa too much and the rest of my family, too, of course. I don't know if I could live somewhere where I had to travel so far to see them. Why, just think of it, I wouldn't get to see Thee or even Green grow up and become men. I wouldn't get to go with Papa on his business trips or help him collect the taxes—"

"Pshaw, Bessie, you won't be doing those things after you're married anyway. You'll have your own family to take care of, your own babies to watch grow up, and your husband to go on trips with."

I hadn't thought about it that way. Not go on business trips with Papa, not watch for him to come home every evening and run to tell him about my day, not hold Thee or Green on my lap and hear them laugh or see their eyes grow heavy when I told them bedtime stories? I eyed the empty saucer. Maybe I'd been wrong to try for a fortune I wasn't even sure I wanted.

Aunt Belle stuck her head in the door. "Girls, come on out here and let's get started on these quilts. Ellie has thirteen tops that need to be finished before her wedding. We've got our work cut out for us."

Thirteen quilts was the traditional number for a bride to take into marriage with her. Ellie and her mama had probably been working on them for years. After each top was completed, it was carefully folded and packed away until the time came to quilt them, usually during the month before the wedding when the bride was sure she would be married and the quilts would be used instead of just moldering away in a chest. I wondered if it was bad luck to quilt them before a girl had actually captured a beau.

Sally grabbed my hand. "Come on, Bessie, I bet Ellie has some new quilt patterns we've never seen before."

I didn't say anything to that since the only quilt top I'd ever tried to piece ended up in Mama's rag bin. It hadn't seemed important to me because up until last weekend I hadn't even considered the idea of marriage. Loney, on the other hand, already had the chest that sat at the end of her bed stuffed full with quilt tops, napkins, and tablecloths. She even had a few dainty little gowns for the babies she'd have one day. It seemed she'd been dreaming of getting married since she was born.

In Aunt Belle's living and dining rooms, all the furniture had either been moved to the porch or pushed to the wall to make room for the quilting frames. Some of the women had pulled up chairs but others stood as they plied needle and thread on the quilts. I could hear some of the younger girls talking and laughing out in the kitchen as they watched over the babies and small children.

My sewing abilities, or I should say, inabilities, were well known to all the ladies of Hot Springs. I couldn't sew a straight line to save my life and in quilting that's very important so Aunt Belle had me moving around and about the frames, threading needles for the quilters. I didn't mind. My eyesight was better than most of the older women and it gave me a chance to hear all the latest gossip. Besides, it was much better than being stuck in the kitchen with the babies.

I'd done this before at other quilting bees and had perfected a sort of routine which allowed me to listen to all the gossip. It was easy to tell when a juicy bit of news was being passed around; the women around the frame would lean in and the storyteller would lower her voice as if she didn't want the other quilters to hear what she was talking about.

The story would make the rounds from frame to frame, so if I kept moving around, threading needles and for the most part keeping my mouth shut, I would hear the whole thing. I might miss a word or two here and there, but if I stuck with it, I'd be rewarded with the latest tittle-tattle.

That day, the ladies were all abuzz about two of the members of our church choir, Hattie Bristow and Homer Stanton.

I just happened to be standing beside Mrs. Aiken when she asked the ladies in her group, "Have any of you seen Hattie's baby yet?"

I pretended to have trouble threading a needle so I could stay where I was. This was bound to be good. Rumors had swirled around Hattie Bristow and Homer Stanton for nigh on a year now.

Aunt Belle looked up, eyes wide. "She had the baby?"

"Oh yes, she did." Mrs. Aiken lifted her nose in the air and sniffed. "Land sakes, I don't know how she'll have the nerve to show her face around town after this."

"Why? Is something wrong with the baby?"

"No, he's as healthy as a baby can be but..." Mrs. Aiken lowered her voice even more and leaned farther over the quilting frame. She waited a moment, probably savoring the attention she was getting. The needles came to a standstill as all eyes watched her. "He has red hair."

The eyebrows of every woman lifted as one. I was surprised when I didn't hear an accompanying whoosh.

Hattie's baby having red hair wouldn't be so bad if she or her husband had the same color. As far as I knew, everyone in the Bristow family and in Hattie Wilson's family, for that matter, was a brunette. Homer Stanton, the man she'd been coupled with in all the rumors and who sang with her in the church choir, however, had a full head of rich, red hair.

The silence lasted for maybe half a minute and then Madora Stevens jabbed her needle in the quilt, covered her mouth with her hands, and giggled. After that, the ladies were off, talking so fast I couldn't keep up with them so I moved on to the next frame where, much to my delight, the women were discussing the same thing.

This would keep the gossip mill grinding for months, a red-headed baby sprung from the loins of parents who both had hair as dark as night. Mrs. Aiken was right, poor Hattie would never again be able to hold her head up in town.

I went into the dining room and helped Mrs. Cooper untangle a knot in her thread, hoping the rumor of Hattie's baby would have made it this far but didn't hear anything of interest so I kept circulating around the rooms, threading needles and catching more and more talk of Hattie and Homer's indiscretion here and there.

We worked on the quilts until the sun started to go down, finishing most of them. The men came in to take the quilting frames down and move the furniture back while the women admired the quilts they'd worked on that day. After that, we shared a potluck supper, and when most of the men went outside to the porch to smoke or drink or whatever it was they did out there, it was time to try our fortunes.

I stood back, letting the other girls go before me as I grappled with what I wanted my fate to be. The memory of Fletcher Elliott standing shirtless over the molasses vat might make my heart race but the thought of marrying anyone and leaving Papa was too much to bear.

I watched as Loney's finger landed in the saucer with the

sudsy water. She would marry a widower. Then Susie Howell and Lola May Phillips both chose the saucer with the clear water. Sally Gibson was next. Behind her back, she crossed the fingers of her left hand and reached out with her right, landing in the saucer with the soapy water. A widower for Sally, who would be relentless in her pursuit of a husband. I pitied all the widowers in our town, particularly one Mr. William Goforth.

When my time came, I tied the blindfold on myself and allowed Loney and Susie to spin me around then lead me over to the table. My hand hovered over the saucers I knew were below but I couldn't bring myself to lower my finger. I heard Loney giggle behind me and someone shushed her as I slowly lowered my finger and touched...the table.

Well, so much for trying my fortune. Nothing I'd done in the past week had given me an answer and now the one thing I'd placed all my hopes on had failed me, too.

"Do it again, Bessie," Loney said.

I shook my head and placed my hand behind my back.

Someone took my arm and turned me around once, twice, three, four times. "Now try it, Vashti Lee."

It was Mama, and for some reason, her voice calling me by my given name was all I needed to hear. I brought my hand around and lowered my finger. This time, instead of the tablecloth, I hit one of the saucers with water in it. The only question now was; which one?

Mama untied the blindfold and I met her eyes. She smiled and nodded. I looked down and saw I'd chosen the one with the clear water. I didn't know whether to be happy or not. Perhaps the fact that I'd bungled the first try meant there would be a delay before I'd marry and maybe by then I'd be more accustomed to the idea of leaving Papa for another man. That was what I told myself anyway.

Chapter Seven

Fall 1897

That girl's just naturally horizontal.

Fletcher Elliott stayed on my mind, harder to get rid of than a burr. I pondered on what it all meant over the next few weeks. Though I didn't realize it, I must have grown quieter with my thoughts because even Papa mentioned it one day when I went with him to collect taxes from some of the families that lived outside of town.

He cast a curious glance my way. "You've been awful quiet lately, Bess. Something on your mind?"

I didn't know what to say. I could talk to Papa about anything, and I usually did, but this was different somehow. It was almost as if I'd be asking for his help in finding another man to replace him.

I opened my mouth but nothing came out so I just shrugged my shoulders, safe in the knowledge that Papa wouldn't reprimand me for not acting like a lady.

Papa smiled. "That cat's had a hold of your tongue for the last month or so. Did something happen at Ellie's quilting bee?"

"No, Papa, it's only..."

"Only what? Come on, girl, you can tell me."

"I know, but..." I shook my head. I had to say something so blurted, "Papa, what's going to happen when I marry?"

He cut his eyes at me and flicked the reins to get the horses to speed up. "Maybe that's something you should ask your mama."

I could feel the heat in my cheeks and looked down at my

hands in my lap in an attempt to hide the blush. I could probably draw him away from what was really bothering me by talking about the physical side of marriage but figured I'd end up more tongue-tied than ever so I set that thought aside. "No, I don't mean that, Papa. I mean what will you do when I get married?"

He laughed but like me skirted away from the question. "You got your eye on someone?"

"Yes, no, I don't know really." I took a deep breath. I couldn't tell Papa I suspected I'd found the one man who could possibly take his place in my heart. There wasn't much chance he'd let me off the hook now so, again, hoping to distract him, I changed directions. "I mean, there was all that stuff with the girls at the quilting bee, you know, trying our fortunes, and I was talking with Sally about getting married. She wants to marry one of those rich tourists that come to stay at the hotel. Well, really, she wants to marry anybody, as long as he wears pants and can grow a little facial hair—and I'm not so sure about that last one. Could be, the pants-wearing part's the only thing she cares about. It's about all she ever talks about, but me, I haven't really given it much thought. Loney has about fifty quilt tops tucked away in her hope chest for the day when she finds a husband and I haven't made the first one nor do I want to. Does that mean I'm odd in some way?"

"Well, you know Loney's not happy unless she has a needle and a piece of material in her hands. As for Sally, she's what my granny would've called naturally horizontal."

I laughed. "Oh, Papa, that describes her perfectly."

"I wouldn't say the fact that you haven't given marriage much thought means you're any different from any of the other girls except that maybe you're just not ready yet and you're sensible enough not to let yourself be rushed into anything." He took the reins in one hand and put his arm around my shoulders. "Not every woman grows up at the same rate and marriage is a serious thing. It's probably better that you take your time and find the right man for you. Why settle for just the biscuit when you can have the gravy, too?"

"But Loney's four years younger than me and she might not talk about it a lot but I'm sure she's thinking about it. Mama was only seventeen when she married you and Aunt Belle was eighteen when she got married. I'll be seventeen in a couple more months. Shouldn't I at least be thinking about it?"

He laughed. "You anxious to leave your papa?"

I smiled. "No, Papa, that's one of the things that has me worried. In fact, that's the most worrisome thing of all. I don't ever want to leave you."

"Well, the time will come when you will but that's just a natural part of life. It'll be hard on both of us, I imagine, but we'll get through it."

I leaned my head on his shoulder. "Where will I ever find a man that can take your place?"

"He won't be taking my place, Bessie, he'll just be sharing it with me. You've got more than enough room in that heart of yours for both of us."

I lifted my head and kissed his cheek. His moustache tickled and I giggled. "Whoever I decide to marry, if I ever decide to marry anyone, I hope he's just like you."

He turned his head and winked at me. "Ain't but one of me, Bessie-girl, but I'm sure when you start looking, you'll find someone suitable. Just make sure he's not a Republican or I may have to shoot him before he gets through the front gate."

"Oh, Papa, you'd never do that. But I promise I'll check out his political leanings before I bring him home to meet you and Mama."

"That's my girl. You feel better now or is there something else you want to talk about?"

"I'm fine, Papa. There's the turnoff to the Masons. Aren't we going there?"

"We'll go out to the Sullivan place first and then we'll stop at Mason's and the others on our way back into town."

I felt better even without telling Papa what had been keeping me quiet for the last month. Mr. Fletcher Elliott would just have to wait until I was ready and then we'd see if he was the right man for me or not.

A shiver ran up my spine and I reached down to get the

blanket Papa kept rolled up and stored under the seat.

"Cold?" he asked.

"A little chilly but it'll warm up when the sun gets a little higher in the sky."

"Gonna be a cold winter this year. Look at all the berries on the dogwoods and the hickory trees are hanging full of nuts."

I smiled. "We'll probably have lots of snow, too. Remember all those foggy mornings we had back in August?"

"I surely do, and I bet if you could catch that rabbit Green had his eye on when we went to your uncle's last month, that little scalawag would have an extra layer of fur on his feet."

I laughed. "I never heard that one before, Papa. What are some others?"

"Well, you know about the wooly bear, don't you? I mean the caterpillar, not the black ones. 'Course, if we saw a black bear today, it'd probably have an extra layer of winter coat on it but the wooly bear, now, it tells us by its stripes."

"Yes, a thicker stripe means more snow. Or is it the other way around?"

"Depends on who you're talking to. Some people believe it does and some people believe a thicker stripe means less snow. Some others think it's more a matter of how much of the little bugger is black. The blacker it is, the more snow we'll have. But I trust the squirrels more than the caterpillars. If they stash their nuts close to the ground, it means a mild winter, but if they hide them up high, it means a lot of snow's headed our way."

I looked up at the trees. "I didn't know that. What did they do this year?"

He pointed to the sky. "Up high so I'd say we're in for it. You can also tell by their tails. Next time you see that rascal that has his nest in the oak tree out back of the barn, look at his tail. It's almost as big around as his body this year. That's a sure sign of a bad winter if I've ever seen one."

I shivered again and pulled the blanket up higher. Talking about cold weather and snow seemed to make the day chillier than it really was. "Mama says if we count the number of days to the next full moon after the first snowfall, that'll tell us how many snowstorms we'll get this winter."

"Yep, and judging by all the signs we've seen out here today, we'll have our first snow on the day after a full moon. That'll mean a whole month of snows this winter."

"Well, I guess we should be grateful it won't all come at once. Of course, by the time spring gets here, it'll probably feel like that one month of snow has lasted for years."

"Sure will. If we're out late enough today, we'll probably hear an owl hooting. 'Course it may not be late enough in the year to go by that one but you keep your ears open when we get farther into November, and if you hear one hoot, you can bet on a bad winter. The screech owls, though, they're different; if you hear one and it sounds like a baby crying, that's a sure sign."

I shook my head. "Are you making up signs now, Papa?"

"Nope, that was one I heard straight from my pap's mouth." He fell silent after that and I knew it was because his father had gone off to fight in the Civil War and he'd never heard from him again.

"Do you ever wonder what happened to him, Papa?"

"'Course I do but I guess I'll have to wait 'til I die to find out. Knowing Pap, he was right in the middle of one of the big battles and died on the battlefield. He never was one to run away from trouble. I was just a boy when he left but I remember my mother telling him not to take any foolish chances. He told her he'd do his part to help the South win even though he knew it was a lost cause and he didn't really believe in it. Last thing he said to me was to take care of the women and the farm. Guess I didn't do a very good job of that, though."

I leaned my head on his shoulder. "You did as good a job as you could. You were only a boy, Papa. You couldn't stop those darned Yankees from destroying the farm, and if your father had any sense at all, he knows that."

"Maybe so. I figure it was all meant to be anyway. Just think, if the Yankees hadn't come through and Mama hadn't lost the farm after they all but burned it to the ground, I wouldn't have ever signed on with Mr. Green and not a one of us would be where we are today."

"No, we wouldn't but don't expect me to be grateful to the Yankees. Instead, I'll thank God that he led you here to North Carolina after the war so you could find Mama, get married and have all of us."

"That's a nice way to think about it, Bess." He pulled on the left rein to steer the horses into a pitted lane that wasn't much more than a break in the trees.

"Is this the way to the Sullivan place?"

"Yep, a few miles on this sorry excuse for a road and we'll be there. Don't know why people live so far out from town, but ol' Sullivan seems to prefer it that way. Used to think it was because of his Melungeon wife but she's been dead a couple of years now and he still lives out here in the woods away from everybody. Got a passel of young-uns that help him tend the place, and every time I've been here, they're clean and healthy and seem to love him despite his ornery ways. One thing's for sure, he won't be happy to see us today, so when we get there, you stay in the wagon while I talk to him."

My ears perked up at the mention of a Melungeon wife and I wished she was still alive so I could meet her. Though I'd heard about the Melungeons all my life, I'd never met one and wondered what they truly looked like. I knew only the basics: dark skin, black hair, and blue eyes. That combination sounded strange and I wanted to see one for myself.

But my concern for Papa's safety smothered my disappointment. "He won't hurt you, will he? I mean because you're here to collect the taxes."

"Nah, he's not dangerous, he just doesn't like people. I've never had any problem out of him before and I don't think I will today. Don't you worry, Bessie-girl."

"All right, Papa."

The Sullivan house surprised me. I guess I'd been expecting something along the lines of Miss Cordy's run-down shack where it was rumored a Melungeon boogie-man lived. But this wasn't anything like the shabby house on the edge of town. Nestled in a grove of trees, it almost seemed to be a part of the landscape. It was neat and clean, and even the small front porch looked as if someone made a point to keep it swept of debris and the leaves that covered the yard.

Spying a large garden off to one side of the house and what looked to be a thriving orchard behind it, I said, "Why this is nice, Papa. I wouldn't want to live this far away from town but it looks like they have everything they need."

"Yeah, like I said, Sullivan takes care of what's his, but I agree with you, I wouldn't want to be this far out."

A man I assumed to be Mr. Sullivan came out on the front porch, seven children of varying ages filing out behind him. They all had dark hair and their skin looked to be the same color as mine. Standing as they were in the shadows of the porch roof, I couldn't make out the color of their eyes. "How many children does he have?"

Papa raised his hand and touched the brim of his hat. The children all waved and their father pushed his hat further back on his head. "Nine. The oldest girl's probably inside with the youngest. It was just a couple of days old when Mrs. Sullivan died," Papa said as I waved back to the children.

Mr. Sullivan said something to the children and they all turned around and went back inside the house.

"Mornin', Hubert," Papa called.

He nodded. "Sheriff Daniels."

Hardly anyone called Papa Sheriff but it didn't seem to surprise or bother Papa any. He pulled on the reins and drew the wagon to a halt beside the small porch. "This is my oldest daughter, Bessie. Bessie, Mr. Sullivan."

"Hello, Mr. Sullivan. I'm pleased to meet you."

He touched his hat again but didn't say anything. Papa reached under the seat for his book then hopped down from the wagon and walked around it to the porch. "This won't take very long, Bess, you wait here."

"Yes, Papa."

As they went in the house, I contented myself with listening to the birds singing in the trees and looking at the garden. There were still a few rows of plants growing, some cabbage and collards, but the rest had been hoed and laid to rest for the winter. An old hound dog came around the side of the house and looked at me for a long moment, lazily wagging his tail. When even that got to be too much of an effort, he ambled over to the side of the porch, stretched out and heaved a world-weary sigh before closing his eyes for what was probably his fifth nap of the day.

He didn't move so much as a whisker when Papa and Mr. Sullivan came back out on the porch. Between them, they carried what looked to be a small dresser with a hump in the middle. It was covered with a beautiful blue and white quilt stitched in the Drunkard's Path pattern. Mr. Sullivan didn't look happy, but then, he hadn't looked happy before.

"I'll get the quilt back to you next time I'm out this way, Hubert. May not be for a couple of weeks. That be all right?"

"Keep it. Molly sewed so many of those things that I have more than I'll ever need. I bought her that sewing machine a month or two before she died. Thought it would make it easier on her but she never really had a chance to use it, and every time my oldest girl sits down in front of it, she can't see what she's doing or pump the pedals for crying so it's no use to us right now."

"It'll more than cover your taxes. I'll hold onto the money that's left over, and next time you're in town, you can stop by the office to pick it up."

Mr. Sullivan nodded. "Let's get her loaded. I've got chores to do."

Papa held out his hand. "Thank you, Hubert. We'll take good care of it."

They shook hands, picked up the sewing machine, and brought it to the wagon. As Papa secured it with some rope he had in the back, Mr. Sullivan tipped his hat to me then turned to walk around the side of the house.

"Good-bye, Mr. Sullivan, it was a pleasure meeting you," I called after him. He waved his hand without turning around and continued on his way.

I watched Papa tie the thick rope then tug on it to make sure the sewing machine wouldn't slide or turn over. It wasn't an odd thing for people to pay their taxes with whatever they had to spare. Papa often brought home things he'd collected from people who had run into hard times and couldn't pay with money. When that happened, I'd seen Papa buy everything from shoes to tools to help the family out. And Mama usually got in on the act by putting together a big basket of food for him to take to them.

She would be thrilled with a sewing machine and would probably start adding a few items of clothing to her food baskets. Loney would love it, too, but with my lack of sewing skills, I couldn't see the value of owning such a thing. It was just something else that would need to be dusted.

Chapter Eight

Spring 1899

That boy's more slippery than snot on a glass doorknob.

That winter was, indeed, bitter but I've never known a harsher one than the following year. Cold and snow descended on Hot Springs in mid-November, 1898 and stayed well into March, 1899, grabbing us by the throat and squeezing hard as if to wring the very life out of us. In some cases, with some families, it succeeded.

Our family came through it all right, though Mama spent a great deal of it sick with one illness or another. She had the care of Green and Thee in the mornings and early afternoons, but almost as soon as I set foot inside the door after school, she took to her bed with a headache or some other complaint. I was always sending Roy to fetch Dr. Hudson to tend to her. I swan, poor Doc Hudson spent almost as much time at our house that winter as he did at his own.

I had the best part of the housework and the care of the children on my shoulders during the afternoon. At times, that irksome winter seemed as if it would drag on and on forever. I think the only times I smiled and meant it were the days when Papa would come home, kiss me on the forehead and say, "Damn, Bess, I don't know what I'd do without you, girl."

That helped, but I admit I spent most of my time in a high state of resentment toward Mama for being so weak and sickly. I hated housework and I learned pretty quickly the things that absolutely had to be done; cooking dinner for all the hungry mouths, keeping Thee in clean diapers and the rest of us in fairly presentable clothes. I also learned the things

I could scrimp on without anyone noticing: the corners in the parlor that seemed to sprout cobwebs on a daily basis, the beds which sometimes went for days without being made, and the furniture that often went without seeing a coat of wax for weeks. And I learned what chores I could put off on Loney and Roy.

Loney had a good hand with a needle and thread and, with the sewing machine to make the chore easier, she took care of all the mending and sewing. She also helped with the washing and the kitchen chores. Ever a maternal soul, she tended the baby and kept Green entertained, an intimidating job at times because he was a curious, bright child, always into something or other. For such a little thing, he could move fast and was as slippery as a gob of grease through a goose.

As for Roy, he took a growing spurt that winter, as if stealing the energy from the frozen ground and absorbing it into his body. I swear to Goshen, he ate anything that didn't eat him first and sometimes grew as much as an inch a day. Papa said he was getting his man growth early and it would taper off after a while. By the time the first violets opened in the early spring sunshine, he'd grown almost as tall as Papa and towered over me though I wasn't short by any stretch of the imagination. I didn't like him being bigger than me, except it came in handy for chopping and splitting firewood, keeping a steady supply of it inside for fires, and tending the fires in the fireplaces. He shoveled paths to the outhouse, to the barn, to the street, and even cleared an area for the young'uns to play outside when the weather cooperated. With all that growing and all that work, he was, by the end of winter, shaping up to be a fine specimen of a man. Not that I would ever say as much to him.

I grew, too, though not as much as Roy, and more internally than outwardly. Always having one or another of my brothers or sisters around seemed to bring out the ornery in me. I discovered a longing for time to myself, time to sit, drink in the blessed silence and do nothing but think. I begged for a diary that Christmas and Papa obliged me. Mama disapproved and Aunt Belle told him the only thing a diary would do was make me more broody, but he just smiled and told them to hush.

After that, the old cantilevered barn out behind the house became my favorite place. I spent every minute I could in the dusty coldness of its loft, writing and pondering what I wanted to do with my life. At 18 years of age, the whole world seemed open to me and I loved nothing more than to contemplate what my future would hold. During these cherished moments, my mind often turned to Fletcher Elliott and the feelings I'd had for him. Although much time had passed since I'd first seen him walking toward me, his image would not leave me and I began to wonder if he was truly destined to be my husband, as my cousin Caroline suspected.

Whenever I could, I sneaked out of the house, climbed the sturdy ladder, and curled up on a quilt I'd placed in one corner, where I stared out the loft window at the sky, lost in dreams. A habit, I admit, that stayed with me for the rest of my life. The hayloft became my sanctuary as I practiced the fine art of daydreaming and I'm sure those precious moments alone with only myself for company kept me sane during those long months when I spent most of my time chasing after dust, dirt, and children or fetching and carrying for Mama. Even after the winter ended, the loft remained my favorite spot. I went there many times over the next few years as I grew into a woman. It was there I finally decided what I wanted to be, and the year I turned twenty, it was there I cried over my broken heart and made the decision that almost shattered the heart of the one who'd broken mine.

At Christmas, I tried my fortune again, but as I suspected, I couldn't tell which holly berry popped first when I threw them into the fire. Was it the one I'd named Fletcher Elliott? I hoped so since none of the other men I'd named held any appeal at all for me. We had a stretch of clear weather in January and I went out every night to count nine stars. On the ninth night, I placed a mirror under my pillow and I did dream about Fletcher, but that didn't surprise me at all. I'd dreamed of him many nights since I'd first met him.

I eventually convinced myself of the foolishness of trying

fortunes. If I was meant to marry, I would, and only God knew who He would send to me for that purpose.

When the cold weather finally loosened its grip on the mountains that year, spring tiptoed in on gossamer slippers with a gauzy cloak tossed jauntily over her shoulders for warmth. The days lengthened and the sun grew stronger, burning off the mountain mist earlier and earlier every day. It was then, when spring finally made up her mind to settle in and stay with us for a spell, that Death crept back into my life. Or perhaps, Death never left. Maybe It had hunkered down beside one of the fireplaces or in the corner beside the wood-burning stove in the kitchen and wiled the time away, weaving evil plots and chuckling over the trouble It would bring in the spring of 1899. The snow melting was Its signal, and It rose, stomping and storming like a surly, ravenous bear, just awakened from hibernation, ready to devour the first sign of life It ran across.

It struck on the last Saturday in April, swift and sure, giving us no time to act and leaving us without a single defense against It.

Mama had perked up with the warmer weather and on that Friday evening, perhaps thinking of Mayday which was more or less the official start of spring in the mountains, said we needed a celebration of some sort to welcome spring. Papa suggested we go to the creek in the woods that backed up to our house for a picnic the next day. We could wade in Spring Creek, chase butterflies, pick wildflowers, or do whatever we needed to shake the dust of winter off of us.

The children were excited and pestered me no end that morning as I fried the chicken Roy had killed for our outdoor feast. I guess I'd gotten up on the wrong side of the bed because I was cranky and jumpy.

Just as I took the chicken out of the skillet to let it drain and cool before I packed it in a basket with fresh baked biscuits and some of the jam Mama and I had put by last summer, Mr. Norton knocked on the back door. He wanted Papa's help at the inn with some silly problem I felt sure could have been handled without him. In my eyes, that was reason enough to cancel the entire outing but Papa insisted we go on ahead and said he'd join us at the creek as soon as he could.

I wanted to protest that we could wait on him, but he kissed Mama and Thee, tousled Green's hair, and was gone, leaving me fuming at the stove.

Green, who had spent the entire morning getting under my feet, clapping his little hands in excitement and urging me continuously to "Hurry, Bessie, hurry," latched onto my skirt and yanked, almost pulling me over. I slapped his hand away and threatened to spank him if he didn't leave me alone. He screwed his face up, a sure sign tears were imminent, so I hollered for Loney to come and take him off my hands.

Green, of course, didn't understand my surliness, and though he went willingly with Loney, I could hear him crying out in the backyard for a long time after. I didn't think to temper my ill mood then, though I've regretted it many times since that day.

When the basket was finally packed with food and plenty of napkins to wipe greasy fingers and chins, Roy hoisted it up with a dramatic grunt and we set off to Spring Creek.

"Should we go up to the falls, Bess?" he asked.

I knew by the time we got that far, I'd be carrying Thee and most likely Mama, as well, so I shook my head. "That's too far for Green to walk. Let's just go down where it bends toward town and we'll eat there. Then if you want, you and Loney can take Green for a walk up to the falls."

He nodded and took off for the path to the bend. Loney fell into step behind him, holding Green's hand tight in hers, keeping him from chasing off into the woods after a butterfly or a bird or whatever caught his fancy.

"Hold onto him, Loney, you know how quick he is."

"I've got him." She patted Green's hand as he bounced in excitement beside her. "We're going to have us a picnic by the creek, little man."

Green's smile was bright enough to challenge the sun and his brown eyes sparkled with anticipation. "Hurry!" he demanded and we all laughed at his impatience.

I took Mama's hand in mine while holding onto Thee with

the other and we made our slow way to the creek. As we walked beneath the trees, a chill raced up my spine. I foolishly shook it off, putting it down to the old adage about geese and future gravesites. That got me wondering where my grave would be and I tried to ignore the nerves tangling themselves into a tight knot in my stomach. Just hunger, I told myself. It had been a long time since breakfast. If Elisi had been with me, I would have told her about the feelings and things might have turned out different.

When we got to the creek, Roy spread the quilt beneath a huge oak tree with the leaf buds just beginning to pop open. After I got Mama and Thee settled, I set out the food. It was a fine day, with the birds singing, a breeze blowing, and the creek babbling merrily. I could think of no better place to be than sitting beside the happy creek with its sloping banks dotted with ferns and a few early wildflowers except maybe my hayloft. Still, the creek soothed my nervousness and set me to dreaming about long summer days when I could spend more time in my little corner of the barn.

We had a high-old time while we ate, with Mama telling us stories of her childhood. I begged her to tell about how she met and married Papa. I loved hearing about Papa as a young man and how Mama had first seen him working in the blacksmith shop, shirtless, dirty and covered in perspiration as he bent over the anvil.

He'd taken her breath, she said, and giggled like a schoolgirl. Her cheeks a rosy pink, her eyes gleaming with love, her smile lighthearted and untroubled, I could see exactly why Papa had been so smitten with her the first time he saw her. I wished fervently that she would be like this more often.

"Tell us some more, Mama," Loney pleaded.

"Oh, child, with all this talking, my throat's as dry as a sinner's in a cyclone. Bessie, why didn't you think to bring something to drink with us?"

I shrugged, torn between her calling me Bessie and her complaining that I'd forgotten to pack something to drink. Before Mama could say anything about my shrug, I picked up the almost empty jam jar and handed it to Roy. "Dump the rest of the jam under that Mountain Laurel bush over there for the birds then go wash the jar out in the creek and bring Mama some water. I'll get everything put away and after that we'll take a walk."

"I can wait for a while," Mama said. "You go on, Roy, take Loney and Green down to the creek. I'll stay here with your sister and take care of Thee." She glanced lovingly at Thee, resting his head in her lap, his eyes heavy.

"May we go in, Mama?" Loney asked.

Mama smiled and I knew it pleased her that Loney had remembered to say *may we* instead of *can we*. "Law, girl, that water most likely still has ice chips floating in it. You'd freeze inside of a minute."

"I know, Mama, but can we take our shoes off and wade?"

Mama frowned this time. "'May we, Pauline, may we. I suppose, but just to wade. Don't let Green go out too far and for lands sake hold onto him."

I could see Loney fighting a frown. She didn't like being called by her real name any more than I did. "I'll keep a tight hold on his hand, Mama. I promise."

I stood up, dusted off my skirt. "You and Roy both keep a hold on him. That way he'll be safe and Mama won't have to worry. Now go on."

I waved a hand at them and watched as they walked down to the creek, Roy and Loney holding one of Green's hands in their own and swinging him in the air every few steps. Green's chortling delight made me smile as I packed up the leftover food. Mama smoothed Thee's hair from his face, a soothing ritual that would carry him to sleep. She sang softly, humming when she forgot the words and keeping her eyes lovingly on Thee the whole time. Then Green screamed and her head jerked up but it was only enjoyment that had that disquieting sound tearing out of his throat.

"It's all right, Mama. Roy's teasing him, that's all," I said.

She smiled and went back to watching Thee whose sleepy eyes drooped lower with every pass of Mama's hand.

"Would you like me to leave one of these biscuits out for you, Mama? You hardly ate enough to keep a bird alive."

She looked up and surprised me when she smiled and said, "No, thank you. You're a good girl for thinking of your mama, Vashti Lee." Then she looked back down at Thee.

"Thank you, Mama," I murmured.

I lost myself in a little soul-searching then, thinking maybe I should be nicer to Mama and try to please her more. I'd spent most of the winter holding her responsible for all my displeasure with life. I was getting too old to blame all my problems on other people, and for the first time, I considered that I had been unfair when it came to Mama. But those thoughts wouldn't last long thanks to my contrary nature.

Her soft voice just a whisper on the air, Mama sang her favorite hymn, "Rock of Ages," as she lulled Thee to sleep. Watching her, I couldn't help but wonder if she had ever loved me as much as she loved Green or Thee, who were her favorites, or even as much as she loved Roy and Loney. It seemed to me Mama and I had been at cross purposes since the day I was born. She wanted me to be her perfect little lady and I wanted to be my own person.

To this day, my stupidity about my mother amazes me. It wouldn't be long before I saw her as the woman she really was, but on that day, I still saw her as a fragile, delicate creature. Worse, I often thought of her as nothing more than a constant complainer.

We heard a roar from the creek and then Green screamed, this time in terror, backed up by Loney shrieking in fear and Roy's shouts of alarm. Mama's head snapped up again, her eyes darting to the creek, searching for Green but she couldn't see him because of the slope of the bank. She froze as the color drained out of her cheeks and a low moan seeped out of her throat. Then she threw her head back and screamed, the piercing screech seeming to hit the mountains and echo back to us. Thee startled, jumping so violently in Mama's lap I thought for sure he would roll off. Terrorized by Mama's actions, he began to cry. She held on to him, clutching him to her breast as she rocked back and forth, sobbing as if the world had just ended.

A sick and ugly dread filled me as I watched her and my

blood ran cold. I forced myself to get to my feet and run for the creek. I'll never know if those few seconds I sat there transfixed on Mama could have changed what happened. I asked Papa one time and he said, "No, Bess, nothing and no one would have made a damn bit of difference."

As I topped the bank and went down, I couldn't believe it was the same creek. Spring Creek on most days was a wide, placid trickle of clear water that flowed peacefully down the mountain, gathering into a pool here and there because of a well-placed beaver dam.

That day, mud had turned the water brown, debris floated and bobbed on its murky surface, and it reached a good three quarters of the way up the long, sloping bank. I knew what had happened. Spring storms up in the mountains coupled with that year's abundant snowfall melting in the warm weather had created a flashflood the likes of which I had never seen before.

Green, perhaps hearing the roar of the approaching water or the silence of the birds and frogs that had been singing blissfully all day, must have broken free from Loney and Roy and raced straight for the bank just as the water tore around the bend. Small but as fast as lightning at times, he never stood a chance against that crushing force of nature.

Loney stood frozen, her hands to her mouth, as she watched Roy, at the very edge of the roaring waters, his eyes darting this way and that, searching for our little brother. I thought I caught a flicker of Green's blue shirt far on the other side of the creek before it disappeared in the swirling brown stream. My heart stopped for a moment and I grabbed Roy's arm just before he could jump in to try to save Green. Roy fought like an angry mountain lion but I desperately held on. If he went in, we'd lose him, too.

I had to slap him to get him to settle down and listen to me. Taking his shoulders, I gave him a good shake. When his wide, disbelieving eyes finally focused on me, I yelled, "Go get Papa. You hear me, Roy? Run as fast as you can for Papa."

He looked back at the water, which had started to abate, then scrubbed his hands over his face, wiping at the tears falling from his eyes.

I shook him again. "Roy, do as I say. Go get Papa right now!"

He nodded and turned to walk back up the bank.

"Run," I yelled. He hesitated for a fraction of a second before he took off, stumbling a bit at first before finding his balance as he clambered to the top.

I ran over to Loney, crumpled into a heap against the trunk of a maple. Reaching down, I yanked her to her feet. I didn't have time for her histrionics. "Loney, go up to Mama. Tell Papa to come down here when Roy brings him. I'm going to look for Green. I'm not going to leave him."

She grabbed my hand. "Promise me you won't go in the water, Bessie, promise me."

I shook her off. "Go, Loney, Mama needs you now."

She looked at me, her face pale and streaked with tears, and I heard the words even before she spoke them, "Yes, ma'am."

No one had ever called me *ma'am* before. I wasn't old enough to be a ma'am. A miss or young miss or even a young lady, but not a ma'am.

After Green's death, I would never be a miss or a young anything again.

Death, in Its devious way, not only stole a life that day, It took what was left of my youth with It.

Chapter Nine

Spring 1899

Mad enough to spit in a wildcat's eye.

I ran alongside the crest of the bank watching the flood waters recede, hoping for a glimpse of Green. Winded, I slowed down then stopped, remembering Mama and the others. I prayed Papa would get here soon and help me find my little brother. I glanced behind me, thinking I was a good half-mile away from where Green went in. I studied the winding creek in each direction, my gaze combing the banks on each side, whispering a prayer to myself. I wanted to search until I found Green but knew Mama needed me. Reluctantly, I returned to our picnic area to wait for Papa.

Loney sat under the tree, holding Thee, and Mama lay beside her on the quilt, sobbing. I was fairly certain Loney hadn't said a word to her about Green but Mama knew. Like Elisi and me, she had that extra sense that often told her when things were going to go wrong. Unlike Elisi and me, she had turned away from her gift at a young age and most days paid no heed to it at all. That day, though, there couldn't have been any way she could ignore the inner voice whispering to her that her child was dead. I know mine seemed loud enough that I wondered Loney, who didn't share the sight with Elisi, Mama and me, didn't hear it screaming the dreadful news of Green's death.

I heard running footsteps and looked up to see Roy, Papa and Mr. Norton hurrying toward us. Without paying us any heed, Roy and Mr. Norton ran past us to the creek, both shouting for Green, their voices bleeding away as they followed the water.

Papa knelt by Mama, pulled her into a hard embrace. He pressed his face into her hair and said in a rough voice, "I'll find him, Cindy, I'll find our boy." He rose to his feet, his gaze shifting to me. "Get your mama home, Bessie." He turned to Loney. "Fetch your Aunt Belle. She'll know what to do for your mama."

"But, Papa, I want to help..."

He shook his head. "Not now, Bess. See to your mama." His focus was already on the creek bed as he ran in that direction.

I hesitated, not wanting to leave, wondering if I had paid attention to that chill I'd gotten earlier if I could have saved Green. It was to be the first of many inner battles I carried on with myself over the next years.

As if in a daze, Loney rose to her feet, Thee in her arms. I helped Mama stand. She swayed and I reached out to her but she grabbed onto the oak tree and leaned her forehead against the rough bark. "My baby's gone, Bess," she sobbed. "I can't stand the thought of it."

I bit my lip and swiped at my eyes, telling myself she was wrong, she had to be. Ignoring that horrible inner feeling whispering Mama was right, I told myself Papa would find Greenie and bring him home and everything would be just fine.

Loney hefted Thee onto one hip and wrapped an arm around him, the other one around Mama. She spoke in a soothing tone as she led Mama away.

I cleared my voice then called out, "Papa will find him, Mama. Y'all go home, like Papa said. I'll catch up."

I watched for a moment, Loney so young and small, already carrying the burden of a grown woman. I placed the abandoned picnic basket on the ground then shook out the quilt and folded it carefully, making sure each corner squared up, smoothing the wrinkles from the material, using this rote task to try to repress the image in my mind of raging water crashing over a small blue shirt. When I finished with the quilt, I laid it across the top of the basket. As the breeze picked up, I heard Loney singing a lullaby to Thee to keep him calm, or maybe it was to soothe Mama.

As I followed them, I thought of going back to the creek and watching for Green. Although I knew the chances were slim, he could still be alive, clinging to a tree limb or already washed up on the bank. If not, his body would have to surface sometime and I didn't think it was right not to look for it or be there to see him off on his way to the next life. Maybe sing him a hymn to light his way. Don't think about that, I told myself.

At the turn in the path, I looked back over my shoulder, trying to see the creek and hopefully catch a glimpse of Green's bright blue shirt, but I couldn't see anything beyond the peaceful shady clearing where we'd had our picnic. That was when the tears finally came and I made no effort to stop them.

When I got back to the house, Loney stood in the kitchen, looking helplessly at the shelf with the tins of herbs collected and dried by Elisi for teas and medicine to treat various ailments.

I filled the tea kettle and put it on the stove. "Where's Mama and Thee?"

She swiped at her eyes. "Mama's lying down. Thee fell asleep on the way back. I put him in the bed with Mama. I thought it might help her, seeing..." Her voice broke.

"What are you looking for, Loney?"

She shook her head. "Mama needs something to calm her nerves, but I can't read these. What does that say?" She pointed to a tin.

"They're in Cherokee." I reached up and took down the tin that held the oat straw. Elisi spent a great deal of time gathering herbs and drying them, selling some to the tourists who came to town convinced the warm waters of the springs would cure some illness. Her oat straw tea would soothe Mama's nerves and hopefully let her sleep for a while. Sleep wouldn't cure the hurt, but it would give Mama a measure of peace for a time.

"Here's what you want. This will calm her down and help her to sleep. You go on and fetch Aunt Belle and I'll make the tea."

I took one of Mama's delicate china cups from the cupboard and poured the boiling water over the tea in the teapot. As it steeped, coloring the water soft amber, I got lost in my thoughts. It seemed as if all the color had bleached out of my life except for that pot of tea glowing golden.

Instead of putting the lid on the pot, I cupped my hand over the opening. The steam dampened my palm, reminding me of Green's tears that morning. I lifted my hand to my cheek and rubbed until it was dry again. It bothered me I was the cause of his tears but even more that I had left him in that cold, cruel water. I kept telling myself he could still be alive but my heart knew our sweet little boy was no longer part of this world.

"What are you doing, Bessie?"

I startled at Loney's quiet words and shook my head, embarrassed. "Nothing. Where's Aunt Belle?"

"She's on her way. She needed to send someone to fetch Uncle Ned to help search for Green."

I nodded. "Do you think I should go ahead and take this up to Mama or wait until Aunt Belle gets here?"

"I'd wait if I were you. Aunt Belle will need something to keep her busy or she'll run us all ragged." She hesitated, biting her lip. "Bessie, where do you think Green is right now? I mean, if he..." she hesitated as if she didn't want to say the word "...drowned, has he already gone to heaven or is there some sort of, I don't know, trail he has to walk like Elisi says?"

"You mean to the Darkening Land?"

"Yes. I don't think Green's strong enough to walk for long and what if he gets lost? Will someone be there to help him, to guide him to where he's supposed to be?" She dabbed at her eyes with her apron.

I walked over and took her hand. "Loney, we don't know that he's dead." I stopped and blinked back tears, clearing my throat. "But if he is, I think wherever Green is, someone is with him and will make sure he gets to where he's supposed to be. Angels if it's heaven and the Cherokee Spirit People if it's to the Darkening Land. Why, it wouldn't surprise me at all if God and Elisi's Creator didn't end up in a whopping battle over who gets to keep him."

Her eyes widened. "Bessie, you shouldn't talk like that."

I shrugged. "Why not?"

"Because it's not right, it's…it's wrong, that's all. I mean, that's like you're going against God or something, isn't it?"

I squeezed her hand. "All depends on what you believe. Elisi will tell you that Green's spirit has been taken to the Darkening Land and Aunt Belle will tell you that an angel came down and carried him up to heaven. Mama would agree with Aunt Belle on that one. Even though they're half Cherokee, they turned their backs on their Cherokee beliefs a long time ago when they were baptized in the church. Papa, well, I don't really know what Papa would say. He's never been much of a church-goer or Bible reader. He'd probably tell you to think whatever made you feel better."

"But what do you think?"

I hesitated. This was the first time I'd ever had to put words to my own beliefs, indeed the first time it even struck me that I had a set of beliefs and that those thoughts and feelings could sway others to my way of thinking. Or turn them away from it.

"I believe Papa's right. Every person has to make up their own mind what they have faith in."

A vacillation, of course, but I so wanted to be like Papa who, though he went to church every Sunday at Mama's insistence, never spoke of his own beliefs and never tried to get anyone else to believe as he did. At that time in my life, Papa's way seemed to make more sense to me than the Bible-thumping-you're-going-to-hell-if-you-don't-believe-as-I-do members of our church.

I believed in God, even then, and still do, though we've had our share of differences over the years. But I hadn't solidified my beliefs and it made me uncomfortable to voice them, even to my little sister.

Loney studied my face as if trying to decide whether to listen to me or not. I squeezed her hand then turned to go back to the tea.

"Bessie?"

Before I could answer, Aunt Belle bustled into the kitchen, bringing with her the smell of vanilla and spearmint, a solution she brewed and wore in lieu of perfume which usually had me wrinkling my nose but today was strangely soothing.

She clapped her hands to make sure she had our attention. "Vashti, put that tea on a tray and bring it up right away. She looked around the kitchen and a panicked look came into her eyes. "Where's Thee?"

"I put him in bed with Mama," Loney said.

"We need to move him out of there right now. Lucinda doesn't need to be bothered with caring for—"

I bristled at that. "No. There's no reason to take Thee away from Mama, too. We don't know for sure that Green's dead. We won't know anything until Papa and Roy come back."

"Not dead? How much chance is there of that? The flood swept him up and—"

Loney, usually so passive and submissive, stormed over to Aunt Belle. "There's always a chance the water threw him up on the bank somewhere. Green's a strong little fellow. Maybe he caught hold of a branch and is hanging onto it just waiting for Papa to come save him."

I couldn't stand the thought of being in this house with Aunt Belle spewing her instructions while Mama did nothing but cry. Squaring my shoulders, I said, "I'm going to help Papa and Roy find Green. Mama's got you to help her, Aunt Belle, and Loney can look after Thee."

It seemed to be a day for rebellion. Loney stood up and said, "I'm not staying behind. Aunt Belle can take care of Thee and Mama." She looked at Aunt Belle. "I'm sure Mama will want to keep Thee with her and it'll make it easier for you to take care of both of them if he's in the same room. I'm going to town and get some of the neighbors to help and then I'm going to look for my little brother." She took the tray with the tea from me. "I'll take this up for you, Aunt Belle, then I'll go next door and send Mrs. Culpepper over to help."

Aunt Belle scowled but didn't object to being left alone so I

CC Tillery

went out the back door and headed for the creek. I heard Loney say as I went out, "Are you coming, Aunt Belle?"

Memories of Green ran nonstop through my mind while I walked and I was terrified they would be the last I had of him. Not that they were bad, but he deserved the chance to make more. We deserved the chance to have him in our lives for a good long time to come.

I topped the crest of the bank and gaped at the peaceful scene before me.

The waters had receded almost to their normal, calm level. If the bank hadn't been strewn with limbs and debris, I wouldn't have believed it was the same creek. The water ran clear again and sparkled in the sunlight as if it had never been mud-brown and riddled with broken branches and other detriment.

When I heard Papa shout, I ran toward his voice. It was to be the first time I saw Papa cry. On his knees beside the creek, he cradled Green's limp body, holding it tight to his chest. Tears streamed down his cheeks and I choked back a sob, hearing his anguished cries of pain.

It was just such a waste, such an all-around waste of a life that hadn't even had the chance to get a good start yet. The anger that had been with me since the water carried Green away grew fierce and feral, leaving me mad enough to spit in a wildcat's eye. I looked up at the sky. They say God works in mysterious ways but I just couldn't fathom why He had decided to take our sweet Green away from us. Tears flooded my eyes and my fury overwhelmed me. "Why?" I shouted.

Not bothering to wait for an answer I knew would not come, I turned away, unable to watch Papa grieve for his baby son, thinking it should have been me in that water, not Green. He had his whole life in front of him while I had been graced with more than 18 years. My mind turned to this morning, when I'd slapped his hand and told him to leave me alone. I fell to my knees, sobbing, unable to breathe. Green was so young, so innocent, and I had been so mean to him. I deserved to be in that creek, not my precious little brother. I prayed to God, asking him to turn back time, place my body

80

there, give Green his life back. But, of course, God, if he heard me, decided he wanted Green instead. I couldn't blame him for preferring a sweet, happy little boy over a surly, sulking young woman, although the unfairness of ending such a new, innocent life seemed cruel to me.

I heard footsteps and looked up to see Loney coming toward me. She ran over, helped me to my feet. "Come on, Bessie, let's go home," she said as she put her arm around my waist.

I managed to get myself under control as my sister led me home, her grief borne out by silent tears. Loney eased me into the rocking chair in the kitchen, telling me she needed to feed Thee. I nodded, afraid to open my mouth, fearful I'd start screaming and never stop. The house was quiet and I assumed Mama was sleeping with Aunt Belle watching over her.

Time seemed to stop for me then and my grief carried me away to a dark, dreary place, interrupted when I heard someone approaching from outside. I rose to my feet, wiping my eyes and clearing my throat.

In a parody of the night when he'd brought a dead man home, Papa carried Green back to the house in the creeping twilight and laid him out on our kitchen table covered with an old quilt by someone, maybe Loney or one of the other women who'd come to help. I could hear Loney upstairs, softly singing a lullaby to Thee, and the thought that there would be no more lullabies for Green nearly brought me to my knees once more.

As he had with Mr. Fore, Papa bowed his head for a few minutes in silent prayer. I busied myself pouring water into the kettle to make more tea.

Papa's voice startled me and I almost dropped the kettle. "Bessie, I hate to ask you to do this, but can you take care of him from here?"

I squeezed my eyes shut. I couldn't look at him, couldn't bear to see the agony I could hear in his voice so kept my gaze on my chore. "I'll take care of him as soon as I take some tea up to Mama and make sure she's all right."

Papa touched my shoulder and I turned to him with

reluctance. "I'll go up and give her the bad news and send Loney down to help you." Digging in his pocket, he pulled out two shiny coins. He placed them beside Green's head then stroked his hand gently over Green's cheek. His shoulders slumped and he pressed the heels of his hands over his eyes as if to hold back tears, and I knew he was trying to compose himself before he went to Mama. He dropped his hands and our eyes met, the pain in his mirroring my own. He cleared his throat then turned and walked up the stairs.

I stifled a sob as I set the kettle on the stove, poking viciously at the fire to get it going.

By the time the water boiled, Loney had come in carrying Thee in her arms. She looked so tired I wanted to tell her to go to bed but someone had to stay with Green, so I just said, "I'll be back as soon as I give Mama her tea."

Papa was coming out of the bedroom when I walked up the stairs. His handlebar moustache framed the tight line of his lips and I wondered what Aunt Belle had said or did to make him mad. Knowing her, she probably told him Green's death was his fault because he'd brought death into the house when he'd brought Mr. Fore home on that night long ago.

He didn't say anything to me as we passed each other in the hall. In the bedroom, Aunt Belle sat on the bed, wiping Mama's face with a handkerchief and murmuring soothing words to her. Papa's side of the bed was turned down and there was a dent in the pillow where Thee's head must have rested as he napped. I admit to feeling a small tug of satisfaction that Loney and I had stood up to Aunt Belle about that issue. But that didn't last long. Mama was crying, and I blinked furiously as my own eyes filled again. I must have sniffed because Aunt Belle glanced up and frowned at me and shook her head before looking back at Mama.

"Here, Lucinda, Vashti has brought you a nice cup of hot tea. Let's get these pillows fluffed up so you can rest while you drink it. You know all these tears aren't good for you right now."

I suppose I should have guessed then that Mama was pregnant, but the memories of Green were too strong and the anger at Aunt Belle's suspected words of criticism to Papa wouldn't let me think of anything else. Ignoring her as best I could, I walked over to the bed and set the tray down on the bedside table.

"Here, Mama, lift up and let's get you comfortable. Aunt Belle—"

Mama grabbed my hand and pulled me down beside her. She clung to me like a burr as she sobbed. I was practically sitting on top of Aunt Belle and she had no choice but to slide out from under me.

"Hush, Mama, it'll be all right. Little Green's with the angels now." I said what I thought she wanted to hear, though I myself wasn't sure I believed it. Angels or the Cherokee Spirit People, I prayed someone was with him.

Aunt Belle tugged on my arm, trying to get me to stand up and move out of the way so she could take over the comforting. I ignored her and kept talking to Mama, doing my best to soothe her. Pretty soon, Aunt Belle started bustling around the bedroom, straightening things that didn't need it, adjusting the pictures on the wall and rearranging the silver brush set on Mama's dresser.

I wanted to tell her to go away and leave us alone but knew I couldn't do that. She was, after all, Mama's sister and dearest friend, and I doubted she would leave for a good long time to come. Uncle Ned could starve and wear the same clothes for days at a time. Aunt Belle liked nothing better than being needed, and in her eyes, she was needed more here than at home.

Mama mumbled something, but with her face buried in my shoulder, I couldn't hear what she said. I pulled back a little bit. "What did you say, Mama?"

Aunt Belle tugged on my arm again but I didn't move.

"Mama? Do you want your tea?"

"No, no. I want my baby."

"Thee? Aunt Belle will get him for you."

"No, I want Green. I need to see him, Bessie."

"Oh, Mama, I promise you can see him as soon as he's ready. You know we need to take care of him first."

She sobbed at that. "Johnny, I want my Johnny."

I turned my head, but before I could tell Aunt Belle to go get him, she was out the door, calling for Papa.

"Shhh, Mama, Aunt Belle's gone to get him. Why don't you drink some tea while we wait?"

I reached over for the cup but it had gone cold and I knew she wouldn't drink it like that. Aunt Belle came back in, scowling fierce enough to scare the Melungeon boogie-man himself. She shook her head when I started to ask her what was wrong. Walking over to me, she all but dragged me away from Mama and took my place on the bed.

She put her hand over Mama's ear and crushed Mama's head to her shoulder, in an attempt to keep Mama from hearing what she had to say. "Go down to Rumbough's place and find that no-good father of yours and bring him back here," she hissed. "Drag him by that silly moustache if you have to, but get him here."

I sighed. Papa, when life got to be too much for him, often went to the Annex saloon and drank his troubles away—or tried to. When Mama would fuss at him about drinking so much, he'd grin sheepishly and tell her, "I can't help it, Cindy, the devil's got me." She would, of course, forgive him after a time but this was different. She might never forgive him for getting drunk when she needed him here to deal with Green's death.

I nodded to Aunt Belle then turned and walked out of the room. I needed to find Roy to go with me. Papa could be very uncooperative when he had a few too many drinks in him. He was never mean but he could be as stubborn as two mules.

Roy was in the kitchen with Loney, leaning against the counter, watching as she rocked and sang to Thee.

"Roy, I need you to come with me."

His eyes were red and swollen but he walked over to me without hesitation. "What is it, Bessie?"

"Loney, can you handle things here for a while?"

"Yes, ma'am."

I winced when she called me that. I could practically see the way things would be from now on, me taking on the role of woman of the house, doing my best to raise the children and them coming to me whenever anything needed handling. Mama would be useless and it would fall on my shoulders to make sure the household ran smoothly.

I wasn't ready for that and I sure didn't want it, but I had no say in the matter. Papa, at least for the time being, wasn't going to be much help either, but I was more willing to take on his share of the load than I was Mama's. After all, Papa would eventually stop drinking, but I had a feeling Mama would wallow in her grief for a long time. Probably for the standard year of mourning, at least, and by that time, everyone would be so used to me being the mother of the family that it would never change.

I grabbed Roy's hand and pulled him into the dining room. "We'll be back as soon as we can, Loney."

"Bessie, what's going on?"

I was so mad by that time that I would have not only spit in that wildcat's eye, I probably would have gone toe-to-toe with it and skinned it alive.

Still, this situation wasn't Roy's fault, any more than it was mine or Mama's or even Green's. I took a deep breath before I said something that would end with Roy getting mad and me swinging a fist at him.

"Aunt Belle says Papa's gone down to the Annex and we need to go get him and bring him home. Mama's asking for him."

"Papa's not at the Annex. He's gone to find a tree to chop down for Green's coffin. I tried to go with him, but he sent me back here, said he wanted me to stay in case Mama needed something before he got back."

Well, trust Aunt Belle to assume the worst of Papa. She'd probably taken a cursory look around, didn't see him and decided he'd taken himself off to drink away the rest of the night at the Annex. She never had liked him.

"Are you sure, Roy?"

He nodded. "He said he knew where there was a chestnut tree that would make Green a nice coffin, so he got his ax and a lantern out of the barn and went back into the woods."

"All right, then, you go looking for him and tell him Mama's asking for him. I'll get started cleaning Green up while you're gone."

Roy pushed an angry fist against his eyes. "I wish I could've gotten to him, Bess. I shouldn't have gone for Papa. I should've jumped right into that water and swum after him."

It seemed Roy and I always stayed at odds with one another over one thing or other. But he was my brother and I loved him deeply and couldn't bear the thought he blamed himself for Green's death. I hugged him hard, crying along with him until he abruptly drew himself up and stepped back, wiping his eyes.

"Roy, there was nothing you could do, nothing. The water already had him. If you had jumped in after him, you'd be gone, too. And that would have been even worse for us, don't you understand that?"

Roy looked away but nodded. "I'll go get Papa."

I turned to walk up the stairs to tell Mama Roy was going to get Papa and he'd be here soon, wishing I could give Aunt Belle a piece of my mind but knowing I'd have to hold my tongue.

"Bessie?"

I turned back around and raised my eyebrows at him. He opened his mouth but didn't say anything. After a few seconds, he shook his head and left.

I knew how he felt. There wasn't anything to say. Green's death was a hard blow and it changed every one of us in some way.

Chapter Ten

Spring 1899

He looks like something the dog's been keeping under the porch.

When I got back to the kitchen, I went immediately to Green and stroked my hand over his cheek. Behind me, Loney sobbed and I turned to her, trying to control my own tears. Thee was nowhere to be found and I assumed she had put him to bed. "We need to get Green cleaned up, Loney. I don't want the neighbor women to do it. Can you help?"

Her answer was another sob, so I took a deep breath and went on. "You can do this, Loney. It's important for family to take care of him." She shook her head and I finished with, "You want to send him up to God looking like he does, all dirty like he's been playing in the pig sty?"

She straightened her shoulders at that, using her apron to wipe the tears. "No, I can help, Bessie. I want to help get him ready. What do you want me to do?"

"First—"

Papa and Roy came in the back door.

"Mama's asking for you, Papa. Did you find a suitable tree?"

"I did. Roy and I'll get started on the coffin as soon as I see to your mama."

"All right."

He started for the stairs.

"Papa?"

He stopped and looked at me.

"Do you think we should send someone for Elisi, so she

87

can be at the funeral, I mean?"

He nodded. "Guess we should at that. Roy, run down to Norton's house and ask him if he'd come up here to see me."

"Yes, Papa."

"And come straight back here with him. Don't let him put you off. Tell him it's important."

"Yes, sir." Roy practically leaped out the door.

Papa looked back at me. "That all right, Bess?"

I nodded. "She knows Mr. Norton so it shouldn't be a problem, especially after he tells her why he's there."

He walked up the stairs, leaving Loney and me to conquer the unwanted task of preparing Green's body for the funeral.

"Should I go get Mama, Bessie?"

"No, we'll wait until he's more presentable. I don't think it'll be good for her to see him like this."

Green looked bedraggled with rips in his shirt and pants, twigs and bits of grass in his hair, one little boot on, one lost to the flood, and numerous cuts on his hands. His beautiful dark-brown eyes stared sightlessly at the ceiling and his mouth hung open. I closed his eyes and gently shut his mouth but as soon as I took my hands away, his eyes opened again and his jaw dropped.

I hadn't understood the purpose of the coins but I knew now. I picked them up and placed them on his eyes to hold the eyelids shut.

"Loney, get me a clean handkerchief or a strip of cloth from your sewing basket. The coins will keep his eyes shut, but we need something to keep his mouth closed for now. And check on Thee, maybe take him in to Mama. It might help her to have him to hold. I'll get some soap and rags to wash Green."

She bustled out of the kitchen just as Aunt Belle came in from the dining room carrying the teapot. She took one look at Green and turned as pale as a ghost.

I actually felt a little sorry for her when I saw her hand shake as she lifted it to her mouth and I took the teapot before she dropped it. "Aunt Belle, why don't you go back upstairs and stay with Mama? I'll have Loney bring up some more tea and we'll call you when we have Green ready."

She nodded as she went up the back stairs, something I'd never seen her do before or since. Normally, she would never have thought of using a passage she considered strictly "for the servants' use," even though we'd never had servants and neither had she. The sight of Green's body must have flummoxed her so bad that she forgot herself.

I looked at Loney as she came back in, carrying a lace handkerchief. "You'd better get some tea made and take it up right away. If Aunt Belle goes up the back stairs, you know she needs it."

I almost told her to add a drop or two of Papa's whiskey in the cup but knew she wouldn't do it.

She frowned at me. "Don't give her such a hard time, Bessie. She loved Green and I imagine she's as upset by this as any of us."

I sighed. "I know, but she's always so proper, always acts so prim and respectable that it's strange to see her so unsettled." I brushed my hand over Loney's shoulder then took the handkerchief from her. "Don't pay any attention to me. I don't mean any harm to Aunt Belle and I'm grateful she's here for Mama. She means well and sometimes I wish I was more like her, if only for Mama's sake."

"You hush, Bessie, you're as good as anybody, Aunt Belle included."

I kissed her cheek. Loney was like a she-cat, ferocious and protective, when it came to defending the people she loved. I went back to the job at hand, gently easing Green's mouth shut and tying the lacy handkerchief beneath his chin to keep it closed. "You go ahead and get their tea, and while you're upstairs, get some proper burial clothes for Green from his room. I'll do as much with him as I can to make him presentable and we'll get him dressed before Mama and Aunt Belle come back down."

Loney made the tea and I set to bathing Green for the last time. I tried to keep my mind off what I was doing but I didn't do a very good job of it. By the time I had his clothes off and started the washing, tears were pouring down my face.

When Loney and I had him ready, I sent her to tell Aunt Belle and Mama. I went out to the barn to tell Papa and stood in the doorway for a moment, watching as his tears fell onto the freshly cut wood. Me, I'd about cried myself out and didn't think I could cry anymore, even though the anger hung on like a flea on a hound dog. My belief in a merciful God was sorely tested and I wasn't too happy with the Cherokee way of thinking, either. Elisi had told me the Cherokee think of death as a natural part of life but right then I thought death was more merciless and harsh than natural. I clenched my fists, wishing I could hit something or someone but knowing it wouldn't do any good.

When we got back to the house, Mama and Aunt Belle were just coming into the kitchen. Mama held on to Aunt Belle's arm as if she wasn't strong enough or brave enough to face this alone. When she saw Green, she stumbled toward him, a low, moaning sound escaping her lips. "My baby," she whispered, reaching a shaking hand out toward him, lightly touching his face. "My poor, sweet baby," she said in a louder voice, pulling Green's body toward her, holding him against her and gently swaying, as if comforting a crying child.

Loney flew out the door, a muffled sob following her. I didn't know if I could bear this and looked out the window, cursing God for taking such a sweet, innocent life in such a cruel, violent way.

Aunt Belle touched Mama's arm, saying, "Let's go back upstairs, Cindy. There's nothing you can do for him. Vashti will stay with him."

Mama jerked her arm away and held Green's body tighter. The coins tumbled from his eyes, hitting the table with dull thuds. My heart echoed the sound.

Mama didn't notice. "No! He's my baby. I'll take care of him." Her voice was cold, determined, fierce.

Aunt Belle gave me an imploring look. I turned as Papa came through the door. He stepped over to Mama and gently loosened her hold on Green. I watched as he positioned Green's body on the table, taking care to replace the coins over his eyes. He cupped Green's face in one of his big hands and Mama's howl of agony as he did this was so primitive, so raw, I didn't think I could stand it. I clenched my fists, closed my eyes, and bit my lip, trying to stifle my urge to answer her in kind.

"Cindy, let's get you upstairs," Papa said in a low voice. He wrapped an arm around her, catching her as she collapsed. Picking her up in his arms, he carried her up the stairs, Aunt Belle following behind, her fist to her mouth, tears streaming down her face.

I sat down in the rocking chair. Someone had to sit with Green and it might as well be me. Mama didn't have the strength, Papa and Roy needed to finish the coffin, and Loney would be busy with Thee. I stayed with my little brother through that long, heartbreaking night, remembering all the times I'd held him, played with him, or just watched him doing whatever small children do. I remembered his happiness and curiosity at every little thing, his stubbornness when he didn't get his way, and his all-around goodness. I thought it terribly unfair that he'd been taken from us so soon.

The next morning, the first of our neighbors showed up, Mr. and Mrs. Ludlow bearing a basket of fresh-baked biscuits, the first offering of many over the next few days. I left them with Loney and slipped out the back door and headed to the barn where I could grieve in private. Papa and Uncle Ned had gone to the church cemetery to dig a grave for Green and Mama was upstairs with Aunt Belle. No one needed me at the moment and I craved the sanctuary of my hayloft.

The familiar scent of horses and hay comforted me until I saw the coffin Papa had finished. The sight of it made my knees go weak and I couldn't bear to think of Green spending eternity in that small box. He should be running, jumping, exploring the world but there would be none of that for him now. I wondered how Papa could set aside his grief long enough to find the strength to dig the hole where his little boy's coffin would be placed.

Tears pouring down my face, I stumbled over to the ladder and hauled my trembling body up to the loft. Roy found me there an hour or two later, and though he tried to talk to me, I lashed out at him. He bore my weak punches and cruel words, and when I realized he wasn't going to leave, I turned away from him and buried my face in my arms. "Go away and leave me alone," I told him.

Instead, he sat down beside me and put his arm around me.

"Go away, I said. I don't want you here. I don't want anybody here."

"Too bad. I'm staying."

I looked at him and, try as I might, I couldn't stay mad so buried my face again and let him hold me. Truth be told, it was a comfort having him there but it wasn't enough. Nothing ever could be.

We buried Green that afternoon, as soon as Mr. Norton got back with Elisi. It was a hot day, one that felt more like summer than spring. Sandy Gap Church was halfway up the mountain outside the town and it was a long, solemn trip. With the help of Roy and Uncle Ned, Papa placed the coffin in the wagon and drove it through the town and up the mountain with Mama and Aunt Belle, holding Thee on her lap, riding with him. Elisi, myself, and the other children, along with a good many of our neighbors and town folk, followed along behind. It surprised me when Miss Cordy fell in with the procession as we passed the path to her run-down shack. She walked off to the side, keeping her head down and not talking to anyone, but her bravery touched me. Her name would be on the lips of every gossip in town after this, but she had the courage and compassion to walk with Green to his grave.

When we got to the cemetery, the minister gave a short sermon and we all joined him in saying the Lord's Prayer. Then Papa, Roy, Mr. Norton, and Uncle Ned carefully lowered the coffin into the grave. When they finished, Pastor Bishop read from the book of Genesis while they shoveled the dirt back in.

"In the sweat of thy face shalt thou eat bread, till thou return into the ground; for out of it was thou taken; for thou art, and unto dust shalt thou return. Amen."

After they'd smoothed the dirt and tamped it down, Papa

went to the head of the grave and drove a small wooden cross he'd made with Green's name on it into the ground. Then he simply stood there with his head bowed for several minutes. Mama broke away from Aunt Belle and stood beside him, holding onto his arm, crying, as she, too, bowed her head.

When Mama's tears turned to sobs, Aunt Belle went over and put her arm around her. "Hush now, Lucinda. He's with God now and you need to look to the next one."

My head snapped up as it dawned on me that Mama was pregnant. Aunt Belle confirmed it with her next words. "John, we need to get her home. It isn't good for her to be out in this sun in her delicate condition."

"Delicate condition" could only mean one thing: Mama was carrying again. My heart leaped at the thought of a new baby then settled down when I realized Mama might not carry this one to term with the trauma of losing our beloved Green. She'd lost two babies between Loney's and Green's births, and those were at a time when there was no trauma in her life.

Papa didn't answer Aunt Belle for the longest time. Then he looked at her and nodded. "Your sister's right, Cindy. Let's get you home."

With his arm around Mama's shoulders, he tried to turn her toward the wagon but Mama dug in her heels. "I can't. I can't leave him here all alone, John. I can't. Who'll take care of my baby?" She buried her face in her hands and sobbed.

Poor Papa didn't have a clue what to do and he looked helplessly at Aunt Belle, who only scowled at him. Then he looked back at Elisi, standing beside me. She took my hand and pulled me forward with her. "Come, child, let's help your mother into the wagon and take her home."

"Is Mama carrying?" I whispered.

Elisi frowned at me and I could see she was worried. "It seems she is."

My stomach churned, a feeling that came from nowhere, and I didn't know what it meant. I held onto Elisi's hand. She'd always told me babies were something to be celebrated but she didn't appear to be too happy about this one. A shiver ran up my spine and I gripped her hand harder. "Elisi, what's going to happen?"

She shook her head and directed her attention to Mama, whispering something in Cherokee in Mama's ear as she hugged her. When Mama's crying quieted, Elisi looked at Papa and said, "Pick her up and carry her to the wagon and get her home as quick as possible. Don't wait for us, we'll be along directly. Elizabeth, go with your sister. When you get there, brew her some tea and keep her quiet. All this crying is as bad for her as the heat."

Papa swung Mama up into his arms and took her to the wagon. He set her gently on the seat, climbed up beside her and waited for Roy to help Aunt Belle up. Loney handed Thee to her and stepped away as Papa snapped the reins.

I hung back, gripping Elisi's hand in mine to keep her with me as the others fell in behind the wagon. When everyone was far enough ahead that they couldn't hear us, I said, "Elisi, what did you see?"

"Do not worry, child, your mama will be all right but you and your sister will have to take very good care of her for the next few months."

"When will the baby be born?"

She frowned and looked off into the distance. After what seemed like an eternity, her eyes cleared and she looked back at me. "Usgiyi."

"What does that mean, Elisi?"

"Your sister will be born under the Snow Moon."

"The Snow Moon? When is that, in January?"

"December."

"So maybe by Christmas we'll have a new baby in the house. I'll have another sister."

Elisi sighed. "I hope so."

I grabbed her hand and drew her to a stop. "You only hope, you don't know?"

"No one knows everything. This could be a brother for you instead." She distracted me, putting a stop to my questions by saying, "Open your heart and see if you can tell me."

I shook my head. "I don't have the gift like you do, Elisi. I mean, I have it, but it's not as strong in me as it is in you."

"It will come, Granddaughter. With time, it will come."

That wasn't good enough for me but she wouldn't say anything else. I walked along beside her and thought about the baby sister I would have in December, the month of the Snow Moon.

Chapter Eleven

Spring 1899

Like two peas in a pod.

To my surprise, Papa asked Elisi to stay with us after the funeral. Her agreement stunned me even more. I know it made Papa nervous having her there because she didn't like him. He was uncomfortable around her, but since the only other option was Aunt Belle, he swallowed his discomfort. While she was with us, Elisi did her best to ignore him.

Which wasn't hard because he only came home to eat and check on Mama and the rest of us. While there, he did everything he could to avoid Elisi. He stayed out all one night and Aunt Belle hinted that he was drinking, but I knew he was at the town's small jail guarding a prisoner. When he came home the next day to get the wagon so he could take his captive to Marshall, the first thing he did was go upstairs to see about Mama. Elisi's dark eyes followed him the whole time he was in the room, but she didn't say anything to him, only smiled a bit when he kissed Mama on the forehead and asked her if she would be all right while he was gone. I remember thinking maybe Elisi's time with us would heal whatever rift existed between them.

It wasn't so much that Elisi disliked Papa as she didn't trust him. A part of her life had been spent hiding with her family in the mountains in order to avoid being forcibly moved west. When the government finally gave up on hunting down all the Cherokee people and moving them across the Mississippi, she and her family settled outside the town of Hot Springs, along the French Broad River, very close to where they had been hiding all those years. Her daughter, Mama's mother Elizabeth, married Len Henderson, a white man from Buncombe County, and they settled in the little town of Brevard. Although Elisi didn't attend the wedding, she had been present at the birth of all the children from that marriage, seven total, including Mama and Aunt Belle. Ever since Elisi's husband, my great-grandfather, died shortly after my parents wed, Elisi stayed close to her tiny cabin.

I hadn't spent a lot of time with Elisi up until Papa asked her to stay after Green's funeral, but she had always fascinated me. Although she had the gift of sight, she kept this close to heart, knowing some would look upon her as cursed. The only time I remember being upset with her was one day when she hinted to Mama that Green's death was the price Mama paid for marrying a white man. I sometimes wondered if this biased statement didn't take seed and germinate into a dark reality for my mother, like the lone malignant cell that begins the body's deadly voyage to demise.

Having Elisi with me turned out to be a blessing. She kept me from dwelling on Green's death too much, though I still mourned him as did the rest of the family. The house just didn't seem the same without him. I missed playing with him, telling him bedtime stories, hearing his bright laughter and beloved voice. Even the prospect of a new life didn't cheer us up very much but I hoped it would when the baby arrived.

When Aunt Belle came over, Elisi shooed me out of the house, telling me to take some time to myself. I, of course, headed to the barn and my hayloft. With Elisi there, I found myself able to spend quite a bit of time in my sanctuary, a lot of it thinking about Green and wondering if Aunt Belle's prediction about Death coming in threes would prove true. My thoughts also dwelt on Fletcher Elliott but not as much as before. It seemed with Green's death, Fletcher's hold on my mind and heart had loosened. Or perhaps it was only that I had something new, Elisi and her teachings, to engage my mind.

The second Saturday she was with us, Elisi took Loney and me herb-gathering. Loney didn't have much interest in learning about the different plants the Cherokee used as medicine, so she sat on a quilt under a tree and played with Thee while I carried a basket and followed along behind Elisi as she looked for plants to gather.

"What are we looking for, Elisi?"

She smiled. "Raspberry leaves for after the child is born. It will make a good tea for strengthening your Mama. And nettle. We should give her nettle tea every day before the baby comes. It will make her stronger."

I nodded. "I know where to find both of those but we'll have to go nearer to the creek." I wasn't too sure I wanted to go back there this soon after Green's death.

Elisi waved at the small field of wild oats in which we stood. "First we'll gather oat straw. It's good for your mother's nerves and calms her enough so she can rest."

I already knew that, of course, since that was the tea I'd made for Mama on the day Green died. It relieved me I hadn't given Mama something that might have hurt her pregnancy in some way. But then, I hadn't known she was carrying at the time I made the tea. I'd only been trying to soothe her nerves and calm her down so she could sleep for a bit.

"Elisi, could I have hurt Mama by giving her something without knowing she was carrying?" I asked as I reached out to break off the top of one of the sheaves.

Elisi stayed my hand. "No, not that one, this one over here."

I shrugged. I didn't know why she'd stopped me from picking that one, but since she knew more about the process, I followed her deeper into the field. Besides, I wanted to know the answer to the question I had just asked her.

Elisi hadn't forgotten. "It is always good to know as much as you can about the patient before giving them anything but this time you did the right thing. Most of the medicine plants are safe for everyone and do more good than harm." She looked down at the bobbing heads of the oat straw and spoke in Cherokee before reaching out and picking some.

"What did you say to it, Elisi?"

"I asked permission to take from it and after I will thank it for the gift."

"Is that the way of the Cherokee?" I was curious about this little, wizened old woman, who rarely spoke. My mother had shunned her heritage and never spoke of her childhood, and though I carried one-fourth Cherokee blood in my body, I knew little about them and their ways.

Elisi nodded. "You must always thank the plants." She waved her hand around us, taking in all the bushes, wildflowers and trees, "The Creator's gift to us to heal our sickness, if only we look and listen."

"Is there a cure here for everything, for every illness?"

She nodded. "Yes, everything, if we are wise enough to listen and seek the Plant Spirit's help." She reached into her pocket and drew out a wrinkled leather pouch. She opened it and spilled the contents into her hand. I watched, catching the sparkle of shale, hearing the click of smooth, gray pebbles, bright buttons and beads as they rolled against one another in her small palm. She withdrew a blue bead and placed it on the ground. "A gift," she explained, "for allowing me to take. Now let's go find raspberry leaves." She poured everything back into the pouch, drew the string to close it, and gestured for me to lead the way.

I frowned. "It's pretty far away, Elisi and…and it's down by the creek where Green…"

She waved her hand. "No reason to be afraid of that. He's not there anymore, is he?"

I shook my head. "I guess not."

"Come, I'll tell you a story. It will make the walk go by faster and keep your mind off where we're going."

I smiled. Elisi's "I'll tell you a story" was as good as Papa saying, "Well, if I recall rightly…" And maybe it would keep my mind off Green as we neared the creek that took him from me. "I'd like that, Elisi."

"Long ago, even before the white man came, all the plants, animals, fish, and insects could talk and they lived in harmony and friendship with the People. But as more and more of the People were born, the animals suffered because they were pushed out of their homes. Then the People started making things they could use to hunt and kill the animals for food and clothes. The animals tried to hide and stay out of the way but there were just too many of the People. They would kill with the weapons they had or carelessly step on the smaller creatures and kill them that way. The animals finally had enough and decided to hold a council with one another to figure out what they could do to keep themselves safe."

I took her arm and helped her over a fallen log although she didn't need my assistance. I wanted to show her how much I enjoyed having her with me so held her hand as we walked further into the woods.

"The bears met first, led by the old White Bear Chief, and they all decided to make war against the People but could not decide what weapon to use. Since the People hunted them with bows and arrows, they tried to make their own, using locust wood for the bow. When it came time to make the string, they didn't know what to do because the People used bear entrails to make their strings. One old bear stood up and agreed to be sacrificed so they could use him to string the bow." Elisi held up her hand with her fingers curved into claws. "But when they tried to use the bow, they found that their claws got in the way when trying to shoot the arrow. One bear suggested they trim their claws, but Chief White Bear said no, they needed their claws to climb trees. On and on they argued until they finally broke the council without agreeing on a way to protect themselves, and that is why the People do not ask the bear's pardon when they kill them."

"You mean it's all right for the Cherokee to kill a bear?"

"It's never good to kill the animals without reason, but a bear is better than other animals because they couldn't agree at their council, so there's nothing they can do to keep the People from killing them. The next council was held by the deer, led by Chief Little Deer. He was smarter than Chief White Bear. They decided that unless a hunter asked pardon for the offense of killing them, he would be afflicted with arthritis. The Cherokee were told of this decision, and from that point on, whenever a hunter shot a deer, Little Deer would go to the place of the killing and ask the spirit of the dead deer if the hunter requested pardon. If he had, the kill was considered in balance. If not, Little Deer would follow the hunter to his home where he would strike him with arthritis.

"The next council to meet was the fish and reptiles, who decided to visit dreams of snakes and rotting fish upon the People who hunted them so that they would not want to eat anything and they would die from hunger."

I laughed. "I don't think that would be enough to keep most people from eating. I know it wouldn't stop Roy."

"The fish and reptiles weren't as smart as the deer, but they were a little smarter than the bears. It was the final council, the one among the insects, birds and smaller creatures that made the difference. The Grubworm was Chief of Council on that one and each of them were allowed to voice their complaint. After all of them had their say, the group voted as to the guilt or innocence of the People, with seven votes mandatory for a verdict of guilt. The only creature who spoke in defense of the people was the ground squirrel. This made the others angry and they tore at him with their claws, producing the stripes that remain on his back to this day. The council finally agreed to afflict the people with diseases and this pleased Chief Grubworm."

Elisi stopped beside a bramble of raspberry bushes and looked them over before taking the basket from me and carefully pushing her way into the tangled mass. She asked permission to pick the leaves then quickly stripped some of the branches, tucking the leaves in her basket. I worked my way in beside her and began picking leaves from one of the branches, being careful of the thorns. Before I'd finished, Elisi took out her little bag again and this time chose a sparkling piece of shale which she tucked under the sprawling branches as she gave her thanks.

Fascinated by the whole procedure, I watched her then took her hand again and started leading her to the nettle as she continued her story.

"When the plants, who remained friendly with the People, heard about the councils and what the animals were doing, they felt sorry for the People and decided each herb, shrub

101

and tree would provide a cure for the diseases visited upon them." Elisi stopped, gesturing at the plants and trees surrounding her. "That is why we must care for the plants and bring them gifts in return for what they give us. But when gathering them for sickness, we must not pick or dig the first one or two that we see but wait for the next so that they will not die out and will continue to multiply."

"So that's why you walked into the center of the wheat field before you picked anything?"

"Good, you learn as you go, Granddaughter, as the People did." Looking up at the sky, she closed her eyes then lifted her nose and sniffed. "Storm soon."

I looked up at the sky but didn't see any threatening clouds. "What makes you say that, Elisi? The sky is clear."

"Close your eyes and smell the wind."

I did as she directed and, sure enough, you could smell the rain on the wind. It was just one of the many things I learned from my great-grandmother, knowledge that would stay with me for the rest of my life.

I opened my eyes and smiled at her. "We'd better hurry, rain's coming."

Elisi smiled back and nodded.

"Will I ever be as smart as you, Elisi? I mean, you know just about everything there is to know and I feel so...lacking about so many things."

She patted my cheek. "Time, you just need to ripen a little more."

That made me laugh. It was a good way to think about getting older.

We gathered the nettle which required careful handling to get what we needed without getting full of the stingers. I tried to imitate Elisi, who covered her hands with her skirt and was able to gather the leaves and stems without once getting stung, but I can't say I was anywhere near as good as she was at avoiding the prickly nettles. Elisi knew how to take care of the sting though; it was simply a matter of washing my hands and arms in the creek.

She mumbled something in Cherokee as she washed the

stinging nettles away then patted my skin dry with her skirt. "You will learn a little more every day and one day you'll be full grown and a woman any man would be proud to have."

That naturally brought on thoughts of Fletcher Elliott which, coupled with the thought of a man having me, made me blush. Elisi patted my cheek again. "Still so young but already a woman. You'll have to grow up fast, Ayoli."

I repeated the word slowly, "A-yo-li, what does that mean?"

"Grandchild."

"Oh." I smiled, pleased with the word but I had more questions. "Why do you say I'll have to grow up fast, Elisi? Is something going to happen to Mama?"

She shook her head and stood up, looking off into the forest. "Come, let's go get your sister and brother before the rain falls." She turned and walked back through the trees.

I followed along, in no hurry to end this time with her and wondering why she hadn't told me if she knew what was going to happen. I was never sure whether Elisi already knew what the next months would bring but I think she probably did. With her, the gift was strongest when it dealt with bad things. She could look into the future and more often than not predict when something terrible would occur.

And I don't know if it would have made it any easier to bear if I'd known for sure what was going to happen, as Elisi probably did.

Chapter Twelve

Late Spring 1899

In high cotton.

My upcoming graduation from Dorland Institute on the last day of May of 1899 helped dampen our grief over losing Green a bit, giving us something to focus on and look forward to. Mama had taught herself to use the new sewing machine Papa got from Mr. Sullivan in lieu of taxes and made me a beautiful white dress for a present. Like any young woman, a new dress for a special occasion thrilled me.

The first graduation ceremony at Dorland Institute was indeed special, even more so for our family because I was one of the members of the graduating class. People had begun arriving the day before for this affair and I was excited to see who would be visiting our small town. Other than funerals and church functions, social events were few and far between in the mountains, and the graduation ceremony at Dorland Institute promised to be the most popular of that year. Visitors and family by the hundreds came from near and far, taking the opportunity to tour our town, including the Southern Railway Depot, general store, and popular Mountain Park Hotel with its golf course and swimming pool. Those who didn't stay overnight with the townspeople either roomed at the hotel, one of the town's boarding houses, or at the Institute, which provided beds for the women, with the men either sleeping in their wagons or on the floor of Dorland's ironing room.

I smiled when Papa announced at breakfast that he intended to visit the Mountain Park Hotel that morning. It was a rare thing for Papa to go to the hotel for anything other than to handle a problem. But when there were special events at the Mountain Park or the town in general, he made it a point to drop in at the hotel, his badge proudly displayed on his vest, introducing himself to unknown visitors and chatting with those he knew. Papa liked meeting new people, learning where they were from and what was happening in their part of the country or world. And I suspect he also wanted outsiders to know there was more to the people of Hot Springs than primitive mountaineers, as so many thought. As social as my father, I accompanied him, in awe of the hotel's grandeur and the beautiful people who inhabited it.

Mama wanted to rest before the afternoon festivities, so Loney stayed behind to help with the children. Elisi had taken the opportunity to go home for a couple of days, claiming she needed to make sure things were all right at her house. It was, I was sure, an excuse to get out of town and away from all the people.

When Papa and I set out, Roy walked with us at first but soon became bored with our company and ran ahead to find friends who might be about. As we stepped onto Bridge Street, I noticed hordes of people milling around, chatting in groups or hurrying from one place to another. The road into town was packed with horses and buggies, lone riders on horses or mules, and oxen or horses pulling lumber wagons filled with people sitting on improvised seats made from white oak slats nailed to the frame and covered with a sheet.

Papa stopped to watch one lumber wagon roll by bearing people sitting inside the box in straight chairs, rocking and rolling with the jerky movement. "Lawsy, mercy, Bess, how those people keep from falling all over themselves is a miracle."

I laughed at this, watching everyone sway from side to side, their hands clenched on the arm of the person next to them for support. It was a wonder they didn't tumble over the sides. One thing I was sure the passengers were grateful for was that the wagons were traversing over dry ground. Roads in this part of the country were packed dirt, filled with ruts and runnels. When it rained, they quickly turned to mud and became treacherous to travel.

As we strolled down Bridge Street and over the wooden bridge above Spring Creek, Papa nodded at the men who passed us and tipped his hat at the women. Their reaction to him was, as always, warm and friendly, many stopping to pass amenities. Papa was a handsome man with an outgoing personality and people responded to him in a favorable way. I proudly stood by him, glad to be his daughter.

We turned down the lane to Mountain Park Hotel, rising four stories above the ground, appearing magnificent, like a picture of a large chalet in the Swiss Alps I had once seen in a book. I stopped and stared at it, thinking it had to be one of the most beautiful buildings in the world.

Papa, standing beside me, grunted with a builder's appreciation. "Can you believe there used to be a tavern here, Bess? A place for travelers to stop during the American Revolution or drovers herding their livestock from over in Greeneville, Tennessee down to Greenville, South Carolina." He smoothed his moustache with his finger. "It was a thieves' haven, though. A lot of robberies happened there, as well as murder."

"Really?" I turned to him. "What happened to it?"

"Well, when they opened the Buncombe Turnpike, it somehow got turned into a hotel. Not near as pretty as it is now. The Patton Brothers bought it back in '32, and made it into one of the most beautiful resort hotels in the East. At least that's what I've been told. They called it the Warm Springs Hotel and it had 350 rooms with 13 columns representing the original 13 colonies. The dining room could seat 600 people and as many as a thousand visitors stayed there at a time. "'Course in '38, the stables and the main part of the hotel were destroyed by fire, but they built it back and reopened in '39. After the Civil War, Colonel Rumbough purchased the hotel and made it even grander. That one, too, burned, but it was rebuilt in 1884 by the Southern Improvement Company, and right after that was when they changed the name of the town from Warm Springs to Hot Springs."

I knew the story, of course. This was what inspired me to

change my name when I was eight, figuring if a town could do it, I could, too. But there was nothing I enjoyed more than hearing Papa's version of the town's history. "Why did they change the name, Papa?"

"Well, as I recall, when they were building the new hotel, they happened upon a spring with hotter water than the original springs. Your great-grandmother claims the mineral springs were first discovered by the Cherokee, who believed in their magical healing powers, and I'd say she's right about that. Wonder what they thought when the white man came and just laid claim to it."

"That doesn't seem fair, Papa."

"Nope, it sure don't." He studied me for a moment. "You'll learn soon enough there ain't much in life that's fair, Bessie. And it hurts my heart to think of it."

I leaned against his arm, hoping he wouldn't become melancholy. "Come on, Papa, let's go see who's up at the Mountain Park."

As we walked closer to the hotel, Papa said, "Did you know this hotel's golf course was the first ever built in North Carolina? Of course, it's the bathhouse over the springs everybody comes here for."

"It's so huge, Papa. How many people can stay here?"

"It's got 200 bedrooms, all lighted by electricity and heated by steam." He shook his head. "Ain't we the lucky ones, Bess, out here in these mountains, far away from the rest of the world, with such a modern wonder right here amongst us."

I made a slight sound, envious of this fact. I wondered if we would always have to light our way with kerosene lamps and heat by fireplace and wood stove. What would it be like to spend the night in such a place, surrounded by all that luxury?

Papa's voice interrupted my musings. "The bathhouse has 16 marble pools, Bess, each nine feet long and six feet wide and up to six feet deep. Why, people from all over the country come here just for that."

"Have you ever used the bathhouse, Papa?"

"Nope, never saw the need. I feel right enough, I reckon." He spied someone up ahead and raised his hand in greeting. I sighed. My time with Papa was at an end. It seemed we never had time enough to spend with one another and truly learn what was in our hearts.

I stood nearby while Papa conversed with Mayor Hill, watching the people on the ornate lawns of the hotel until Papa waved me over.

"Come on over here, Bess, and say hello."

The mayor's usual dour expression brightened into a smile when I joined them. "Well, Bess, aren't you looking pretty," he said, nodding at me.

"Thank you, Mayor." I offered a small curtsy.

He rocked back on his heels, tucking his thumbs beneath his suspenders. "I hear this is a special day for you, missy."

"Yes, sir. Today's my graduation at the Dorland Institute."

Papa draped his arm over my shoulder, pulling me closer. "First Daniels to graduate school," he said with a proud tone.

The mayor arched his brows. "What's next, young lady, getting hitched and having babies?"

I stood straighter. "No, sir. I plan to teach."

"Is that right?"

"It sure is."

He turned his head and spat tobacco juice at the ground. Wiping his mouth with one hand, he gestured with the other. "I've got someone I want you to meet, Bess."

A young woman stood near, but I hadn't paid much attention to her. She stepped forward at the mayor's wave and smiled at me. I returned her greeting, thinking how pretty she looked, dressed in a pink and white dress, a large pink bow in her sunny blond hair. Her blue eyes twinkled with health and happiness.

"Bess, this is my niece Alice Hill. She's my brother's daughter from over in Knoxville. She's visiting us this summer and we're trying to talk her into staying and attending Dorland when the fall session starts."

"Oh, you really should consider it. You'd love it there," I told her.

The mayor nodded his approval at my statement. "Why don't you two get acquainted? I've got some business to discuss with John here." Before we could respond, he and Papa walked away, their heads down, talking in low voices.

I turned to Alice. "Papa and I were going up to the hotel. Would you like to walk that way?"

"Oh, yes. It's such a beautiful place, isn't it?"

"Yes, it's wonderful." I studied her, thinking she might be close to my age. "How old are you, Alice?"

"Fifteen." She seemed to consider, then said, "Do you really think I'll like it there? I want to be a teacher, like you, but Daddy says there's no need for a girl to be educated."

"Why, that's backward."

She gave me a shocked look. "Well, he thinks women should marry, stay at home, and take care of their families."

"If she has a mind to, she should. But I don't want that. Not now, at least. I want to travel some, have a career, be independent."

I could tell by her slanted glances my beliefs must be at odds with her own family's views.

I spied Juliette Dorland ahead of us, walking toward the hotel, assisted by one of her sons. I stopped and put my hand on Alice's forearm. "See that woman there?"

Her gaze followed my pointing finger. "The old woman with that man?"

"Yes. That's the wife of the school's founder, Dr. Luke Dorland."

Alice watched Mrs. Dorland for a moment. "Is Dr. Dorland here?"

"No, Dr. Dorland died in 1896. That's her son escorting her."

"Was Dr. Dorland a real doctor?"

"No, he was a reverend."

"Were they from around here?" She gestured at the mountain, thinking, I'm sure, it was such an inconvenient location.

"No. He and his wife came to Hot Springs in the summer of 1886. Dr. Dorland did mission work and needed to rest and heal from his infirmities, so they came here to partake of the springs. Talk was, Dr. Dorland founded a school for Negro girls in 1867 in Cabarrus County, North Carolina, which he started in his own home."

Alice's mouth dropped open. "You mean, colored girls?"

"Yes. I find that such a noble mission but wonder if the townspeople gave him any trouble over it."

Alice stared at Mrs. Dorland's back. "They most likely did."

"Anyway, the Dorlands must have liked Hot Springs well enough to stay here, I reckon. He bought a house on an acre of land on our main street for $800. That sure sounds like a lot of money to me. I wonder if I'll ever have that much during my lifetime."

Alice's eyes brightened. "Do you think a teacher might make that much money, Bessie?"

"Maybe one day." We started walking again.

"Tell me more about the Institute," Alice said.

"Well, at the time the Dorlands came here, there were some three-month schools in the mountains but there wasn't any kind of school here in Hot Springs. When the townspeople learned about the Dorland's background, they asked them to teach their children. Since we didn't have a schoolhouse, they turned their home into a school and ended up with 25 students. The next year, Dr. Dorland used his own money to build a two-story frame schoolhouse on the hill in back of his house and they had 60 students. The third year, almost 90 pupils were enrolled, some coming from far away, so Mrs. Dorland let some of the girls board with them, and they hired Miss Abbie Bassett to teach the older girls to make their own clothes. The fourth year, Dorland had over 100 students, from six to nineteen years of age, and some from as far away as six miles walked to school. That's when Dr. Dorland added two wings to the lower floor of the schoolhouse and hired two more teachers. The school grew so much they built the girls' dormitory the year after Dr. Dorland retired in 1893. That's where you'll stay if you decide to attend."

"What about the boys? Where do they stay?"

"They used to stay in a tobacco barn but now they're boarding in a rental house. There's talk that the Presbyterian Women's Board is going to rent a farm about two miles downriver for the boys next year."

Alice grinned at me. "You sure know the history of the Institute, Bess."

"That's because I've had most all of my schooling there and I've watched it grow."

She gave me an impish smile. "Are the boys handsome?"

Fletcher Elliott flashed into my mind. He hadn't been a student there, and in my eyes, he surpassed the boys I'd gone to school with. "I suppose. I never really paid attention."

She nodded. "Well, maybe I'll see if I can't talk Papa into letting me stay here."

"Wait till you see the girls' dorm. It looks like a castle with crystal chandeliers and beveled glass doors." I stopped. "You're coming to the graduation, aren't you?"

"Yes, of course."

"You'll see then. I'll give you a tour if we have time."

"Oh, thank you. I'd love that."

We caught up with Papa and the mayor, waiting on the steps leading up to the hotel.

"Well, girls, let's go see who we know," Papa said, leading the way.

***

After lunch, I donned the white dress Mama made. We didn't have a cheval mirror, so I had Loney hold our small, round one in her hands so I could see how I looked as I turned this way and that. I liked the contrast between the white material and my dark hair and eyes, wondering if Fletcher Elliott would be present and if he found me pretty.

Mama had made a beautiful corsage for me out of purple lilacs and Papa made a big to-do when he pinned it on my dress. He stood back, smiling wide. "Why, Bess, you're all grown up. I reckon this is the first time I'm seeing it and damn if you didn't turn out to be one pretty young lady."

"John, watch your language," Mama said, but her lips turned upward.

I smiled at her, wishing I could be as beautiful as she.

Roy burst through the front door, yelling, "We better get a move on or we're gonna miss the whole thing."

Since the Presbyterian Institute had no church, the graduation ceremony took place at the Baptist Church next door to the school. Due to the number of visitors, two sessions were held, one in the afternoon and one in the evening. During the afternoon, I sat in the front row, along with the six other graduates, the girls dressed in white, the boys in black, waiting my turn to perform on stage. It was beautifully decorated, with mountain wildflowers and ferns and evergreens lending a stated elegance to the room. Each student of the Institute appeared on stage, some reciting poetry or Scripture, others playing the piano or organ, and some singing. I turned in my seat, looking for Fletcher Elliott, and saw Alice sitting between Mayor Hill and his wife. She smiled and waved, and I returned her greeting. The room was packed and those who couldn't find a seat were lined up along the walls. I glanced outdoors and noticed faces peering in all the windows. The church could fit four hundred people crowded together and there had to be near a hundred outside, looking in. I'd never seen so many people in all my life.

I twisted my fingers together, my stomach feeling queasy, afraid I'd trip when I walked to the stage or throw up in front of all these people. When it was my turn to perform, I stepped onto the stage, biting my lip, trying not to let my nervousness show. I sat down at the piano and placed my hands above the keys, and when I began to play, the world slipped away and my fingers took control. I must have done a fairly good job because everyone clapped when I finished. Some men whistled and stood, showing their appreciation, Papa leading the way. I bowed, my gaze sweeping the crowd, and there, at the back, his eyes searing, stood Fletcher. Our gazes locked and his mouth lifted slightly, his head tilting toward me. My heart quickened and my face flushed as I scurried off the stage and into my seat.

The program ended with the school pastor giving Bibles to the students who had memorized the Westminster Catechism. Afterwards, the guests were invited to wander around and view the student exposition of domestic and science projects, along with selections of their best drawings and handwriting on sheets tacked to the walls.

I walked with Mama and Papa and my siblings, chatting with friends and admiring the exhibits, smiling when Alice caught up with us. After introducing her to Mama, I said, "You ready for that tour, Alice?"

She took my hand. "Oh, yes. It's so pretty, don't you think?" She pointed to the dormitory, standing well above the buildings around it.

"Wait until we get inside but first let me show you the schoolhouse. The two new additions Dr. Dorland added changed its shape to that of a cross. I think that's rather fitting."

As we stepped over the threshold, Alice looked around. "How many classes do you have here, Bessie?"

"Dorland has three levels. Primary is for learning reading and numbers. Students have to be able to read in the Second Reader before they advance into the Intermediate group where they learn basic arithmetic, reading, writing and spelling. Then they go on to the Advanced Department where they learn more difficult subjects such as Latin and algebra. What level do you think you'd be, Alice?"

"Well, I'd say I'd go to the Advanced Department. I'm a pretty good reader and speller but I like arithmetic most of all."

"That's good. Dorland also has what they call industrial training, teaching cooking, cleaning, sewing and home nursing."

"Oh Mama's already taught me all that."

"Some of these mountain girls aren't so good at it at first but Mrs. Dorland says most learn quick enough."

We entered the girls' dormitory which also held classrooms due to the growing number of pupils. "Papa says the dormitory is built in a Victorian style. With its five stories, it looks enormous to most of the mountain folk around here who live in one-story, sometimes one-room homes."

We started up the winding stairway and down the wide hallway on the second floor. I pointed out to Alice the long hardwood benches and showed her how the top sections lifted up for storage. "They're on each floor so students can store their coats and extra blankets." Everything glistened and all the rooms were tidy and I explained that the students were required to clean the dormitory and keep it neat. Alice's eyes shone with delight as she strolled through the rooms, exclaiming at this or that.

Walking down the staircase, she squeezed my hand. "Oh, Bessie, I do hope Daddy will let me attend the Institute. It's just beautiful."

I hoped so, too. I liked Alice's merry nature.

As we stepped outside, the Institute's superintendent walked toward us. In a low voice, I said, "There's our principal, Miss Julia Phillips. When she first came to Dorland, a lot of the mountain people didn't like her because she stopped the Dorlands' custom of giving away donated clothing. Instead, Miss Phillips insisted on treating it as what she called a business transaction. Since many of the folks from around here are poor and have no money, they bartered with the only things they had, produce from their gardens or butter made from their cows' milk, which turned out to be a good thing because it helped the school feed its students. Since each recipient benefits from this system, Miss Phillips is pretty popular here in Hot Springs now."

I smiled when Miss Phillips joined us, introducing Alice to her and telling her Alice might be attending in the fall.

"We would be glad to have you, Alice," Miss Phillips said with a smile. She reached out and hugged me. "We're going to miss you, Bessie. You're one of our smartest students. I know you'll do well in life."

My eyes misted and I managed to thank her without openly crying.

Alice squeezed my hand as we walked away. She leaned close and whispered, "That Miss Phillips talks funny. She isn't from around here, is she?"

I shook my head. "She came all the way here from New York. Her sister Miss Amelia has tuberculosis so they moved to Asheville to be near the treatment center which is located there. Miss Phillips taught at the Asheville Normal and Collegiate Institute for Girls until Dr. Dorland decided he wanted to retire and then she came here." I searched the grounds but didn't see Miss Amelia. "If you attend Dorland, you'll like Miss Amelia. She's one of our best teachers."

Mayor Hill called to Alice and she gave me a quick wave before leaving to join him.

I caught up with Papa and Mama, my gaze darting this way and that, looking for Fletcher. From time to time, I caught sight of him, and it seemed as if he would turn his head just as my eyes met his. I hoped to run into him so we could at least exchange greetings, but whenever I headed in his direction, he would go the opposite way. I wondered if he was avoiding me.

When refreshments were served, we sat on a blanket on the lawn, drinking lemonade and eating ham sandwiches and lush, ripe cherries. The evening session started at eight o'clock and this focused on the older students, with the boys giving orations and the girls doing Whittier exercises. Sewing certificates were handed out and the closing address was given by an out-of-town speaker, to whom I barely listened, I was so confused by Fletcher's obvious efforts to stay away from me.

Afterwards, we returned home, Papa holding Thee in his arms, Mama walking close to him, her arm grazing his, Loney and me holding hands. Roy ran ahead of us, shouting and teasing his friends. I climbed into bed, wondering what lay ahead of me. I wanted to teach but there was no position open at the Dorland Institute. Miss Phillips had heard there might be a new school opening up the following year in Black Mountain but that was some distance from home. I would miss Papa and Mama and my siblings but vowed to myself that if that's where I was needed, that's where I would go. Whether Fletcher Elliott came with me was something I dared not hope for.

Chapter Thirteen

Fall 1899

The Trail Where They Cried.

In late September, shortly after school started up again, Dr. Hudson ordered Mama to bed and told her to stay there. There had been some problems with early labor pains and a little bit of bleeding, and he was hoping to keep the baby from coming prematurely. Mama, being Mama, didn't mind being confined to bed, and since Elisi was there and could handle just about anything that happened, I felt comfortable leaving her.

Miss Phillips had asked me to fill in at the school until her sister returned after a round of treatment from the center in Asheville. It was my first job and one that set me on the course of a profession I continued in for many years. I loved teaching and Dorland Institute was the perfect place for me to start since I was working with teachers I knew and students eager to learn. Still, I told Papa I'd stay at home and help with Mama if he thought it best.

"I know you will, Bess, but I'd rather you not do that. Your great-grandmother can handle things during the day and your aunt will probably spend more time here than at her own home until the baby's born."

Papa was right about that. Many a day I'd come home and find Mama and Aunt Belle curled up on Mama's bed reading, sewing, or just sharing the latest gossip.

Elisi spent most of her time in the kitchen, cooking, working with her herbs, or brewing up different remedies to make Mama feel better. She seemed happier and more comfortable doing that than she did spending time with her granddaughters but always had time to talk to me and explain what she was doing and how it would help Mama.

Between Elisi's home-made concoctions, Aunt Belle's gossiping, and Loney's coddling, Mama was, for the most part, comfortable and content. But she did have terrible bouts of tiredness and seemed to sleep an awful lot. Dr. Hudson told me that could have more to do with her grief than the pregnancy and Lord knew I could empathize with that. The house seemed like a funeral parlor at times without Green's happy laughter.

Elisi and I continued our habit of herb-gathering on Saturdays with Loney and Aunt Belle staying at home to take care of Mama. Those times in the woods, along with the times Elisi sent me to my hayloft to, as she said, "find my peace," were my salvation during those long months between Green's death and the baby's birth.

I sometimes thought I learned more from Elisi than I had from going to Dorland Institute. The teachers there were smart and accomplished in their field and I would use many of the things they taught me in the years to come, but as far as learning about the more practical side of life, Elisi was the best teacher I could have. She knew so much more than any school or instructor could ever know and was generous and patient enough to share her knowledge with me without making me feel as if I were learning anything at all.

Elisi taught me the true history of the Cherokee, something most people, even the academics who wrote the history books we studied at school, didn't know, and how to diagnose and heal most illnesses using the gifts provided by nature. By the time that summer was over, I could recognize the many plants the Cherokee had been using for years to treat sicknesses.

In the woods, Elisi showed me how to gather 'sang, or ginseng, one of the wild herbs she sold and the one which brought her the most money. There she told me about a "whistling woman and a crowing hen" and I decided that was exactly what I wanted to be. And it was in the woods that she told me the story of her childhood which gave me a clue as to why she didn't like Papa. As I suspected, it was more a matter of distrust than dislike, a general distaste for the "white man" because of all they had done to her people.

Elisi was old enough to have lived through the Indian Removal back in the 1830's, when the Cherokee and other Native American tribes were gathered up and moved to the west. She didn't walk the Trail of Tears, or the Trail Where They Cried, as she called it. Her family went into hiding after the Indian Removal Act was enforced and the soldiers started taking the Cherokee people from their homes and moving them to camps. I was grateful her father foresaw what was going to happen and took them into hiding or who knows where I would have grown up or even if I would have existed at all.

Her family lived through those terrible years always afraid that someone would find them and make them leave. I can't imagine what it must have been like for them. When they finally were able to come out of hiding, it was to a world that had grown so crowded with the "white man" that they had a hard time adjusting.

Hearing her stories of what they'd endured made me equal parts sad and furious that human beings could treat their brothers and sisters like that.

One day as we walked into the woods, Elisi reached up, snapped off a leaf and held it out to me.

I knew what she wanted and said, "It's a sourwood or a sorrel tree. The leaves can be brewed into a tincture to treat a number of digestive problems and the sap can be boiled down into syrup. The residue from the sap is called sour gum and can be chewed to treat mouth sores. You can also use the sap or the inner part of the bark to treat rashes."

She smiled. "Good, good." Her smile turned mischievous. "Want to eat?"

I took it from her, made a face when I remembered the tree got its name from the sour taste of its leaves and handed it back. "You first."

She puckered her lips as she shook her head. "Too sour

for an old lady like me. Come, we need to find a buckeye tree for when the baby's born."

"I thought we had everything we needed to help Mama when her time comes."

"We do but buckeye bark can be brewed into a tea that will help ease the pain. In case the raspberry leaves don't work."

Still holding onto the leaf, I twirled it by the stem as I followed along beside her. I knew she wasn't finished talking about what happened to her family when the government decided to move the Cherokee west but with Elisi I often had to bide my time to get the full story. She wasn't like the women at the quilting bee, spilling everything they knew in the hopes of being the first to spread the news. But then, this was her life she was talking about and she had learned at an early age that silence was often the best course when it came to dealing with people.

We walked for several minutes before she said, "When I was a girl, not much older than your sister is now, my father came home one day and told us we would have to leave our home. My mother didn't understand. She'd lived all her life among the white people and there had never been any trouble.

"Father told her that things were different now because Andrew Jackson had taken the side of the white men and could no longer be trusted when it came to the Cherokee. The whites all wanted us out, mostly so they could have our lands, but they'd recently found gold on the Cherokee land in Georgia and they wanted that, too. They started building holding forts to take us to. Then when the forts got too crowded, they built internment camps.

"To keep from going to one of the forts, we had to pack up and hide where the soldiers couldn't find us. And so, even though we didn't walk the real Trail Where They Cried, we walked our own trail just as every Cherokee did who decided they weren't going to be forced out of their homes. We packed up everything we could carry and started out without knowing where we would go. But go we did and over the next few weeks walked through the trees, up and over the mountains, and finally stopped by the French Broad River near where I live now. Father led us to the Painted Rock and left us there for a few days while he looked for a place where we would be safe. When he found it, he came back to get us and we left the rock behind to walk some more. The place he found was well hidden and by a creek so we built a home far back in the trees. And there we stayed until it was safe to come out again."

"How long did you hide, Elisi?"

She waved her hand. "Doesn't matter. We made it through and waited to come out until the time was right. We'd heard tell that the government had changed and Cherokee people were being given money and land if they agreed never to talk of their heritage again."

"Is that why you speak English so well?"

She shrugged. "We had to learn. If we didn't, who knows what they would have done to us? I don't know if they would have taken our home again and sent us out west anyway but we weren't willing to take the chance of that happening. These mountains have been home to the Cherokee for thousands of years and they shouldn't have been able to take them from us but they did. Many were angry but we had to live and so we accepted the new way of life, except many of us were still Cherokee at heart and what the government didn't know was that we continued on with our traditions, speaking our language when no white men were around, living our lives the way we'd been taught.

"I was the first in my family to fully learn the white man's way of talking and I tried to teach the others. We went on for a while without any problems because the white men thought we could be trusted and they didn't seem to really care that we were Cherokee. And many of us did our best to take on their ways, hoping not to call attention to ourselves."

She stopped, turned and looked at me with an expression so fierce it scared me. "We changed but we didn't do it for them. We did it for ourselves and we held the strongest parts of our heritage deep in our hearts so that we could teach our children what it is to be Cherokee."

I took her hand. "I'm proud to be Cherokee, Elisi, and I'll tell anybody I see just that."

She smiled. "You have white blood in you, child, but I think that drop or two of Cherokee blood is strong and it will serve you well. I can't imagine something like that happening to us again, especially now that the white man has moved on to another people, but if it does, we'll need strong daughters like you to preserve our way of life."

"What do you mean they've moved on to another people?"

Elisi snorted. "White men always have to have someone to plague just because they're different. Your uncle came home last year and told me about the latest group to catch the white man's eye."

"Who?"

"The ones who call themselves Black Dutch or Black Irish, the Melungeons."

"You mean like Mama's Melungeon boogie-man?"

"There's no such thing. That's just something white women made up to scare their children into behaving."

"Papa told me the same thing."

Her eyebrows shot up. "Well, that's one thing we agree on. I don't know why your Mama says things like that. Her own family went through the same thing that I see coming for the Melungeons."

"You mean they're going to round them up and make them leave?"

"No, I don't think they'll do that, but they will make it hard for them to continue to live here. Why, there's even some talk of fixing the young ones so they can't have any babies."

I was appalled that people could treat other human beings that way just because they were a little different from them. "But Elisi, they can't do that, can they?"

"Why not? They took our land when it wasn't theirs to take and they made a great many of us move a far distance away so we couldn't do anything about it. Look what they did to the Negroes, they took them from their homeland and brought them over here to live and work like animals. It took a war to set them free, and even with that, they struggle to live to this day. The Melungeons are the latest to catch the white man's attention, and it wouldn't surprise me a bit if they do start rounding them up and butchering them." She spit on the ground. "White men always have to have someone to hate and torment. They're not happy unless they do."

"But Elisi, not all white men are like that. Papa's not and I don't think any of the other men in Hot Springs are, either."

"You might be surprised."

"Don't say that. Papa would never hurt another living soul. It just about killed him last fall to shoot Mr. Fore and Mr. Fore was a very bad man. Why, if Papa hadn't shot him first, he'd have shot Papa and no telling how many others."

"Shh, I don't think your Papa would ever do what other white men do but there are those in this town I wouldn't turn my back on."

"Who?" I demanded.

She shook her head and wouldn't answer no matter how much I pestered her. Finally, I gave up but I never forgot her words and found myself watching the men in town closer than I ever had before. Elisi had lived a long time and I figured she knew more about the ways of men than I did.

She brushed her fingers over my cheeks, catching one of the tears that I couldn't seem to stop from falling.

"Don't cry, ayoli. I'll tell you the story of the Cherokee rose."

It seemed I cried at the drop of a hat since Green died. I wiped my hands over my cheeks. "I don't think you ever told me that one, Elisi. I didn't know the Cherokee had a rose bush named for them."

"When our people were forced out of their homes and made to walk the Trail Where They Cried, the Elders were worried because the mothers couldn't stop crying. Unlike the white man, women are revered by our People and are held as the head of the family. They hold much power within the different clans and are free to choose or reject their mate. The Elders knew there was no hope for the People if the women didn't make it to the new land. They prayed to the Creator, asking Him to give the women strength. The Creator heard, and the next morning when the soldiers made them start walking again, He told the Elders to tell the women to look back down the trail where they'd walked the day before.

"When the women turned and looked, they saw a plant growing so fast it almost covered the trail behind them as they watched. In a little while, far less time than it should have taken, the plants started blooming. Beautiful white roses, each with five petals and with a golden center that the Creator said represented the white man's greed. The stems had seven green leaves, one for each of the Cherokee clans, and were covered with sharp thorns to protect the beautiful flower and keep anyone from trying to pull it up or move it.

"Seeing that, the women felt hope again. They knew they would survive and their children would grow and flourish in the new land. It is a strong plant, the Cherokee rose. I've heard it covers the entire trail now. Some say that for every tear drop a Cherokee mother shed on the trail, a rose bush sprang up, and to this day, the trail is lined with the Cherokee rose."

I looked down at the ground and wished I could see a rose bush spring up where my tears fell.

"Cherokee women are strong and have endured much, Granddaughter. You will need to let your Cherokee blood take over in the days to come."

"What's going to happen, Elisi?"

"If I knew for sure, I would tell you. The only thing I know right now is the next few years will be a trial for you. In the end, your heart will break, but you're strong enough to deal with that, and when you look outside yourself to mend it, you will find the right person to help you."

"Elisi," I said as we walked home, "what do you think was the worst part of the removal?"

She looked up at the sky and I was afraid she would put me off as she had when I'd asked what she knew about Mama and the baby that was on the way. She took a deep breath and said, "For the ones who stayed behind, I think it was probably staying in hiding and knowing that they couldn't help the ones who were unlucky enough to be caught and forced to walk the trail. For those that walked the trail, it was probably the uncertainty of going to a new land without any of their possessions or the possibility that by the time they finally got to where they were going there wouldn't be any of their family left."

"Then maybe the ones who died on the trail were the lucky ones, if it could be said that any of the Cherokee were lucky."

She shook her head. "Maybe they were, but for the ones who lived, it was a bad time whether they made it to Oklahoma or stayed behind."

"I don't understand how people can do that to each other."

She shrugged. "Human beings always seem to look for someone to torment. They've been doing it for many years now and I expect they'll continue to do it as long as there are any people alive."

We'd reached the house and Elisi went upstairs to check on Mama. I turned my mind to fixing supper as I thought about all Elisi had told me. When Papa came home that night, I ran to meet him and blurted out, "Would you ever force someone to leave their home just because they're different from you?"

"Damn, Bess, can't a man even get in the door before he's met with such a question?"

"No, Papa, this is too important. Elisi says there are men here in town that would make us move if they knew we're part Cherokee."

Papa sighed. "Your great-grandmother is living in the past. No one is going to make you leave town just because you have a drop or two of Cherokee blood in you."

"But it makes me different and white people don't like people who are different."

"No, it doesn't make you different. Hell, for all we know, everybody in town is part Cherokee or part Negro or part something or other that makes them different. I'd stake my life on the fact that most of the town people have at least one ancestor, if not more, that isn't purely white. Besides, everybody in town knows your mother is part Cherokee. It isn't a secret."

"Did you know before you married her?"

"Of course I did, and before you ask, your Uncle Ned knew your Aunt Belle was part Cherokee before he married her. What kind of garbage has Elisi been telling you that has you so het up?"

"She told me about what happened when she was little and the government tried to make them move out west."

"Damn, Bess, that was sixty years ago and she was only a young girl when it happened. She can't remember it that well. It's nothing for you to worry yourself over now."

Maybe not, but what if I had Melungeon blood in me? Would the government try to take away my right to have children?

Chapter Fourteen

Late Fall 1899

Barking up the wrong tree.

Although Elisi predicted Mama would have the baby during the time of the Snow Moon, the baby had other ideas. Mama's time came on the first Saturday in early December, under the new moon instead of the full moon which wouldn't arrive until two weeks later. I often wonder if things would have been different if Jack hadn't been so eager to be born and waited until the full moon when most people say things just naturally seem to turn out better.

To my consternation, Aunt Belle banished me from the bedroom simply because I wasn't married. I didn't think that was fair since I'd seen animals giving birth and knew pretty much what it was all about so decided to find Papa and complain to him. From past experience, I knew where he'd be and sure enough I found him pacing in Mama's front parlor. He carried a whiskey bottle in one hand and had a worried look on his face.

"Papa?" I spoke in a near whisper but he still jumped.

"Damn, Bess, what are you trying to do, scare me into an early grave?"

I laughed. Papa always got jumpy when Mama gave birth. He'd paced and worried when Green, God rest his soul, had been born and had done the same thing when Thee came into the world. As far as I could tell, he would only have one drink, but as soon as the baby arrived and Papa got a look at it, he'd take off for the Annex saloon to celebrate. Before the night was over, most of the men folk in town would have heard the news and made their own journey to the saloon to congratulate Papa and have a drink or two with him.

Mama might not understand Papa's imbibing but I thought I did, at least when it came to the babies. That first shot of whiskey was because he loved her so much and felt helpless in the face of childbirth. It numbed those feelings of vulnerability when she was birthing. As for the ones after, they were in celebration of a new child, something Papa always said was a joy and a miracle.

I understood and this time found myself wishing I could join him. I was convinced Elisi was hiding something bad about the birth and had feelings about this one myself. Similar to the day when Green died, they weren't strong and I couldn't put my finger on them but they were there. Right then, I would have loved nothing more than to down a few glasses of whiskey and drown those feelings of apprehension as Papa could. Since I couldn't, I decided to do my best to take Papa's mind off what was going on upstairs.

"Can I make you some coffee, Papa, or maybe something to eat?"

He looked down at the bottle in his hand then up at the ceiling as if he could get a look at what was going on upstairs. "I guess you'd better make it coffee, Bess. It promises to be a long night."

I took the bottle from his hands and set it on the piano. "She'll be all right, Papa. Elisi and Aunt Belle are with her and Dr. Hudson will be here as soon as he can. They'll all take care of her. I wonder what it'll be this time. Elisi says a girl because of the way Mama was carrying, but I'm hoping for a boy."

"Why do you want it to be a boy?"

"I don't know. I guess it just seems right what with Green being gone and all."

Papa squeezed my shoulder. "Maybe you're right but whatever we get we'll all love it."

"Oh, I know, Papa, and I don't really care one way or the other. I just thought another boy would make you happy."

"Damn, Bess, I don't need boys to make me happy. I've

got Roy and Thee, don't I?"

"Yes, you do, but doesn't every father wish for a boy to," I waved my hand, "carry on the family name or take care of him in his old age or something like that?"

Papa laughed, which was exactly the reaction I had been hoping for. "Boys, girls, makes no difference to me, as long as the baby and your mama come through it all right. Besides, I have you to take care of me when I get old. You're going to live to a ripe old age yourself so I won't have to worry about anything. You will take care of your Papa, won't you?"

I laughed and then shivered as a clear picture of Fletcher Elliott popped into my mind and I remembered Sally's words at the quilting bee. Would I have to choose between Papa and Fletcher if we married? I couldn't imagine it.

The back door slammed and Roy raced from the kitchen to the parlor. "Is it here yet?"

Covered in dirt from head to toe, he looked like he'd taken a bath in a pig sty. "What have you been up to?"

He hooked his thumbs in his pockets and grinned. "Baseball game down at the Mountain Park. We sent those Northern sissies back to their fancy rooms with their tails tucked between their legs."

Loney came to the door of the parlor. "If you think I'm cleaning up that trail of mud you left from the back door to here, Roy Scott, you'd better think again. Go get cleaned up yourself and then get busy cleaning up that mess."

Roy sneered. "That's women's work. You or Bessie can do it."

I raised my fist at him. "I'll show you what a woman can do if you don't clean it up yourself."

Loney moved over to stand beside me. "And I'll help her."

Papa chuckled as he joined us. "And if that doesn't do it, I'll show you what a man can do."

"Aw, Papa, you're supposed to be on my side," Roy said.

"No sides here, boy, just common sense. You're as able as your sisters and since you made the mess you can clean it up. You better get it done by the time your mama's up and about or I'll hold you while she tans your backside."

"Aw, Papa…"

"Go on, do as your sister says, but wash the dirt off yourself first. Then get busy on those footprints."

Roy scuffed the toe of his boot on the floor, leaving behind a muddy mark. Papa grinned. "That's just one more thing you have to clean. Better get busy, boy."

I was fighting back laughter by that time. Roy's face had fallen almost to his knees and he shoved his hands in his pockets before turning and walking back to the kitchen, carefully placing his feet on the prints he'd left when he came to the parlor.

Papa put one arm around me and the other around Loney. "Now, why would you think I'd want another boy, Bess? Nothing but trouble and dirt, the lot of 'em. I'll take my two girls over a whole passel of boys any day."

I let the laughter out. "I can't imagine why I ever thought that, Papa. I must've been touched in the head for a minute there."

My amusement and Papa's smile faded when we heard a scream from upstairs. It cut off abruptly and Papa took off at a run for the steps then stopped when Aunt Belle came out of the bedroom.

"Nothing to worry about, John, just Lucinda expressing her frustration at the way this baby is taking its own sweet time being born."

"Is she all right?"

Aunt Belle smiled as she came down the stairs, stopping about halfway to the bottom. "Yes, Elisi's with her and asked me to tell Vashti to brew up some of the buckeye they collected."

"Buckeyes? What good will buckeyes do her now?"

"Not the buckeyes, the bark from the tree. It'll help with the pain a bit. Loney, while your sister takes care of the tea, you should start thinking about supper for everyone. We're going to be a while yet."

"Can I see her?" Papa asked.

"You better not just yet. Let her get the birth over with and then we'll clean her and the baby up and introduce you properly to your new child." She looked down and saw Roy's muddy footprints. "Sakes alive, what happened to the floor?" Before anyone could answer, she waved her hand and said, "Never mind, just be sure it's cleaned up before Cindy sees it."

"Damn it, Belle, I want to see her," Papa said.

Aunt Belle frowned at him then turned to go back up the stairs. "Well, you can't. Cindy would never forgive me if I let you in that room right now. You just go and do whatever it is fathers do at a time like this and quit acting like a fool." When she got to the landing, she turned and looked at me. "Vashti, bring that tea up as soon as it's ready."

Papa opened his mouth but didn't say anything. It wouldn't have done him any good anyway since Aunt Belle had disappeared behind that same closed door that hid the secrets of childbirth from me. Papa looked miserable as he came back in the parlor and picked up the bottle from the piano.

"I'll make you some coffee while I'm brewing Mama's tea, Papa," I told him, but he didn't seem to hear me, so I added, "You don't want to be drunk when you see Mama and the baby, do you, Papa? It'll only upset her."

He shook his head and set the bottle back down. "Damn, Bess, this is hard on a man."

I smiled and patted him on the arm. "I'm sure it is. Maybe you should be glad it isn't you up there in that bed. It's much harder on Mama than it is on you."

I heard him mumble another "Damn" as I walked out of the parlor.

When I took the tea upstairs and knocked on the bedroom door, Aunt Belle pulled it open and motioned for me to come in. I hesitated, surprised to be allowed into the inner sanctum, so to speak. As I walked over to the bed, I realized I was also scared. When I got a good look at Mama, my heart almost pounded out of my chest. She looked as if she'd gotten caught in a rainstorm and ran all the way home, her hair wet and tangled around her face, her nightgown damp and wrinkled, and her breath coming in quick little pants. But her eyes were bright and with her flushed cheeks she looked more beautiful than I'd ever seen her before. Elisi said something to her in

Cherokee and Mama gripped the bedpost with one hand, tight enough to turn her knuckles white. Elisi slipped a piece of leather between her teeth but I could hear her pain even though she bit down hard.

Maybe I didn't want to be here, after all.

Mama's grip loosened and she spit the strip out. She drew in a deep breath, letting it out slowly before giving me a weak smile.

I did my best to smile back, but I was both amazed and scared, and I couldn't get my lips to cooperate. I'd never seen Mama like this and couldn't believe she was the same delicate creature I'd often thought of as more child than woman. That was the first inkling I had that I had truly been wrong all those years when it came to my mother.

Aunt Belle saved me, coming up beside me and taking the cup of tea from my lifeless hands before I dropped it. She handed it to Mama. "Here, Cindy, drink this, it'll help with the pain. Vashti, wet that cloth in the basin and wipe your mama's face for her."

I stood there, dumbfounded. If this was what having a baby did to a woman, I didn't ever want to have one. And I could understand even more why Papa drank while it was going on. If I could, I would bolt from the room and join him in the parlor for a drink myself.

"Vashti, what's got into you, girl? Can't you see your mama needs your help?"

"Posh, Belle, don't fuss at her. She's never been in on this part of it before." Mama held out her hand to me. "Come over here, child."

It was the same hand that gripped the bedpost so tight the knuckles had gone white. I found myself reluctant to chance the flimsy bones of my own hand in its powerful grasp. Elisi walked over and nudged my back to get me going. Aunt Belle slapped the wet cloth in my hand before I got to Mama's side.

Elisi took the teacup from Mama as I knelt beside the bed and gently washed her face while she spoke words I would have never imagined my fragile mother speaking. "It's not as bad as it probably looks to you. I won't lie and say it doesn't hurt, because it does, but if you keep your mind focused on what's to come, the pain's bearable. Just think, Vashti Lee, when all this is over, we'll have another baby to coo over and maybe we'll all be able to get past losing our precious Green. Oh, I'm not saying any baby could ever replace him, but it'll help to have new life in this house, don't you think?" She took the cloth from me and wiped my face. "This is a time for smiles, not tears."

Like the other day with Elisi in the woods, I hadn't realized I was crying. I tried to muster up a smile, but before I could, Mama dropped the cloth and took my hand. Her grip was gentle at first but tightened with each second that passed. Elisi moved up beside me, picked up the leather strip and slipped it between Mama's teeth.

"Breathe, Lucinda," she said.

Mama gave a jerky nod.

I wrapped my other hand around Mama's. "Grip harder, Mama, if it helps."

Her fingers clasped mine tight enough to bruise, but I gritted my teeth and bore the pain. It was nothing compared to what Mama must be going through. Besides, I couldn't have let go if I wanted. This was the closest I'd ever come to admiring her and I hoped she knew what I was feeling. As her hold loosened, I stroked her hand then raised it to my lips and kissed it.

"Are you all right now, Mama?"

She didn't answer, her gaze seeming distant and far away.

Elisi took my arm and helped me stand up. "It's time."

Confused, I looked at her then my head snapped back to Mama, who said, "I have to push." She sat up, raising her knees, and hunched over, grunting with effort.

Aunt Belle snapped to. "Vashti, sit down behind her and brace her shoulders. When she pushes, you support her. Elisi and I will take care of the rest."

I could feel the excitement growing in the room.

"How do you know?" I asked Elisi when Mama relaxed against me.

She shrugged. "It's just a feeling. You'll know when you have a child."

"Oh, no, I'm not ever having a baby. I couldn't go through that," I blurted without thinking.

Mama gasped as she leaned forward again. I did as instructed and wished I could do more. Everything seemed to happen in a blur after that and all I remember is Mama pushing and gasping, working hard to deliver her baby.

Long before the baby arrived with an ear-shattering wail, I knew without a doubt I'd been like a hound dog barking up the wrong tree for most of my life. That day, I had a new respect for my so-called delicate Mama and found myself thinking I needed to spend more time around her. If I did, maybe someday I would be a better woman for it.

The baby's first cry shocked me because I had been so engrossed in watching Mama's face that I hadn't paid any attention to what was going on at the other end of the bed. Mama laughed when she heard it and I was crying again, but these were tears of joy, if not tears of discovery...or tears of regret at the wrong I'd done to my mother all these years. Elisi immediately whisked the baby away to the wash basin. I couldn't see if it was healthy or even if it was a boy or a girl.

Mama lay back in my arms, exhausted. "Frances Ann," she said as if she knew without being told. "We'll call her Frances Ann."

That was how I found out I had a baby sister.

While Elisi washed Frances Ann, Aunt Belle hurriedly took care of the mess on the bed. I didn't move but sat beside Mama, hugging her and wondering at this miracle that had just entered our lives. Not only did God bring us a new baby that day, He showed me my mother in a new light. When Aunt Belle finished tidying up the bed, she shooed me away so she could tend to Mama, and I walked over to get my first look.

"Why, she looks like a miniature Papa."

Elisi grunted as she swaddled Frances Ann in a blanket before handing her over to Mama.

"You're right, Vashti, she does look like my Johnny."

Mama sounded a little disappointed and I laughed. "At

least she doesn't have red hair."

Even Aunt Belle laughed at that and Elisi chuckled. I had told her the story of Hattie Bristow and her red-headed baby.

Mama smiled. "No, no chance of that. There's not a single person in our family that has red hair." Frances Ann let out another wail and Mama looked down at the baby. "She's your father's child, there's no doubt of that."

I jumped when someone thumped on the door.

"Better let him in, Belle, before he breaks it down," Mama said.

Aunt Belle went over and opened the door. Papa rushed by her then slowed to a walk as he neared the bed and stopped completely a few feet away.

"Are you all right, Cindy?"

She smiled at him. "Why, yes, John, I'm fine."

"And the baby?"

"She's as right as rain. See for yourself." She moved the blanket away from the baby's face as Papa stepped to the side of the bed. "She looks a lot like her father, don't you think?"

Papa grinned when he got a look at her and I laughed. "Proud Papa, don't you even want to know her name?"

He shook his head. "Doesn't matter, I'm going to call her Jack."

"Why, John Daniels, you'll do no such thing," Aunt Belle said. "Her name is Frances Ann. If you call her Jack, you'll have people thinking she's a boy."

"I'll be sure to set them straight if they do. Can I hold her, Cindy?"

Mama handed her to Papa as Roy and Loney, holding Thee's hand, came into the room and crowded around the bed to see their new sister.

Downstairs, someone knocked on the door. "That must be Dr. Hudson. Go on down and let him in, Roy," I said.

Roy, surprisingly enough, did what I told him without his usual protest.

"No need for a doctor now," Elisi said.

Mama nodded. "You and Belle and Vashti did a wonderful

134

job, but we'll let him take a look at her anyway. Hand her back to me, John. She's probably hungry."

Papa gave the baby back then kissed Mama on the cheek. Now that he'd seen for himself that all was well, I knew he wanted to get to the Annex and spread the word.

Mama smiled as he left the room and I wondered why she didn't object. She had to know where he was headed but seemed too taken with the new baby to say anything.

It had been a day of surprises for me and I decided to enjoy the newfound respect for my mother and the happiness that had my heart swelling like a bubble in my chest. I would have a very short time to bask in the glow of that miraculous day before my world shattered around me, leaving me scared, miserable and full of regret.

Chapter Fifteen

Late Fall 1899

She's resting at peace in the marble orchard.

The week after Mama gave birth to her sixth child was a busy one in our house. Not only was Jack a fussy eater and didn't want to nurse, which worried Mama no end, but Thee and Loney came down with a horrible cold. Elisi had Papa bring home some of the local moonshine for her homemade cold remedy. She heated the moonshine then added honey and rock candy to sweeten the taste. It worked so well that I took some to Miss Phillips for the students at Dorland and I've never been without it in my life since.

Even though the medicine made Thee and Loney drowsy, Elisi worked so hard during the day while Roy and I were at school that when we got home in the afternoon I felt it only fair for us to take over as much of the care and feeding of Mama, Jack, Loney and Thee as we could. Of course, Elisi never complained but I could see the work was wearing her down. She was, after all, in her seventies, and by all rights, she had raised her children and shouldn't be asked to do it all over again. When I said as much to her, she replied, "One day you'll know that your child is your child for all of her life and that responsibility never ends, no matter how old she gets. It works the same for grandchildren."

"Maybe so," I answered, "but you've done enough for today so sit down and rest your feet while Roy and I do the fetching and carrying for a while."

She sat down but even then insisted on having her mortar and pestle in easy reach so she could crush some of the herbs we'd gathered and dried.

I figured it was enough for her just to be off her feet for a while and went back to preparing supper. It was Jack's one-week birthday and I was in the mood for a celebration. The pall that had hung over the house since Green's death seemed to have dissipated with a new baby, and though Mama was still in bed, she seemed to feel better and stronger with each passing day. I had been worried about her dying in childbirth but she'd made it through without any problems so I cast my qualms about her aside.

If only I had known.

Elisi grunted as she pressed down on the pestle and I glanced at her. "Tough herbs, Elisi, or are you tired?"

She looked up and smiled. "A little of both."

"Why don't you put those aside and I'll do them for you later? You should rest while you have the chance. Mama, Thee, and baby Jack are all napping, Loney's trying to catch up on her schoolwork, Roy's mucking out the barn and I'm taking care of supper. There's nothing else that needs to be done so why don't you go lie down and rest for a while? I'll call you when supper's ready."

She put the pestle down and brushed her fingers over the cedar I'd cut and put in a glass jar on the center of the table. "I'll tell you a story instead. It'll make your work and mine go faster."

I smiled, always happy to be entertained by one of her stories. "What's the story about?"

She looked out the window though I can't imagine she saw much of anything. The sun had set and evening shadows were slowly growing larger. It wouldn't be long before the gloaming turned into full dark.

"Night and day and how the People once thought it would be better to have all of one and none of the other, how the atsina tlugv, the cedar tree, got its name and why you must always remember to honor it."

I didn't say anything, although I thought that out of all the things Elisi had told me about her people, honoring a cedar tree had to be one of the strangest. The Cherokee were a peculiar lot indeed. Still, if Elisi had taught me anything at all about them, it was that they believed in the goodness of all of God's creations and that all people should respect them.

"A long time ago," she began, "when the People were still new to the world, they decided life would be much better for them if they could have daylight all the time, so the Elders approached the Creator and asked if it would be possible never to have night anymore but to have only day.

"The Creator listened, and because He loved his people, He agreed to give them their wish, always light and no darkness at all, and the People were happy. But with all that daylight, the plants and trees soon started to grow and it became difficult for the People to move around because the earth was so crowded with plants. They couldn't find the paths they had always walked and they had trouble keeping the weeds from overtaking their gardens. With the sun always out, it was hot, and with no night, they couldn't sleep, so they grew short-tempered and were always fighting and arguing with each other."

I laughed. "Good thing Roy wasn't around back then. He's meaner than a striped-eyed snake when he misses his sleep."

She smiled. "Most men are like that and it didn't take very long at all for the People to change their mind about having daylight all the time. So they went to the Creator again, told Him they had made a mistake, and asked Him to change it so that it was night all the time instead. The Creator asked them if they were sure. After all, He reminded them, all things were created in twos, life and death, good and evil, day and night. The People, though, were tired of day and wanted only night so the Creator indulged them and made it dark all the time.

"It wasn't long before the plants stopped growing which meant they didn't have much food. It was cold all the time, and since there was no light, they couldn't see to hunt and they grew very weak without even the energy to gather wood for their fires. Many died and finally the People knew they had made another mistake so they went to the Creator again and begged for Him to bring back the daylight, to make it as He'd intended it to be, with both day and night."

"I bet the Creator wished His People would make up their minds and quit bothering Him all the time."

"Could be, I guess, but the Creator loved His People and so He gave them what they wanted. Day was day again and night was night, the weather improved and the crops began to grow. The People could see to hunt and they had enough to eat so they didn't get sick and die. They stopped all the fussing and fighting and instead treated each other with respect, as they should. And they were so grateful to the Creator that they thanked Him every day for all His blessings. The Creator accepted their gratitude and was glad to see His People happy again but He regretted that so many had died during the time of all darkness. Because of that, He decided to create a new tree to honor the ones who had died, and so the cedar tree was born. He named the new tree atsina tlugv."

I smiled. "The cedar tree. So we honor the cedar tree because it reminds us that God—or the Creator—knows best."

"Yes, and because the Creator felt so bad about the People who had died, He placed their spirits in the new tree He'd made." She reached out and touched the cedar again. "So whenever the People smell the cedar or look at it, they remember they are looking at the spirits of their ancestors and that life works best when it's in balance."

I sighed. "You tell the most wonderful stories, Elisi."

She fingered the medicine bag that hung around her neck. "It's more than a story to our People. It's a way of life. The cedar tree holds powerful spirits and many carry a small piece of its wood in their medicine bags, just like I do." She pointed at the door. "If you hang some over the door, it will protect against evil spirits coming into the house."

My mind immediately went to Green. Could we have saved him by the simple act of hanging a sprig of cedar over the door? Would that have kept Death out and allowed Green to go on living?

I wiped the biscuit dough off my hands with my apron then walked over to the table and plucked one of the cedar twigs out of the jar. Its pleasant aroma wafted up around me as Elisi nodded.

"Honor your ancestors, child, and they will do what they can to protect you."

"And my family, too?"

The baby started crying and Elisi didn't answer my question. She patted my shoulder before she left the kitchen to go see what was wrong with Jack. Apprehension tingled up my spine as I walked over to lay cedar on top of the door jamb and I wondered if it was a warning of some kind like the one I'd been given the day Green died. I'd ignored that one and look what happened.

If so, I hoped the cedar sprigs would lessen any danger to my family, but just to be safe, I plucked another one from the arrangement on the table and added it to the one already resting on the jamb.

After that, I took a couple more to the front door and did the same there.

As I stuck my hands back into the biscuit dough, Elisi rushed into the kitchen. She went straight to the herb shelf which, due to her diligence, was jam-packed with the dried plants we gathered over the summer. As she rummaged through the jars and tins, she mumbled to herself, so low that I couldn't hear what she said or even whether she spoke in Cherokee or English.

"Is something wrong, Elisi? Is the baby sick?"

"Not the baby, she's fine. It's your mama."

A chill ran over me and I think I knew deep down in my bones what was going to happen. I didn't dwell on it as I wiped my hands on my apron then went over to help Elisi search for whatever she was looking for.

Before I got there, she found what she was after at the back of the shelf, hidden behind blackberry leaves and buckeye bark. When I saw what she had in her hand, that icy feeling ran through me again, leaving me weak and shaking.

The tin held pokeroot, a common herb for the treatment of many ailments, chief among them, milk fever. Milk fever could be bad, but if we'd caught it early enough, there were any number of herbs that could be used to treat it. Maybe Mama would be all right.

"How bad is it, Elisi?"

She frowned. "Fever, tenderness, no leaking yet, and she says she's tired, but that could be because she just had a baby."

"She's not vomiting or sick to her stomach?"

Elisi shook her head. "No, not yet. You need to go up and sit with her while she nurses the baby. It's going to be painful until she gets better."

"But Elisi, should she be nursing? Shouldn't I see if I can get Jack to take some cow's milk or send Roy to the Andersons to see if they can spare some goat's milk?"

"No. Better for her to nurse. It'll help your mama get over the fever."

"But if Mama has a fever, won't Jack get sick?"

Elisi smiled as she laid her hand on my shoulder. "Already questioning your teacher. That's good, but in this case, it's better for your mama to continue to nurse. I promise you it won't hurt the baby."

"All right. Should I send Roy for the doctor?"

She shook her head. "No, he won't be any help with this. He'll treat her the same way we're going to treat her and then he'll charge your papa for it."

"He won't know anything else we can do?"

"I doubt it but send Roy for him if it'll make you feel better."

I shook my head. "No, I think Mama will be more comfortable if you treat her. She trusts you and so do I. And besides, you never know when Dr. Hudson will get here. He's so busy these days, he might not consider this important enough to put his other patients aside."

Elisi set the pokeroot down on the counter and turned to me. Her eyes were clouded with worry. "I'll do what I can to make her better but I can't promise you I will."

I hugged her before stepping back. "I know that, Elisi. We'll just have to treat her with the Cherokee remedies and pray for the best."

"Yes, prayer will be good. Go see to your mama now and sit with her while I get this ready. If the poke doesn't work for the fever, we've got a few other things we can try. But poke is usually best so we'll go with it first."

I rushed upstairs and when I stepped in Mama's room saw she had Jack at her breast, and for once, Jack wasn't being fussy about nursing. Just yesterday, Mama would have been smiling at Jack's eagerness, but today, her face twisted in pain as Jack suckled.

I forced a smile on my face so Mama wouldn't see how scared I was. "Elisi's fixing some poke for you, Mama. She says it'll help."

She shifted the baby and I could see that her breast was red and slightly swollen but I couldn't tell if the swelling was from the milk fever or the natural effect of having a child. Her cheeks were flushed. Not knowing what else to do or say, I placed the back of my hand on her forehead.

"Not much of a fever but you are warm. Elisi will be here soon. Can I get you anything or do anything to make you more comfortable?"

Her eyes, when she raised them to mine, looked weak but she didn't seem to be scared. I guess I had enough fear for both of us that day.

"As soon as Frances Ann finishes, a hot compress might be nice. It'll help with the swelling and should ease the pain a bit." Then she looked down at the baby and smiled even as Jack pulled on her breast. According to Elisi, it was painful for a woman to nurse a baby when she had milk fever, but Mama didn't seem to think of pain when it came to doing something for her babies.

It was then that it hit me. Mama was exactly what she wanted to be. Maybe she chose a different path than I would, but that didn't matter. She was the woman she was meant to be. Why hadn't I seen that before?

I sat down on the bed beside her, stroked my hand over Jack's downy cap of dark hair. "Do you want me to go get Papa for you?"

"No need to bother him. There's nothing he can do here except worry. You know your papa's no good when it comes to illness."

"No, he's not, but I thought it might make you feel better to have him here."

"Laws, child, this isn't anything to get so het up over. It's just a little case of milk fever and Elisi knows how to treat it. I'll be better in no time at all."

I would remember those words in the days to come as Mama continued to get worse and nothing Elisi or I did seemed to help. We called in Dr. Hudson, who surprisingly complimented Elisi on everything she'd done and told her he would have followed the same treatment she had. I don't know why Mama didn't get better. We tried everything, poke weed, cone flower, madder root, even dandelion, but nothing seemed to help. The infection raged through her body, and after a couple of days when it was obvious she wasn't getting better, Papa set his job aside and stayed home. He refused to leave, spending every minute with her, and was with her in the end when the infection took her life.

She died early one morning with her family around her, Papa sitting on one side of the bed, holding her hand, Elisi and Aunt Belle on the other, doing likewise. Loney hovered in the doorway, holding Thee, occasionally leaving when she couldn't stand Aunt Belle's hysterics any longer. Roy and I stood at the foot of the bed, arms around one another, tears streaming down our faces. Jack slept in the crib beneath the window.

I'd given up on praying and now cursed my God—again—for taking another life from this family. At times, Roy's arm tightened around my waist with such force, I had to bite my lip to keep from crying out loud. But I welcomed the pain, a distraction from my agony as I watched Mama, delusional with fever when she was conscious, calling for her Johnny to go get Green and bring him to her.

And at the end, before she breathed her last breath, she smiled the most beatific smile I'd ever seen, opened her eyes, looked at Papa and said, "Green's here, John. Do you see him?" Her eyes seemed to glaze as if she were looking beyond us, at some unknown thing, and said, "Oh, my little Greenie, my precious boy, I've missed you so. Come here to your mama, let me hold you." She held her hands out as if picking up her baby boy, then her body relaxed as her spirit left her, but that smile remained, and I was glad for that. I hoped she did see Green and that they were together now.

Papa bowed his head, making a guttural sound of such pain, it brought me to my knees, and I buried my face in my hands as Roy collapsed beside me, openly crying. Aunt Belle stumbled out of the room, sobbing as she pushed past Loney, who had turned her back on this excruciating scene. Elisi chanted something in Cherokee over Mama's body, her voice calm but her face bearing such grief I wondered that it didn't just break apart.

Papa was, of course, devastated but rallied long enough to help Elisi and me clean Mama up and change her into a fresh nightgown. He carried her downstairs to the kitchen table, tears streaming down his face, then went out to the barn, hitched the horses to the wagon, and drove to the lumber mill in town to buy wood. When he came back, he called Roy to come help him and they started on her coffin. A few hours later, he left the job to Roy, went to the Annex saloon and got drunk.

If it hadn't been for Elisi's calming presence, I don't think I could have survived. Poor Thee constantly asked where his mama was and Jack cried nonstop for her. Loney took it upon herself to look after the two of them, entertaining Thee with stories and games and feeding Jack, first from one of the new-fangled bottles with a nipple, and when Jack didn't take to that, with an old pap boat Mama had used with us.

Late that afternoon, I sent Roy to the Annex Saloon to find Papa and tell him he needed to sober up and buy Mama a dress to be buried in. Roy, glad for a reason to be out of the house and away from all the sadness, took off like a jackrabbit. He returned with the news that Papa said he'd take care of it.

As it turned out, Papa, in his misery, ordered more drinks and never did buy Mama that dress. He stayed drunk for a week and didn't set foot inside our house until long after Mama's funeral. I had Roy check on him every now and then but Roy always returned with the news that Papa was still drinking and refused to come home.

We buried Mama the next afternoon. Elisi, Loney and I dressed her in her finest dress, a soft yellow silk with white collar and cuffs. Tears streamed down my cheeks as I brushed her thick dark hair and left it falling softly around her face. Papa always complimented Mama on how much he liked looking at her with her hair down and I agreed with him. It seemed years fell away and she more resembled a young, beautiful girl with her life ahead of her than the mother of six children. I bit back a sob. After today, I'd never see her and she had no future left.

Every few minutes, I glanced toward the door, hoping Papa would walk through, strong and straight without the odor of liquor hanging about him, carrying a fine new dress for Mama, but he didn't appear until we began the funeral procession to Sandy Gap. Roy enlisted the aid of Uncle Ned and several neighbors to load the oak casket in the back of the wagon. Aunt Belle rode beside him as we made our slow way up the mountain with most of the township of Hot Springs following behind. I cradled Jack in my arms and Loney held Thee's hand. Elisi walked in silence beside us, tears falling. As she had when we buried Green, Miss Cordy fell into step with us when we passed the path to her house. Dark-gray clouds hovered above us and the wind slapped at our faces with a biting chill. A fitting day for a funeral, I thought.

Papa joined us at the graveyard, stepping out from behind the church and standing well back from the crowd. I looked at him for a moment then turned from him in anger and anguish. His clothes were disheveled, his face unshaved, his eyes bloodshot and swollen, the pain on his face unbearable. I knew he grieved Mama more than anyone else but could not understand why he turned to liquor at such a disturbing time in his children's lives. He stood there wringing his hat as the minister spoke over Mama's grave. He watched in solemn silence as Roy, Loney, and I placed a sprig of cedar on top of her coffin but turned away when Roy and several men began to lower her into the ground. Aunt Belle cried the hardest and I knew her grief was sincere. She and Mama had been friends as well as sisters and loved one another deeply. When we turned to retrace our steps to Hot Springs, Papa had vanished, and I knew if we looked when we got back to town, we would find him in the Annex Saloon drinking himself into oblivion.

I caught sight of Fletcher Elliott standing among the crowd but paid him no mind, such was my grief. I had only begun to really know Mama and appreciate her before we lost her so suddenly. I didn't have the chance to tell her how much I loved her. The unfairness of her death weighed on my heart and at times I wondered if I could get through it. I wanted to scream myself senseless, beat my fists against something tangible until they bled but forced my mind to calm, my hands to still. My brothers and sisters needed me, and since Papa wasn't there to help, I must do what I could for them.

I had a hard time forgiving Papa and it seemed to me I stayed mad at him for one reason or another for the next year. Just about the time I decided I needed to forgive him, I found a runaway hiding in our barn and, in my eyes, Papa did yet another unforgivable thing.

Chapter Sixteen

Winter 1899 – Summer 1900

Scared as a sinner in a cyclone.

Christmas fell one week after Mama died but none of us were in the mood to celebrate. We observed the holiday quietly and at home with only the family.

If it weren't for Elisi and me, we probably wouldn't have done even that. Elisi wasn't much for celebrating Christian holidays but she agreed with me that we needed to at least observe Christmas for the children's sake. Thee, the only one of an age to really care, was unusually subdued except when he saw the small Christmas tree Roy brought home and set on the little table in the parlor.

And when he glimpsed the presents resting beneath the tree on Christmas morning, his eyes lit brighter than the candles on the tree. It was all we could do to keep him from opening them until after we got home from the early-morning church services.

It seemed to me that Loney had cried nonstop since Mama died but she actually smiled as we watched Thee tear into his gifts, a toy set of tools and a handful of clay marbles in a small bag that Loney made. Roy, of course, still being more boy than man, joined in Thee's happiness as the presents were opened and even knelt down on the rug to show him how to shoot the marbles but after that brief moment of diversion wandered off outside to the barn.

On Old Christmas Eve, Elisi and I cooked a big dinner in silence as we worked to salvage something of this first Christmas season without Mama. None of us had much to say as we all sat around the table eating ham, sweet potatoes and biscuits we didn't really have an appetite for. As soon as Loney and I started to clear the table, Papa scooted his chair back and stood up. He bowed slightly then thanked us for the dinner before turning and walking out the door. I knew he was going to the Annex saloon. He spent more time there than he did at home. As he left, I vowed then and there that next year the holidays would be a time of celebration and joy again for my family.

Elisi, as if reading my mind, put her hand over mine and said, "Next year will be better."

I didn't know if she was just saying that to cheer me up or if her sight told her so but I smiled and clasped her hand. "Well, it can't be much worse than this."

Things settled down for a while after that. Winter reluctantly gave way to spring and spring to summer. As the weather warmed, Papa spent less and less time at the Annex. Mayhap, he finally realized he had children who needed him. Elisi and I kept the house and took care of the children during the day. Amelia Phillips had returned to Dorland over the Christmas holidays, her health much improved, so I was no longer needed at the Institute. I missed teaching and the students and constantly dreamed of the day when I would have a full-time job in a school of my own. I didn't give much thought to Fletcher Elliott or trying my fortune or much of anything except getting through one day and moving on to the next.

But still, he was there in my mind at times and I remembered him standing shirtless in the sun stripping the cane for the molasses. So much like when Mama first saw Papa, I considered it a sign of sorts. He had been working at the sawmill for some time now, and when I caught sight of him around town, I told myself it wasn't meant to be. If he'd been interested, he would have found a way to talk to me.

On a hot summer day, I climbed the wooden ladder leading to the barn loft, inhaling deeply, enjoying the intermingling odors drifting in the air. The lingering, bitter smell of the tobacco leaves that had once hung from the rafters blended with the sweet comforting aroma of golden hay stored above and the warm soothing whiff of the horses from the cribs below. I hesitated, one foot on a rung, the other in midair, and sniffed deeply. Another scent, one I could not identify, sharp and a bit tangy but barely there. Maybe one of the cats lurked nearby or a varmint lay in hiding.

I walked along the planks, dust motes dancing in sunbeams shining through the slatted shutters. I unlatched them and pushed gently, watching as they swung outward on well-oiled hinges. Leaning over the sill, I looked down and, as always, felt a slight sense of disorientation. From the outside, the cantilevered barn had an odd look, built so that the floor of the loft was larger than the ground floor. Standing in the eaves looking down, I saw only grass and dirt with no evidence of any supporting structure beneath my feet. I closed my eyes and imagined I floated on air.

I felt a slight prickling at the base of my neck. The air up here seemed disturbed as if I were not the only one in the loft. I wheeled around but saw nothing out of the ordinary in the deep, dark recesses. With a shrug, I crossed over to the left front corner to dig beneath a small pile of hay. I removed my journal and returned to the window where I sat cross-legged on the floor. The journal opened to a fresh page marked by the chewed pencil I used to record my life's moments. Rustling sounded behind me and my head snapped around.

"Who's there?"

No one answered.

"I swear, I'm acting about as nervous as a cat in a room full of rocking chairs," I muttered. I stuffed the pencil sideways in my mouth and bit down as I contemplated what I would write in my journal today. My gaze noted the sun's position in the sky, halfway between the noon spot and the neighboring mountain's peak. Around two o'clock. I didn't have much time. Chores had to be done before I needed to help Elisi fix supper. I sighed, my mind turning to my mother and the fine meals she prepared while alive. Would I ever stop missing her? Would the hurt ever go away? And would Papa and I ever get beyond what he'd done? I shook my head at this thought.

The unfamiliar smell I noticed before seemed suddenly stronger and much closer. I swiveled my head to look behind me and froze. Was that a face among the bales of hay stacked against the far wall? I shot to my feet and hurried across the room, more out of curiosity than anything else. It didn't occur to me there might be danger there.

As I drew near, the face disappeared. "Hey!" I shifted the hay bales, stopping when a girl around my own age fell to the floor, wrapping her arms around her stomach as if in pain.

I knelt beside her and touched her shoulder, resisting the urge to pull my fingers away. Through her dress, her skin burned as if on fire. I noted the sharp acidic smell of fever.

"Are you all right?" I asked in a gentle voice.

She made a moaning sound.

"What is it? Are you sick?"

"My stomach," she groaned. "It's been giving me a fit. I can't hardly stand straight anymore, it hurts so."

"Here, let me help you." I eased her back against the hay, watched her draw her knees up against her abdomen. "Maybe it's the gripes you've got. Did you eat something bad?"

She squeezed her eyes shut and shook her head. "I ain't had nothing in so long I can't remember when or what I 'et."

I studied the girl, who seemed a darker version of myself with her deep olive skin. Her cloudy blue eyes were a contrast to my own dark brown. Although we shared raven black hair, mine was straight and fine while hers was coarse and curly. We were about the same size, too, both slightly built.

"I'll be right back." I hurried down the ladder and ran outside. I rounded the side of the barn, heading for the paddock. There, I snatched a rag hanging off the pump handle and dipped it in the water trough. The water felt cool and fine as silk against my hand. I squeezed the excess moisture out of the rag and hurried back to the barn. In the loft, I bathed the girl's face, noting the ashen tone underlying her dark complexion.

"What's your name?"

"Druanna. What's yours?"

"Bessie."

Druanna lay on her side, her legs to her chest.

I touched her shoulder. "Do you want some water or something to eat? Well, maybe you better not eat just yet."

Druanna's hand clutched my forearm. "I'm thirsty as a mule. Could you bring me something? I'd be ever so grateful. And after, I'll leave you be. I just needed a place to rest till my stomach feels better."

I watched her as she talked, studying her features, and with a slight jolt remembered everything I'd heard about the Melungeons; blue eyes, dark skin, dark, coarse hair. I drew back.

"Are you a *Melungeon*?"

Druanna's eyes grew wide with alarm. She closed them as another spasm gripped her stomach. "No," she grunted. "I'm Cherokee."

"No you're not. I'm part Cherokee and I don't have blue eyes. And I don't recall ever meeting a Cherokee with blue eyes. Go on, now, tell the truth."

Tears slid down Druanna's face. "Please, you can't tell anyone I'm here. You don't know what they'll do to me if they find me." With difficulty, she sat up. "I'll leave. Right now. You won't have to bother about me no more."

"Oh, don't go on so." I pushed gently against her shoulder, urging her to lie back. "I won't tell anybody I saw you. Now, you close your eyes and rest. I'll go fetch you some cool water and a biscuit. Well, maybe just the water till we see if you can keep something down."

"Thank you kindly," Druanna murmured, closing her eyes.

As I climbed down the ladder and headed toward the house, I wondered if Elisi would intuit the same thing I had when I touched Druanna. I didn't know what it was really, a darkness that lay over her spirit like a heavy blanket, but I sensed it wasn't a good sign for her.

Elisi took one look at my face when I burst through the kitchen door and asked me what had happened. I grabbed her hand and told her about the sick girl in the barn.

"Please Elisi, you have to help. She's in awful pain and I'm afraid she's going to die."

"Shh, now, let me take a look at her," Elisi said.

I poured a cup of water from the water jug and returned to the barn, Elisi in tow. Druanna was where I left her, lying on her side, knees drawn up to her chest. I knelt beside her and urged her onto her back.

I helped her sit up and put the cup to her lips. "Take small sips." When she lay back, I answered her inquisitive glance toward Elisi. "I've brought my great-grandmother. She's Cherokee and knows a lot about healing. She can help."

Elisi knelt on the other side of Druanna but didn't say anything.

"It's her stomach, Elisi. She's been throwing up and it hurts her to straighten up."

Elisi put a hand on Druanna's abdomen and pressed. Druanna screamed in agony, curling herself into a fetal position.

"Look at me, child," Elisi said, using her apron to wipe perspiration off Druanna's forehead.

When Druanna opened her eyes, Elisi drew back. She turned to me, her dark eyes filled with concern and a trace of fear. "Bessie, she's Melungeon. She needs to go." She made a shooing motion with her hands.

"No."

"This girl is a Melungeon. You can't have her here."

"No," I repeated. "She's sick. We can't turn our back on her, Elisi. Why, that would make us no better than the white man you hold in such contempt. We need to help her. When she's better, she can go."

Elisi regarded both of us for a long moment. She gave a curt nod and stood. "Come, we need to go into the woods for medicine."

I leaned down and patted Druanna on the shoulder. "We shouldn't be gone long. Do you need anything before we leave?"

"No, please, just hurry," Druanna grunted.

Without saying anything else, Elisi climbed down the ladder. She didn't speak as we made our way into the woods.

"What are we looking for?" I asked.

"Beech tree bark. We'll make tea from that to start with. If that doesn't work, there are some other things we can try."

"Will that stop her from throwing up?"

Elisi nodded as she marched deeper into the cool embrace of the forest.

"Don't we have some back at the house, Elisi?"

"We used most of it when your little brother was sick last month. We need more."

We walked quite a way before she found a beech tree she thought worthy enough to sacrifice its bark. She spoke to it in Cherokee before taking only what she felt we would need. I waited as she chose a small stone from her bag and placed it at the base of the tree.

When she finished, she turned and started back through the trees but I put my hand on her arm and stopped her. I could see she was tired and I had something I needed to say. She would never admit to fatigue so I pointed to a fallen log. "Can we sit for a minute, Elisi? I'm a little tired."

She handed the bark to me and her sigh as she sat down was enough to confirm my suspicions.

"I want to apologize to you, Elisi, for being so snappish back at the barn."

She shrugged. "You were right. It was wrong of me to want to send that poor girl away simply because she's different. I wasn't thinking of her as a person but only about what your papa would say. I'm sorry, too."

I smiled. "You want to know a secret? Sending her away was my first thought when I saw her, but I remembered what you said about how your people were treated and I just couldn't do it."

"You've learned much. Before long, you'll be smarter than your teacher."

"Oh no, that will never happen. You know so much and there's so much more that I need to learn, but I'm thankful I have you to teach me."

She nodded, stood up, and held out a hand to me. "Come, we should get back. I'll tell you a story as we walk."

I stood up and kissed her cheek. "That's a fine bit of bribery, Elisi."

She smiled. "Long ago when the world was still new, the People didn't know about selfishness and greed. All the tribes lived together without arguing, happy to share their hunting and fishing grounds with their neighbors. But men being men, selfishness and greed soon came into being. The People started quarreling with a tribe to the east and it seemed nothing could resolve their differences.

"Finally, the tribal chiefs decided to meet in council and try to settle the quarrels of their people. They sat around the fire and smoked the peace pipe for seven days and seven nights but never could agree on a solution. Instead they just kept arguing and that was when the Creator got mad because men are not supposed to smoke the pipe until after they make peace.

"The Creator decided to teach them a lesson. Looking down on the old men sitting around the fire, He swirled the smoke around them and turned them into grayish flowers, which we now call Indian Pipes. To remind the People not to quarrel anymore, He made the flowers grow wherever the People argued and He made the smoke hang over the mountains until all have learned to live together in peace."

She pointed to the mountains in the distance, shrouded in mist. "I guess the People haven't learned yet. I wonder if they ever will."

I squeezed her hand. "Probably not but we can bring peace to our little corner of the world, Elisi."

"That may not be possible when your father finds out about that girl in the barn. But we'll do the best we can by her and maybe she'll be well enough to leave before your papa gets home tonight."

A chill ran over me at the thought of what Papa would say if he found out but I couldn't just turn Druanna away. She was too sick and I didn't want her death on my conscience.

I clutched the beech bark in my hand and vowed no matter what happened I would help this girl.

Back at the house, I poured water into the tea kettle while

Elisi shoved kindling into the belly of the wood stove, stoking the fire that simmered there. As soon as she had it going good, I set the kettle on to heat. Elisi shredded the bark and tied the pieces in a muslin bag.

As we waited for the water to boil, Elisi stared up at the spray of cedar I'd nailed over the door and told me another story.

"When the Creator first made the plants and animals, He told them to keep watch and stay awake for seven nights. Almost all the animals stayed awake the first night, but the second night, some slept, and the third night, more slept, and on the seventh night, only the panther and owl and maybe one or two others were still awake. To reward them, the Creator gave them the power to see in the dark and hunt animals that sleep at night. Only holly, pine, spruce and cedar trees were awake by the seventh night, so the Creator's reward to them was to stay green always and have the greatest power for medicine. But others lose their hair each winter as punishment."

She went to the stove to pour the boiling water over the bag of bark in the tea pot. "Let it steep for a few minutes and then you can take it to the girl."

"Will it help?" I asked.

"We'll wait and see," she replied, turning her back to me and stirring the stew simmering on the stove.

After the tea steeped, I poured it into a cup and took it out to the barn for Druanna, pulling myself slowly up the ladder with one hand, holding the cup of tea in the other. At the top, I set it on the loft floor and climbed up the rest of the way.

She hadn't moved but watched me with frightened eyes as I walked over to her and knelt down. "This should settle your stomach." I helped her sit up and held the cup for her. After she drank the tea, I put my arm around her shoulders and eased her down onto the floor. She rolled to her side and drew her legs up to her stomach again. "I'll be right back," I said, before going over to the corner of the loft and getting the quilt I kept there. I shook it out beside Druanna and helped her move over onto it. She curled on her side, shivering, so I folded it over to cover her. Her body shook with another chill and her teeth chattered.

"Maybe I should go fetch the doctor," I said, more to myself than her.

She clutched my forearm with her fingers, her skin so hot it burned through my sleeve. "No, please. They'll send me back. They won't help me."

I patted her hand. "Don't worry. I won't let anyone take you." Back to where, I wondered as I sat down beside her.

She closed her eyes and I studied her face, so delicate and exotic-looking. I had never seen a person with dark skin and light eyes and found the contrast quite beautiful. "Is the tea helping any?" I whispered.

She nodded. "A little. I should be better by tonight. I'll leave once it's good and dark."

"Why are you so afraid for anyone to know you're here?"

She opened her eyes and stared at me. "Do you know about the one-drop rule?"

I had heard Papa mention it; something about segregating white people from colored people. "But you're not colored." I hesitated. "Are you?"

She shook her head. "It doesn't matter. I'm not considered white and that's what counts. Your great-grandmother was right. I'm Melungeon but we don't know what our heritage is. We're hated and I don't know why. We aren't allowed to own land, we can't vote, we're spurned wherever we go. We hide so they can't find us. Those of us who can, pass for Cherokee."

"But why are you hated so?"

"I don't know why. No one does and no one ever talks of it." She shuddered. "Now there's even talk of sterilizing us."

I gasped, remembering Elisi telling me the same thing.

She clutched my skirt, her eyes pleading. "Please, don't tell anyone I'm here. They'll make me go back to Virginia. I can't go back there."

I patted her hand. "But where will you go?"

"There's a school in Asheville that accepts Melungeons." She grimaced with pain. "Have you heard of it? It's called the

Pease Home and Industrial School, run by a Presbyterian minister named L.M. Pease."

I shook my head. "Maybe Papa's heard of it. He has to take prisoners to Asheville sometimes." A horse nickered outside and I hurried over to the window and glanced out. Papa, home from working on his latest house. I returned to Druanna and knelt beside her. "Don't worry, Druanna, I won't tell anyone you're here." I piled bales of hay around her so Papa wouldn't see her if he climbed the loft for some reason. "I'll be back after supper," I said before sliding the last bale into place. "I'll bring you some more tea and something to eat."

Druanna nodded her head weakly. I didn't like the glazed look in her eyes, her pale countenance.

I flew down the ladder and into the yard. Papa stood by the water trough, dipping his handkerchief into the cold water and running it over his face.

"Papa," I said, giving him a hello kiss on the cheek. "Here, let me take Bob. I'll unsaddle her, brush her down for you."

Papa's eyes flickered with amusement. "Damn, Bess, you must have done something awful bad to be so willing to take care of a sweaty old horse."

"Just helping out," I said with a smile.

He cast me a suspicious look before turning toward the house.

After I took care of Bob, I went into the kitchen, where Elisi was putting a pot of stew on the table. I leaned close to her and whispered, "You won't tell Papa about Druanna, will you?"

She gave me a long look before offering a curt nod. "For now."

I hugged her and set to work placing plates and silverware on the table.

After supper, I helped Elisi wash dishes, alert to the whereabouts of my father the whole time. He sat in his favorite chair in the parlor, listening to Loney play the piano, belting out gospel songs she had learned in church. He held Jack in his lap, who alternated between groping for his moustache and running her pudgy fingers over his shiny badge. Thee, on the floor, played with a wooden horse.

I filled a bowl with stew, placed a corn muffin on top, and poured the tea Elisi had made into a tin mug. After glancing into the parlor, making sure Papa was still being entertained, I made my way to the barn. Druanna sat near the window, the breeze stirring her dark, curly hair. She gave me a weak smile when I topped the ladder.

"How are you feeling?" I asked, making my way to her, careful not to spill the tea or drop the bowl.

"A little better. I can sit up now." She took the bowl from me with a thankful nod. I placed the mug beside her and sat. After taking a couple of bites, she put the bowl down. "I guess I don't have much of an appetite."

"Drink the tea. It will help your stomach."

She dutifully put the cup to her lips and swallowed, then set it aside.

"Try to drink it all, if you can, Druanna. Elisi says it should help you get over your stomach problems."

While Druanna sipped at the tea, I stared out the window at the sky, wondering if I could fly, how long it would take me to reach the closest star. I darted a glance at Druanna, curious as to her heritage, wondering why the Melungeons didn't know where they came from. Was it some sort of horrible secret? What would it be like to live life as an outcast, forced into hiding? To be cast aside as some sort of boogie-man used to threaten small children into behaving? Druanna seemed perfectly ordinary to me, a young woman who should soon marry and have children and live her own life, who shouldn't be traveling the mountains of western North Carolina, seeking refuge at the only school in the area that would accept her kind.

Druanna caught me staring and gave me a tentative smile. I decided I'd like her for a friend.

"You could stay here."

She shook her head. "It's too dangerous. I'd be forced to go back."

"But why? This is America, after all. You're free. You shouldn't have to hide anywhere, be forced to live in one area. It isn't right." My voice rose with indignation.

Druanna lay back. The dark aura I initially sensed hovering around her had steadily gained mass throughout the afternoon and now resembled a black, boiling cloud. I didn't know it then, but this was Death, waiting for the designated time to lay Its claim to her soul.

I scooted closer. She reached out and took my hand. The fever was back, it felt as if I held a burning lump of coal.

"There may be a warrant out for my arrest."

I jerked my hand back in surprise. "What? For you? What happened?"

"I was working as a maid for a woman in Virginia. A very rich woman." She shook her head. "She was a horrible person and only hired me because no one else would work for her." She closed her eyes and sighed. She didn't speak for a long moment and I began to worry she might have fallen unconscious, but she stirred and her eyes opened and rested on me. "She misplaced her favorite piece of jewelry, a diamond-and-sapphire brooch given to her by her husband. She was a terrible enough person when he was alive, but after he died, the meanness of her spirit took over what goodness there was in her and she became an angry, bitter, vengeful old woman." Druanna's gaze drifted toward the window and her voice lowered.

"When she couldn't find the brooch, she said I took it since I had cleaned her bedroom the day before. I denied it but what right did I have to be heard? She insisted I had taken it and had my room searched by her cook. The cook didn't find it, so the old woman demanded I strip down to prove I didn't have it on my person. When I refused, she sent the stable boy for the sheriff. I was so scared, Bessie, I didn't think. I ran as soon as I got the chance."

I didn't want to but I had to ask, "Did you take it?"

She grasped my hand in both of hers and drew it to rest against her heart. "I swear I didn't."

"Why didn't you go for help? To your family or a friend?"

Keeping my hand clasped to her breast, she said, "I couldn't. It would only get them in trouble with the sheriff, too, and I couldn't do that." She took a deep breath. "She had a man whipped once..." her eyes darted toward me "...a Melungeon. She claimed he disrespected her and the sheriff believed her story. We all knew she wasn't telling the truth but what could we do? We were at the mercy of her and the sheriff."

She closed her eyes once more and said, in a tired voice, "I'm sure they're looking for me. I won't go back there, I'll die first. She'll have me thrown in jail, have me taken away to some strange place, among people I don't know."

I took out my handkerchief and mopped her face, red and perspiring from the fever. "I won't let anything happen to you, Druanna. I promise you that."

I don't think she heard. She had fallen into a restless sleep, muttering to herself. I stayed with her for awhile then went back inside before Papa missed me.

Papa was in the kitchen when I stepped through the doorway. "Where you been, Bess? I've been looking all over for you."

"I was out in the barn, Papa."

His eyes twinkled. "If I go look, I won't find some young fella hidden among the hay bales, will I?"

My face grew hot. "Papa!"

He laughed. "That's my Bess."

I felt guilty for deceiving Papa about Druanna but had promised I wouldn't tell anyone else about her. And Papa might see fit to take her back if he found out. "Where's Elisi?"

"In the bedroom putting Jack to bed. You best go see if she needs you for anything." He picked up his hat. "I'm going down to the saloon for a bit. I won't be gone long." His look conveyed his own sense of guilt. Elisi, like Mama, wouldn't be pleased to hear this and I would probably be the one bearing the news. I felt a brief tug of resentment toward Papa but quickly squelched it. He worked hard. He should have his pleasures, too.

I smiled at him as I walked out of the room and stopped in the hallway, worrying about Druanna. Hopefully, she would be sleeping and Papa wouldn't hear her while he was in the barn saddling Bob. I looked up when Loney and Roy tromped down the stairs toward me.

"Where you been, Bessie?" Roy asked.

I ignored the question, taking in Roy's combed hair and tucked-in shirt, Loney without her apron. "Where are you two headed?"

"Loney's trying out for the church choir so I figured I'd walk her over," Roy said, not looking at me.

I nodded, figuring if my brother was so interested in accompanying Loney, there must be a pretty girl he had an interest in seeing. I kissed each on the cheek. "Have fun and good luck, Loney."

I found Elisi in the rocker by the bedroom window, the cool breeze playing over her face, Jack nestled against her bosom, starting to doze. She smiled when I stepped into the room and for the first time I saw the resemblance between Elisi and Mama and realized they were both beautiful women. Although Mama's countenance had so often been worried or flustered and she rarely smiled, when she did, her face brightened and smoothed so that she resembled a very young girl ready to go out into the world and make her place. I had her dark eyes and dark hair but my face resembled my father's more than hers. I used to envy her the looks other men cast her way when they didn't think she was looking, the jealous glances other women gave her as they passed her in church or on the street. I opened my mouth to tell Elisi Papa had gone off to the saloon, but before a sound passed my lips, I heard my father's loud, "What the hell?" coming from the barn. Oh, no!

Chapter Seventeen

Summer 1900

***He couldn't pour rain out of a boot with a hole in the toe
and directions on the heel.***

Elisi jumped when Papa yelled and Jack began wailing. Thee
came pounding toward us, a look of alarm on his small face.
Elisi soothed Jack, running her hand over the back of her
head, making shushing noises, as she gathered Thee against
her. She cast a quick glance at me. "Go see what's got your
papa so disturbed, Bess."

I ran to the kitchen, flew out the door and into the yard.
Papa walked toward me, Druanna in his arms. I retreated onto
the porch and held the door open for him. He pushed through,
pausing long enough to stare at me, anger flaring in his eyes.
"Damn, Bess, what the hell have you done?"

I followed along as he took Druanna into the parlor and
laid her limp body on the sofa. "I was trying to help her, Papa."

"Help her? Who is she and why would you want to help
her?"

"She's sick, Papa. Her name's Druanna. She wanted to
sleep in the barn tonight then move on tomorrow when her
stomach was feeling better."

He pointed his finger at her. "Is she a runaway?"

I hesitated, unsure what to say. I didn't want to tell him
Druanna might be wanted by the law.

"What's she running from, Bess?"

"She just needed a place to sleep, Papa. She's so sick, I
didn't know what to do for her."

Papa ran his hand through his hair. "Where did she come

from? How did she end up here?"

"She's from Virginia and was trying to get to Asheville, to a school there for Melungeons."

"What's she...she's a *Melungeon*? Damn, Bess."

Elisi stepped into the room and crossed over to Druanna. She put the back of her hand on the young woman's cheek and quickly withdrew it. When she looked at me, I clearly heard her voice speaking in my head. *This girl is dying. She won't live through the night.*

I turned to Papa. "Please, you have to go get the doctor. She's so sick. She'll die if we don't get help for her."

Papa shoved his hat on his head. "I'll get him, all right, but she's going back where she came from, Bessie."

I watched him leave, terrified. What if there was an actual warrant for her arrest? If so, Papa would have it in his office. He'd see it and would feel it his duty to return her. She'd be jailed, maybe go to prison. I couldn't stand the thought of it.

The front door opened and a female voice trilled hello. Oh, no. Aunt Belle. I hurried out of the parlor, hoping to waylay her before she saw Druanna.

She noted my flushed cheeks, flustered expression, and instead of stopping moved toward me at an alarming speed. "What on earth is wrong with you?"

I forced myself to stand still, control my breathing. "Nothing, Aunt Belle. Just trying to take care of a few things. You know how it is with the young'uns around bedtime."

She studied my face before giving a sharp shake of her head. "What are you trying to hide? Is your father passed out drunk again?"

She stepped around me and I followed her, trying to think of something to say, anything that would keep her from going into the parlor. But she was light on her feet and seemed to fly into the room, stopping short when she saw Druanna on the sofa.

"What in the world?"

I knelt beside Druanna, took her hot hand in mine. "She's sick. Papa's gone for the doctor."

Aunt Belle stepped closer and stared at Druanna. A

horrified look crossed her face. "Is she Melungeon, Vashti?"

"That doesn't matter."

"You can't have her in the house, girl. It's not right. She has to leave."

"She's sick, so sick she passed out. We can't move her, not till the doctor gets here and treats her."

"She'll place a curse on this house," Aunt Belle shrieked, her cheeks crimson, spittle flying from her mouth.

Loud wails from the bedroom reached us: Jack and Thee, startled out of sleep by Aunt Belle's outburst.

Elisi hurried from the room, casting a look of reproach at her granddaughter as she passed by.

Aunt Belle pointed toward the door. "Remove her, now, before the curse takes hold. Get her out of here, Vashti."

I rose to my feet and crossed over to stand in front of my aunt. "You need to leave. You're upsetting the babies."

Aunt Belle drew herself up. "I will not leave, not until she's out of this house."

"Yes, you will, and now. This is not your house, you don't have the right to tell me what to do here. Only Papa has that right and he's gone to get help for Dru—for that girl."

Aunt Belle's eyes widened. "You know her? How in the world do you know a person like that, Vashti?"

"It's none of your business. Now, please, leave." I put my hand on her elbow and steered her out of the room.

"You're making a terrible mistake, Vashti," she said, her voice low and husky. "She's Melungeon. They're cursed. Now you're cursed."

I stopped, my hand on the doorknob, and stared at her. "Don't you understand, Aunt Belle, this house is already cursed. Was cursed long before Druanna got here. And we've got two lives cut short to prove it."

Her eyes hardened. "I'm just glad your Mama isn't here to see what you're doing."

"Mama wasn't like you. She didn't have your hard heart. She would have helped." I pushed her out the door and slammed it shut.

"You're cursed, Vashti Lee Daniels," she yelled at me from

the other side. "You've cursed everyone in that house."

I rushed into the kitchen, found a clean rag, and dipped it into the water bucket. When I returned to the parlor, Druanna was moving restlessly, moaning in her sleep. I washed her face with the rag, horrified at how quickly it grew hot. How high could a temperature go, I wondered, before it killed someone? I hoped Papa found Doctor Hudson and returned soon.

Elisi stepped into the room and gave me a questioning look. "I can handle this. You go on, take care of the babies," I said. She nodded and was gone.

Every few minutes, I returned to the kitchen to dip the rag into the water bucket then back to the parlor to bathe Druanna's face. I talked softly to her, not knowing if she could hear me, but hoping my voice might be some comfort to her. I prayed she would wake up, free of the fever and free of the gripes, but that black cloud I had seen earlier was thick as molasses around her body. I hated that cloud, hated my ability to perceive it, and asked God to take it away but leave Druanna with me.

The front door burst open and heavy footsteps sounded down the hall. Papa stepped into the parlor and I noted his eyes glittered with cold anger. Doc Willoughby followed him in, shuffling along like an old man. With his wide girth, bowed head, droopy shoulders and shambling gait, he reminded me of a wooly bear. When his eyes met mine, I noted his were bloodshot and heavy lidded.

I clenched my fists with frustration. Doc Willoughby spent his days more drunk than sober. About the only people who went to him for medicinal purposes were the poor people that lived in Tiger Town and Clinch Row, the two slums in Hot Springs.

Papa put his hand on Doc's back and pushed him toward the sofa.

I rose to my feet, caught the bitter aroma of whiskey wafting off the man from five feet way, and shoved him back. "You're drunk." I looked at Papa. "We can't let him take care of her like this. Why didn't you get Doctor Hudson?"

"I tried. He's off delivering a baby or something. We got no choice, Bessie. Doc Willoughby's all she's got."

"He's drunk, Papa. We should wait till Doctor Hudson can come."

Ignoring us, Doc Willoughby dropped his medical bag on the floor and bent over Druanna. He lifted each closed eyelid before straightening and giving Papa an accusing look. "You didn't tell me she was Melungeon." His words were slurred but clear enough.

"That shouldn't matter to you, old man," Papa said, his voice low and growly. "You're a doctor and all that should concern you is your patient and what you can do for her. Her color or anything else about her shouldn't factor into this at all. Now do your damn job and quit lollygagging, you old drunk."

Doc stared at Papa for a long moment before turning back to Druanna. "This girl's burning up with fever," he said, the back of his hand on her cheek.

I stepped closer, holding my breath against the stench of sweat and liquor surrounding the man. "She's got the gripes, I think. Her stomach hurts something awful. She said she can't stand to lie straight or stand up, it hurts so much. Elisi and I gave her some herb tea and it helped at first but now she's worse than she was to start with." I tugged at his sleeve. "Can you help her, Doc Willoughby? We tried, but she's been out since Papa found her, hasn't come around at all."

"Got the gripes, huh? Maybe she ate something she shouldn't have." Doc put his hand on her abdomen and started prodding, moving about in a circular motion. Druanna drew her knees up and screamed. A loud wail answered from the bedroom. Jack. Awake again. I hoped Thee wouldn't join in.

Doc straightened up and turned to Papa, his movements slow and measured. "It's her appendix, looks like. Not much we can do for her but wait."

Papa's eyebrows drew together. "You can't give her some medicine?"

Doc shook his head. "Nope. Hate to say it, but in most of these cases, the outcome's not good."

I glanced at Druanna. That black cloud was thicker than ever now, boiling over her entire body. "What do you mean?"

Doc pinched his lips together. "Most likely die, I'd say, from the looks of her." He scratched his jaw, his blunt fingernails rasping over the gray whiskers. "Of course, I read recently about an operation for this kind of thing they're doing up North. New York City, I think. Believe they call it an appendectomy." He squinted his eyes at us before adding, "Removal of the appendix. Have to cut her open to do it."

I stepped in front of Papa. "He's drunk, Papa. He can't operate on her, he's liable to kill her. The shape he's in, I wouldn't trust him to take a splinter out of my finger, much less cut me open."

Papa glanced at Doc. "Can you do it? Or do you need to sober up first?"

Doc licked his lips He raised a shaky hand to wipe sweat off his brow and this movement seemed to knock him off course. He stumbled forward a couple of steps before Papa put a hand against his chest to stop his momentum.

"Be best to do it sober, but I don't know if she'll make it till then."

Fear tingled along my spine. "Papa, can't we wait for Doctor Hudson? This," I waved my hand in Doc Willoughby's direction, but didn't finish what I'd started to say. Papa wouldn't tolerate disrespect for any man, even from me. "Isn't there someone else? He can't even stand on his own two feet."

Papa gave me a considering look and finally said. "Bess, there are times in life when you've got to take what's there at the time for taking. That girl's bad sick and Doc's right here. If it's her appendix, I don't think we have time to wait for Hudson and God knows there's no time to ride to Marshall and bring back one of their doctors."

Doc put his hand to his mouth and belched softly. "That's right," he slurred. "We don't have much time at all. If the appendix ruptures, it's certain death." He glanced back at Druanna. "Course, that may have already happened. Won't know till I open her up."

Papa looked around. "Where do you want to operate, Doc? What do you need?"

"I reckon your kitchen table's the best place."

I plucked at Papa's shirtsleeve. "Papa, please, don't let him do this. He'll kill her. He isn't sober enough to tie his own shoes. He'll kill her."

"I ain't got much choice, Bess." Papa bent down and picked Druanna up in his arms. I followed along to the kitchen. He waited for me to clear everything off the table then gently laid her down.

Elisi came into the room. Our eyes met and I knew she had heard everything spoken in the parlor. I sent her a pleading look. She put her hands over Druanna's body, hovering inches above her abdomen, chanting in the Cherokee tongue.

Papa watched her, his eyes hooded. He and Elisi had no love for one another, and at that moment, the animosity between them seemed almost palpable.

Doc shambled in and placed his medical bag on the table. He rolled up his sleeves, his hands shaky and frail.

Elisi glared at my father as she pointed at Doc Willoughby. "Your doctor there will kill her."

"We don't have time for this," Papa said, his voice gruff.

"Your doctor is drunk. He isn't in his right mind. He'll kill her as soon as he touches her." Her voice rose shrilly.

"Papa, please. Listen to Elisi. She knows these things." I hesitated then plunged ahead. "And I do, too. He'll kill her, I know he will. You can't let that happen."

Papa's gaze shifted from me to Elisi, then back to me. "Bess, you and your great-grandmother need to mind the babies. I'll help Doc Willoughby." He put his hand on my back and guided me away from the table. "Don't you worry none. I'll make sure Doc doesn't do anything wrong. Hell, I'll cut her open if I have to. But we got to get that thing out of there or she's liable to die, like Doc says."

I turned back to him. Our eyes met. "There's no other way," he said. I knew from the tone of his voice he had made up his mind, and once Papa did, there was no turning back.

Elisi took my hand as we walked up the back staircase. Upstairs, I leaned against the wall, slid down to the floor, holding my arms around my middle. My body shook, my head hurt. I closed my eyes. "She's going to die."

Elisi sat beside me, pulled me into her arms. "She will die anyway, my child. He'll just help her begin her journey sooner."

I turned to her. "Did you see the black cloud, Elisi? Did you see it?"

Her eyes sharpened. "You saw it, too?"

"Yes."

"Oh, child, I am sorry."

I didn't know if she meant the certainty that Druanna would die or my ability to perceive death.

We held each other for a long time, listening to Jack and Thee's slow, steady breathing, the background of deep murmurs from the kitchen. I put my head on Elisi's shoulder and mourned for my mother and my brother, both dead too young and for no just reason. When the men's voices rose in the kitchen, I knew Druanna had departed this life. I closed my eyes and said a prayer for her soul. Elisi began chanting in Cherokee and somehow her soothing tone comforted me.

Elisi squeezed my arm. "Her spirit is free, she has begun her next journey, but she is not *not*." She put her hand under my chin and turned my face to her. "You understand? Her body is dead but her spirit lives on. Try not to grieve too much for her. She will continue."

I wiped my eyes. Even though I had only known Druanna less than a full day, I felt a connection to her. I wasn't sure if it was because we were both young females in a cruel, hard world, or simply that our souls had linked on a deeper, more enigmatic level.

I straightened up. "I hope so, Elisi, truly I do." I took a deep breath. "But he killed her. Doc Willoughby. And Papa let him do it." For the first time in my life, I hated my father, hated him more than I thought possible.

Chapter Eighteen

Summer 1900

He's so windy he could blow up an onion sack.

The circle was complete. The arc that began with Papa bringing a dead man home and laying him out on our kitchen table, continued with first Green's death and then Mama's, came to an end with Druanna's death on that same table. I could only pray Death had had Its fill and would meander back to wherever It came from, leaving us in peace to mourn the ones taken.

Papa, perhaps out of guilt or maybe as a gesture of reconciliation to me, wrapped Druanna up in one of Mama's old quilts, fashioned a quick casket out of leftover wood he had in the barn and took her up to Sandy Gap cemetery. After he dug a grave and buried her close to Mama and Green, marking the spot with a wooden cross, he sent Mr. Norton to Virginia to try to find her family.

When he told me this, my aching heart eased a bit, but I was still hopping mad, and though I thanked him for doing it, I couldn't bring myself to forgive him.

After Mama died, I didn't think I could be any angrier with Papa but I was wrong. My rage with him over Druanna's death grew a thousand-fold when he asked my grandmother to leave. When I questioned this, he brusquely told me he felt I was old enough to handle the household and Elisi needed to get back to her life, and there would be no further discussion about it. I knew, though, this decision stemmed from the events that took place the night he allowed Doc Willoughby to kill Druanna. Now the animosity between my father and Elisi was such that Elisi could no longer bear to be in the same room with Papa. The two made wide berths around one another when passing and the air became thick with tension when they were forced to speak. Although Elisi and I did not discuss that night—after all, what more could we say?—and she never made disparaging remarks to me about my father, my feelings mirrored hers. Even though I had been raised to show respect, it was all I could do to speak to Papa in a civil manner. My efforts to curb my tongue exhausted me and I spent a lot of time in the barn loft, writing in my journal, trying to find a way to purge the resentment and frustration from my whirling mind.

The one bright spot in my life at that time was that I had been asked to play during the sermons at our church. The Sunday after Druanna died, I sat at the organ, waiting for the congregation to file in and take their seats, humming a hymn to myself as I watched the people milling about. When Papa stepped through the doors, anger spiked in my brain and I clenched my fists with unvented outrage. To take my mind off this, I focused on stories I knew about some of the more colorful citizens of our town.

I smiled when I saw Evvie Hall, her head held high, strutting down the aisle toward her favorite pew. Her husband Luther followed, hat in hand, eyes downcast, his hair looking like a cat had been sucking on it. Luther must have sensed my thoughts because he licked the fingers of his other hand and tried to slick down the cowlick sticking up from the crown of his head. I wondered, not for the first time, if Evvie wasn't one of those Christian hypocrites, because it seemed every time the church doors swung open, there stood Evvie, Bible clutched in one hand, hymnal in the other. Or maybe she thought it might atone for the fact that she was married to a heathen; at least that's how the pastor referred to Luther. It was rumored Luther loved Evvie best but moonshine came in a close second. Luther made it known he didn't agree with some of the principles of Christianity but recent events brought him here, and I wondered how long this relapse would last.

I bit my lip so I wouldn't laugh out loud over Evvie's

version of Luther's latest near escape with death when Luther got hold of some moonshine that had been stored in a galvanized container. If Luther had any sense, he'd have known that would turn the liquor to poison. I shook my head with derision. What was it Evvie said one time? Oh, yes. Luther was so useless, if he had a third hand, he'd need another pocket to put it in. Luther barely made it home after he drank the concoction and stumbled through the door yelling for Evvie. He lay on the floor, holding his stomach, gasping with pain, telling Evvie he was going to die, he knew it for sure this time, and asked her to pray for him. Evvie commenced to praying over Luther, asking God to spare his drunken life, to forgive his sins. Right in the middle of all this, Luther raised up and said, "Hell, woman, don't tell Him I'm drunk!" A giggle escaped at that and I put my hand over my mouth.

So here Luther was, back in church, and I was fairly certain Evvie was the reason behind this latest appearance. I figured it wouldn't be too much longer when the need for moonshine would overcome the need for Evvie.

The choir filed into the room and mingled a bit while everyone found their place. Mr. Stanton's more-orange-than-red hair drew my gaze, reminding me of a freshly-picked carrot. I watched him give a secretive wink to Mrs. Bristow, whose lips turned upward at the attention. I searched the congregation for Mr. Bristow, wondering if he noticed. There he was, sitting near the back, his attention on his red-headed son who sat in his lap, clapping his little hands together when he saw his mother.

Gertrude and Arthur Ramsey stepped over the threshold, Gertrude holding her baby in her arms, Arthur looking proud as a peacock. The women at the quilting bee predicted wrong. Hattie Bristow didn't hang her head in shame for long before she'd been replaced by Gertrude Walland and Arthur Ramsey and their rush to the altar. The town gossips buzzed for months about those two, and sure enough, not long after their wedding, Gertrude started gaining weight. A mere six months later, she delivered a healthy nine-pound baby boy. As the women said, Gertie and Arthur ate supper before they said grace.

Doc Nanny ambled up the aisle toward me, a wide grin on his face, looking at no one in particular. I considered him a much better musician than myself but everyone in town thought he was touched in the head. The pastor had, in what I considered an unchristian manner, forbidden him to play during church services. Most people couldn't remember Doc's real name or how he'd gained the nickname. Even Doc claimed he couldn't recollect what his given name was. I asked him once if his mother hadn't recorded it in their family Bible, but he said none of them knew how to read or write, so he reckoned not. Doc's brother Horace strolled along behind him, his eyes focused on Doc's back. Horace, as usual, had his head wrapped in a dark-green turban, looking like a native from some exotic country. He'd taken to wearing the turban when he got his hair cut down at the barber shop and the barber snipped it too short. Ever since then, well over two years now, he kept his head covered. I wondered who actually didn't have all his marbles in that family.

When the Bearing sisters and their brother Tommy crossed over the threshold, I turned around and faced the organ, pretending to organize my sheet music. I couldn't help but steal a glance behind me, watching the sisters fuss over Tommy as they herded him toward a pew, then all three hovered around him after he sat down, making sure he was comfortable and didn't need anything. Tommy accepted the attention like a king sitting on his throne being catered to by his servants. No wonder he thought the sun came up to hear him crow.

The crowd thinned out at the door and a beam of sunshine shone through. My eyes were drawn to that light and standing there in the doorway, silhouetted against the sunbeam, stood Fletcher Elliott. He took off his hat and held it between both hands, staring into the dim sanctuary as if unsure he wanted to come inside. His dark hair fell forward onto his forehead and his blue eyes looked solemn and brooding. An inch or two taller than me, his wide shoulders and powerful arms belied an otherwise slim frame. My heart sped up and my breath came in quick little gasps. Lord, he was one fine-looking man, although a bit standoffish.

I wondered if he was a Democrat because Papa wouldn't let a Republican past the front gate. No matter, Papa wouldn't like him anyway. Since my graduation, he had begun his quest to see me married to a well-to-do man and Fletcher Elliott was nowhere near high-falutin' enough for Papa's tastes.

Pastor Bishop entered from a side door and strutted to the pulpit. With a sigh, I placed my fingers on the keys and began the introductory notes, signaling everyone to be seated and the choir to come to attention.

After church, I started walking toward home but changed my mind and veered into the woods to look for wildflowers. When I'd picked enough for three small bouquets, I wandered back to the graveyard to lay them on Mama's, Green's and Druanna's graves. I settled on the grass nearby and talked to them for a good two hours as if they were all sitting right there in front of me instead of resting beneath the ground.

I bid them farewell and took my time walking back toward home. I couldn't face returning to that house, filled with such antagonism. Papa, I knew, would be there, putting the finishing touches on a new outhouse. Elisi would be present, minding the children and preparing for her journey home. She would be leaving tomorrow and the thought of losing her filled my heart with such pain. Tears sprang to my eyes and I brushed them aside, clearing my burning throat. I would miss my great-grandmother terribly. Since my mother's death, Elisi had stepped into my life as a well-loved substitute for her.

It was mid afternoon by this time, and still I dawdled. When I realized the path to my right led to Miss Cordy Etheridge's small place, I stopped and considered. Although she attended church regularly, most shunned her and some were afraid of her. At the very least, everyone thought she was odd, especially since she'd started carrying her prize hen, Elsie, with her wherever she went, except to church and only because Pastor Bishop banned her from doing so. Curiosity led me up the rutted path and I hid behind a bush, remembering Aunt Belle's comments to Mama about her. The front door banged open and Miss Cordy stepped out on the porch. She sat on the top step, crying into her apron.

At church that morning, she had seemed distraught, not her usual reserved self, but I had been so consumed with my anger and grief, I only noticed her peripherally. Some people called her a witch but she didn't look so scary to me and I wondered why she was crying. Giving in to my inquisitive nature as I remembered Elisi's words about Miss Cordy being a whistling woman and that she had trailed along at both Green's and Mama's funerals, I decided to pay her a visit. Maybe she would feel free to share her concerns with me. Perhaps if I heard someone else's problems, I wouldn't feel so awful about my own.

Still weeping, Miss Cordy got up and walked back into the house. That decided me.

I stepped into the yard, looking for Elsie, who Miss Cordy treated as a member of her family. More like a domesticated animal than fowl, Elsie followed Miss Cordy around as a cat or dog might do. When Miss Cordy sat, Elsie flapped her wings and waited for Miss Cordy to place her in her lap, where she stroked the hen like a prized pet. Not spying Elsie, I surmised she must be in the house. I stepped up onto the porch and knocked on the wooden door, sensing something amiss. There was an air of dejection about the place, a feeling of doom. Something terribly wrong had happened here.

After several moments, I heard shuffling movements inside then Miss Cordy opened the door. Her eyes were bloodshot, her hair disheveled. "Miss Cordy, are you all right? Are you sick? Is there anything I can do?" I pushed the door open and grasped her arm.

She wiped her eyes with her apron then forced a smile on her face, her lips trembling from the effort. "Come on in, child."

Without waiting, she turned and walked away. I followed her to the kitchen and sat at the table while she poured me a cup of strong herbal tea.

I looked around. "Where's Elsie, Miss Cordy?"

She broke into tears and I sprang from my chair. "Is she all right? Has something happened to her?"

Miss Cordy collapsed in the chair, sobbing into her apron.

I knelt beside her, hugging her slightly, making comforting noises in my throat.

After a while, she straightened up, wiping her nose and streaming eyes on the apron. "I kilt her," she said, her voice choking.

"What? Oh, but it must have been an accident, Miss Cordy. I know you wouldn't do it on purpose."

She shook her head. "No. I had to. Didn't know nothin' else I could do."

Scooting my chair closer to her, I sat down and took both her hands in mine. "What happened, Miss Cordy?"

She blew her nose on her apron before speaking. "Today was my day to feed Pastor Bishop." She wrung her hands together. "I didn't have nothing a'tall to offer the man. Not even squirrel or possum for a good stew. I ain't been feeling so well lately and haven't been able to go huntin' or nothin'."

It dawned on me what she meant. I felt my mouth drop open. "Oh, no, not Elsie."

"I didn't have nothin' else to feed him." She burst into tears once more.

I waited for her to calm down. In my mind, a good cry was exactly what Miss Cordy needed. After a while, I asked, "Where's Hunter?" referring to her son.

"Why he's gone over to Asheville way, thought he might could get work there. He left last month and I ain't heard nothin' from him since."

"Oh, I'm sorry. I didn't know. I would have helped if I'd known, Miss Cordy. Why didn't you say something in church?"

She straightened a bit. "My problems are my own, I don't want nobody feeling sorry for me or like they got to help me." Her voice shook with strong emotion and I couldn't help but think of what her pride had cost her: her prized pet.

"That's not what I meant. Why, you'd help me, wouldn't you, if I needed help?"

"Of course, I would. I'm a Christian woman."

"It's the same with me."

Her eyes teared up. "I had to feed him something. I didn't

know what else to do."

I sat back in my chair, feeling awful. That poor woman and her sweet chicken. Elsie had been like a child to Miss Cordy, a substitute for a family she never really had. Her husband died when Hunter was a baby and Hunter grew into a man who preferred being outdoors with other men rather than inside with his mother. He liked to go hunting with his buddies, stay out drinking. Even when Hunter was around, he wasn't much account. Miss Cordy put up with his ways because she had no one else to help her.

"Is there anything I can do?" Tears streamed down my cheeks. "Anything at all?"

She put her hand on my arm. I noticed how very old her skin was. Like parchment stretched thin over thick blue cables and speckled with brown spots. She seemed so frail to me, then, so very old and infirm.

"You're a sweet child," she said, her voice shaky. "It's enough that it matters to you."

A spike of anger shot through my mind as I thought of Pastor Bishop. He probably ate every last bite of Elsie, not even paying attention to Miss Cordy and her distress. Probably couldn't have cared less, anyway. He strutted around town, preceded by his amply rounded belly, expecting families to provide his meals instead of taking it upon himself to feed his portly body. I hated it when he came to Sunday dinner. He was narrow-minded and opinionated and didn't mind espousing his point of view to anyone within hearing distance. Although he called himself a Christian, I had a hard time correlating his vicious gossip, bigoted expressions, and arrogant manner as such. I often thought if God's heaven was filled with creatures like him, maybe that's not where I wanted to end up.

I sat there, watching Miss Cordy cry, wiping at my own tears. If only I had known, I would have done something. And could not stop the small voice speaking in my head: You should have talked to her this morning, Bess, instead of wallowing in your grief. Well, I'd have to make it up to her in some other way, I decided. And I would.

As I walked home, it occurred to me that I had accomplished what I hoped to by my visit to Miss Cordy. My troubles, indeed, had been forgotten. I just wished it hadn't been over the death of her poor, sweet hen. Thoughts of Elisi and her departure on the morrow flitted through my mind and I pushed them aside, instead concentrating on what pet I might find for Miss Cordy to care for. I kept an eye out for a stray dog or cat, chicken, or even a pig, an animal needing a good home and a caring owner, but had no such luck. With a sigh, I stepped onto our front lawn, thinking I'd begin my search tomorrow, after Elisi left. Biting my lip, preparing myself for an emotional evening, I opened the door and stepped inside.

***

Early the next morning, Loney and Thee clung to Elisi, begging her not to go. Roy stood a bit away, ramrod straight, trying to project the image of a man disciplined enough to control his emotions, but the constant swiping of his eyes belied this. Papa looked on with a cold eye, his mouth set in a grim line. I held Jack, blinking back tears. When it was my turn to tell Elisi goodbye, I thrust Jack at my father, my cold glare meeting his, watching as his eyes warmed, now showing sympathy and a bit of guilt for the plight of his children.

I threw myself into Elisi's arms, sobbing, my heart breaking with pain. "I wish you'd stay," I whispered in her ear.

She pulled back, cupping my cheek with one weathered, calloused hand. "You will do well enough without me, ayoli." Tears trailed down her brown, lined cheeks. "Besides, I will always be with you. You remember that." She kissed the corner of my mouth and turned to mount her horse. I threw my father another dark look. The least he could do would be to travel with Elisi. But I knew the decision to make the journey by herself had been hers alone. At least Papa had seen she had a good horse to see her home.

Elisi settled the commodious saddlebag behind her then waved at me and the other children before nudging the horse with her heels and trotting away. I watched her small figure swaying in the saddle, her long, gray braid trailing down her back, and prayed she would have a safe journey.

When I turned, Papa was beside me. He held Jack out to me. I took her in my arms and settled her on my hip.

"It's for the best," Papa said. He turned and walked toward the barn.

"Maybe for you," I called after his back.

He hesitated for a moment; Papa wasn't used to backtalk from me. But he apparently thought my sass not worth commenting on and continued on his way.

Roy followed after Papa and I herded Loney and Thee into the house, instructing Loney to look after Thee while I put Jack down for her nap.

The next few days went by in a blur as I transitioned from sister to mother to my siblings. Most of my days were spent in the kitchen, either preparing meals or cleaning up afterwards. When Roy and Loney weren't at school, they helped with the chores. I spoke to my father only when he addressed me and otherwise pretended he didn't exist. I had lost a friend and the most important woman in my life because of him and doubted I would ever forgive him for such. I made the decision during that time to seek employment as far away from Hot Springs as I could. That way, I could escape my father and my caretaking responsibilities. Papa made enough money that he could afford to hire a woman to take care of the children and household. I had no desire to carry that burden on my shoulders for long.

After a couple of weeks, we had settled into some semblance of order. Twice a week, I took Loney, Thee and Jack with me to visit Miss Cordy, always leaving behind eggs, fresh vegetables from our garden, and meat. I told her these were given to my father in payment for his carpentry services and we had too much food for us to eat. On the afternoons we didn't visit Miss Cordy, after Loney arrived home from school I left her in charge of Thee and Jack and walked into town on the pretext of shopping or doing an errand but in reality taking a break from the drudgery of housework and child rearing.

The construction of a new Presbyterian chapel for Dorland Institute held my interest and I made a point of visiting the site on my daily walks to see the progress being made. When completed, it would be a beautiful building, one that would serve the town and its citizens well. Situated on Bridge Street, the main thoroughfare through town, I could see it becoming an added attraction for the tourists who came to Hot Springs for the waters. It couldn't compete with the grandeur of the Mountain Park Hotel, of course, but it promised to be a popular spot. Many of the parishioners of Sandy Gap, including Papa, were already talking about joining the new church so they wouldn't have to travel so far for Sunday services. I had met the pastor and I liked him much more than Pastor Bishop, so I hoped Papa would switch.

One Friday afternoon, as I strode by the sawmill I saw Fletcher Elliott kneeling beside a dog, running his hands over the animal's side as if inspecting him. I stepped closer and watched for a moment, admiring the muscles in his upper arms as he flexed them with each movement. My attention eventually turned to the dog, a small mutt with shaggy brown fur which appeared to be bald in places. The dog bore the examination stoically, although I could see from his eyes he was not in the best of health. Ribs stood out in stark relief against his fur and his tail drooped as if he had lost all hope in the world.

"What's wrong with that dog?" I asked.

Fletcher twitched, as if startled, and looked over his shoulder at me. Those intense blue eyes of his bore into my own and a thrill ran through my body. He turned back to the dog. "He's got the mange, I think."

I walked over to have a look. "Oh, poor thing. Can it be fixed?"

"Probably."

I grew annoyed he didn't have the backbone to look into my eyes. I straightened and said, with a great deal of irritation, "I would appreciate it, sir, if you would look at me when you speak to me."

He glanced up and I saw a hint of amusement in those eyes, crowded with a margin of anger. "I said, probably."

"Well, are you going to fix him or not?"

"Can't do it. The boss means to put him out of his misery."

A cold chill crept up my spine. "What exactly does that mean?"

"He's gone inside to get his gun. I reckon he's gonna shoot him."

"Why in the world would he want to kill a living, breathing thing that isn't doing any bit of harm to anyone in the world?"

"It's on his property, I guess. According to him, that gives him the right."

"Well, we'll see about that." I stepped forward and picked the dog up in my arms. It trembled against me and my heart went out to it. "As of now, this dog belongs to me and I dare anyone to try to shoot him. Why, they'll have to shoot me first."

Fletcher stood up and stared at me as he took off his hat and wiped the sweat from his forehead with the back of his arm. He turned at the sound of footsteps coming toward us. His rigid posture told me his boss must be heading this way.

I hightailed it toward the street, making sure I was off the sawmill property. The owner, Gerald Dunlap, called after me but I ignored him until I was far enough away I'd have a good head start if he got it into his head to come after me.

I turned back to him, the dog clutched against my bosom. "You called me, Mr. Dunlap?" I said, my voice icy sweet.

"I reckon you better bring that dog back on over here, Miss Bessie. He's got the mange and needs to be put out of his misery." He lifted the gun up to show me how he intended to do it.

"You're not going to kill this dog, Mr. Dunlap. I'm going to save him."

Fletcher, his back to his boss, grinned at that. He quickly wiped the back of his hand over his mouth.

"He's liable to give it to you," Dunlap said, nodding his head sagely.

"Well, if he does, he does. I see no reason to kill an animal that can be saved, Mr. Dunlap. Why, a proper Christian would have fed the poor thing, taken care of him till he got well, then found a good home for him."

Dunlap bristled at that. At church, he was one of the loudest at proclaiming his faith and didn't like his conviction challenged.

"That dog can't be saved," Dunlap roared. "He's got the mange and he's gonna give it to you. Bring him on over here so I can take care of the matter."

I backed further away. "Mr. Elliott, what can I do to treat this poor dog?"

I waited to see what Fletcher Elliott would do. If he kowtowed to Mr. Dunlap, took the side of murdering this sweet animal, I swore then and there I would never look at him again. But Fletcher never even glanced at his boss. Instead, he stared straight into my eyes and said, "Kerosene's the best I've seen. Wash the dog then put kerosene on the bald patches. He should be well enough in a few weeks."

"Thank you very much, Mr. Elliott." I nodded my goodbye to Mr. Dunlap and went on my way, the dog lying passively in my arms.

Out of sight of the sawmill, I had no idea what to do with the dog. I could take him home but we had more than enough animals running around the place, as Papa liked to proclaim. Besides, I was angry with Papa and asking if I could keep the dog, at least long enough to get him well, would mean having to have an actual conversation with him. The thought of having to ask him for something tasted bitter on my tongue. Then I remembered Miss Cordy, living up there by herself, no pets to take care of after sacrificing her beloved Elsie to the sanctimonious and uncaring Pastor Bishop. I reversed direction and went back down the street, staying on the opposite side when I passed the sawmill. They were back to business over there, but I kept my nose in the air and my head high as I passed by, resisting the urge to glance over at Fletcher Elliott.

Walking the path to Miss Cordy's house with the dog in my arms was a commodious task but I managed to do it. The poor thing wasn't that heavy but maneuvering up a rocky pathway carrying a bundle in my arms proved to be awkward at best. When I finally arrived at Miss Cordy's, I was out of breath and starting to see dots in front of my eyes. I climbed the porch steps one at a time in slow motion and leaned beside the door for a minute to catch my breath.

Miss Cordy must have heard my footsteps crossing the porch because she opened the door and looked out. She caught sight of me and her eyes opened wide. "Bess, what are you doing here? You was just here yesterday."

I held the dog out to her. "They were going to kill this poor thing, Miss Cordy, and I thought maybe you could help me get him back to health so I can find a good home for him."

Miss Cordy opened the door and ushered me inside. "Come on into the kitchen and let's have a look." Her eyes, dull and lifeless when she opened the door, now brightened and were practically glowing.

I laid the dog down on the kitchen floor. He was too weak to move other than to raise his head to lick my hand and wag his limp tail in a half-hearted wave.

Miss Cordy knelt beside me, studying the dog's patchy fur. She ran her hands over the protruding ribs. "My, my," she said, in a low voice. "Who would want to starve a pretty little thing like you?"

The dog whimpered in answer.

"That Mr. Fletcher Elliott told me you can use kerosene to cure the mange. He said to bathe the dog then put kerosene on the bald patches."

"Why that's pure torture." Miss Cordy gave me a look. "I have my own remedy for the mange. My own little recipe made from herbs I grow." She rose to her feet. "I'll go get it right now."

I petted the dog until Miss Cordy returned, running my hands over his back and stomach. The dog lay there, eyes closed, seeming comforted by my touch.

Miss Cordy sat on the floor beside the dog and put his head in her lap as she spoke to him. "Now, I'm going to be a-puttin' a salve on you to help you get better. It won't hurt none, I promise. And after that, we'll have us a little something to eat."

I jerked at that. I had forgotten Miss Cordy's dilemma with food.

She must have noticed, for she looked at me.

Understanding dawned on her face. She patted my cheek. "Don't you worry about that. You've brought me more than enough food to stay me for awhile, and I'm well enough now that I'm able to hunt a bit and work in my garden. We'll get by."

"I hope you don't mind that I bring you food, Miss Cordy. We have way more than we need."

She smiled at me. "You're a sweet child." She patted the dog on the head. "And Little Bit here's going to be a big help to me when I hunt. Why, you'll tree me some coon and possum, won't you, sweetie?" she said to the dog.

Little Bit opened his eyes and panted a smile.

Joy surged through my body and I laughed with delight. "Are you saying you want to keep him, Miss Cordy?"

"Oh, child, it's not me that wants to keep him. It's him that wants to keep me." She glanced up at me. "You're too young to understand that yet, but when it comes to animals, more times than not, they choose us. God brought him to you, then through you to me. He's meant to be my Little Bit." She smiled down at the dog. "And don't you worry about him, Bess. I'll give him a good, loving home."

I squeezed her hand. "That's why I brought him here, Miss Cordy. I knew you would."

Chapter Nineteen

Fall 1900

Shucking corn.

Even though it had been almost a year, the Thanksgiving after Mama passed was a sad affair. Papa didn't take Roy on their annual wild turkey hunt and Roy's heart wasn't into going alone, so we made do with baked ham. Loney and I fixed the traditional side dishes, sweet potatoes, green beans we'd canned during the summer, and biscuits, but without Mama there, it seemed more a chore to get through than a family event. The sun shone bright in a sky so blue it ached to look at it for long and the air had a bite to it, although it seemed a bit warmer than Thanksgivings past. I wished Mama were here to enjoy such a beautiful day and reached out with my mind, hoping to connect with her spirit, sighing with disappointment when she didn't answer.

I had by this time forgiven Papa for Druanna's death and sending Elisi home but could not forget these things and there now existed a wariness between us that had not been present before. I knew Papa grieved Mama even more than I did but could not find it in myself to give him the comfort he needed. I missed her terribly and resented having to care for the household. My dreams had been put on hold and I wondered if I would ever be able to have my career as a teacher or maybe to travel as I had hoped. But such was my fate and I had resigned myself to it.

Knowing Miss Cordy's son Hunter was still away and she had no family to spend the holiday with, I invited her to join us and was warmed by her happy response. She arrived early afternoon with Little Bit in tow. The small mutt had blossomed under her care and was quite a handsome dog with silky fur and bright brown eyes and a tail that rarely stopped wagging. Now, instead of a pet chicken following her about, Miss Cordy had Little Bit, who generously gave her the love she had never received in life, and I was happy to note that each benefited from their affectionate relationship. Miss Cordy's eyes shone with health and happiness and she seemed in good spirits.

Little Bit turned out to be a blessing to our Thanksgiving. Thee and Roy romped and played with him as Jack watched, shrieking with glee at their escapades. Even Papa let loose a chortle now and then. It was good to hear laughter in the house once more and I silently thanked God for Miss Cordy and her sweet dog.

At dinner, Miss Cordy asked if we would be attending Gerald Dunlap's corn husking party, which took place each year on the Saturday after Thanksgiving. Unlike most of the mountaineers who planted their corn in rocky terrain, yielding sparse results, Mr. Dunlap planted acres of corn on rich bottom soil along the French Broad River. On the Friday after Thanksgiving, the sawmill employees gathered up the corn in his fields and moved it to his barn in preparation for the biggest corn shucking party in Madison County. Mr. Dunlap's wife Louise prepared delicious dishes and most of the women attending brought food, as well. On Saturday, large wooden tables set up along the barn's inner walls bowed under the weight of platters of baked hams, fried chicken, sweet potatoes, beans, pickled vegetables, cornbread, biscuits and a multitude of fine desserts. Kegs of sweet cider sat near the tables and Luther Hall could be counted on to provide the moonshine, although I was sure he would take a lot of ribbing over what kind of container it had been stored in. Luther, an affable soul, would probably laugh along with the men while peeking about, hoping Evvie wasn't anywhere near.

I glanced at Papa, waiting for him to answer. We hadn't discussed it, although in years past, we always attended the party. Papa put down his fork and sat back, rubbing his lips with a napkin. "Well, Miss Cordy, I hadn't thought about it. If everybody wants to go, I reckon we will."

Roy and I stared at one another for a moment before Roy said, "I think it'd be good for us all to go, Papa. We haven't had any fun since..."

"Yes, Roy's right. We should go," I said before everyone's minds turned to Mama's death.

"Well, then, we will." Papa leaned back in his chair, patting his stomach. "That was a mighty fine dinner, girls. Why, I'm chugged full."

Loney giggled at this.

I turned to Miss Cordy. "Are you going, Miss Cordy?"

She reached down to pet Little Bit, staring up at her with adoring eyes. "I'm not fer sure I'll go this year. After all, it was that Mr. Dunlap that wanted to kill my Little Bit here just for havin' the mange. Don't know as I'm feeling particularly well toward the man."

Papa picked up a piece of ham and tossed it to the dog. "I reckon he'd been misinformed about the mange, Miss Cordy, thinking there wasn't a cure for it." He glanced at me and his eyes glimmered. "I'm sure he's better educated about the subject now."

I couldn't resist smiling back. I hadn't known Papa was aware of my confrontation with Mr. Dunlap.

Miss Cordy snorted. "That man don't know nothin' about nothin' unless it has to do with that business he runs or showing up at church every Sunday acting all religious, shouting his amens and hallelujahs loud enough for the Lord Jesus above to hear."

Papa threw back his head and laughed.

"You should go, Miss Cordy, and bring Little Bit. Show Mr. Dunlap what Christian loving and kindness can do."

She gave me a beatific smile and squeezed my hand. "Why, Bess, I just might do that." Tears shone in her eyes. "I can't thank you enough for bringing him to me. He saved my life, Bess. I want you to know that."

I patted her arm, my own eyes misting. "You did the same for him, Miss Cordy, and it does my heart proud to see the two of you together."

Roy, always uncomfortable in the presence of emotion, rubbed his hands together. "What's for dessert, Bessie? I left room enough for a plate or two, I reckon."

***

Saturday morning, Papa and Roy helped me cart the dishes I had prepared out to the wagon. My mind dwelt on the party and Fletcher Elliott, who, as Mr. Dunlap's employee, would be there. By this time, I had resigned myself to a lost relationship with him. He seemed to have developed a dislike for me and had become expert at disappearing whenever I appeared nearby. I couldn't fathom what I had done to warrant this sort of behavior but accepted that he wanted nothing to do with me. I vowed to myself to make as much of an effort to stay away from him as he did me.

When we finished loading the wagon, Papa stepped back and pretended to wipe sweat off his brow. "Law, Bessie, I ain't never seen so much food from one household." He sniffed the air. "I reckon this might be what heaven smells like." He smiled at me, a twinkle in his eyes.

I smiled back and for a moment the tension between us faded. I hugged him hard, wishing we could get back to where we used to be.

Roy clapped his hands and said, "Let's get a move on. I'm near starved to death."

Roy, Loney and Thee sat in the bed of the wagon while I rode beside Papa, holding little Jack in my arms. She was a good baby, cheerful and content with her world. I held a finger in front of her, watching as she grasped it and pulled it to her mouth. She looked so much like Papa, with his dark hair and sparkling eyes. I wondered what would happen in her life. Would she marry and have children? Would she be happy? I prayed so.

Loney, easily bored on trips, moved to sit behind Papa. "Tell us a story, Papa, about when you were little."

Roy and Thee moved closer. Papa's tales about his childhood were always entertaining.

Papa sat in silence for a moment, "Did I ever tell you about my grandma Daniels?"

A chorus of "No's" responded.

"Well, if I recall rightly, when Granny Daniels died, we were all beside ourselves with grief." He darted a smile my way. "Granny Daniels had a joyous nature but was a bit of a spitfire like you, Bess, so I reckon you come by it honest."

I couldn't help but feel proud, hearing this.

"I wasn't but a young'un then, no older than Thee, I reckon. So, the family got together and discussed it and decided to set Granny Daniels out in the sun and let her dry out real good, then store her in the closet. And when we wanted to visit with her or spend time with her during holidays, why, Pap'd take her out, soak her in saltwater for a few hours, and she'd be good as new."

Thee's eyes gleamed with excitement. "What'd you do when you was done visiting, Papa?"

Roy barked a laugh at this. I caught myself before I shook my head. Let Thee believe the story until he grew old enough to know better.

"Well, son, Pap'd put her back out in the sun till she shriveled back down. Then we'd hang her in the closet again."

I tried holding my laughter back and ended up snorting. Roy had a good chuckle over that.

When we calmed down, Thee said, "Whatever happened to her, Papa?"

Papa paused for a dramatic moment. "Why, you know something, Thee? We moved away from that house during the war when the Yankees come. Never thought about it before but I reckon we left Granny Daniels behind in that closet. Why, I bet she's still hanging in there waiting for us to soak her in saltwater for a visit."

"You reckon so?" Thee breathed.

Papa winked at me. "Yep, I reckon so, 'less, of course, them Yankees did somethin' with her. I would've liked to see their faces when they opened that closet door and come across that withered body."

Roy, Loney and I burst out laughing again, and by the time I got myself under control, tears were streaming down my face.

"Here we go," Papa said, pulling into the Dunlap barnyard. Wagons were parked every which way with lone horses and mules hobbled in the nearby meadow, grazing. Papa found a place for our wagon, set the brake and hopped down. I waited for him to come around and take Jack, then held his hand as he helped me climb down. Loney took Jack out of Papa's arms and headed toward the barn, anxious to show her baby sister to her friends. They loved nothing more than to fuss over little Jack like a baby doll come to life.

I helped Papa and Roy carry our dishes inside and place them on one of the tables. Papa headed outside and around the barn to join the men drinking moonshine. I didn't blame him for that. Papa hadn't enjoyed much since Mama died. He needed the companionship of other men and a drink or two to help him relax. Roy saw friends from Dorland and headed toward them with a wave and shout.

Mr. Dunlap bade me a warm welcome. I was glad he held no malice toward me over our conflict over Miss Cordy's dog. Alice, the mayor's niece, rushed over to greet me. She and I had become quick friends and I was thrilled her father had agreed for her to be educated at Dorland Institute. Alice seemed happy there and I truly hoped she would graduate. So many students never reached that point. Too many were forced to quit school to help at home while others lost interest or couldn't see the value of an education.

Her eyes glistened with excitement. "Oh, Bess, isn't this the most wonderful thing?" She waved an arm in the direction of the corn, piled high in the center of the barn. "I've never been to a corn shucking party but it sounds like it's going to be such fun." We both looked at a small stage set toward the front of the room, guitars and banjos laid about. "And there's to be dancing afterward. Oh, I can't wait to write home to Mama and Daddy about this."

"It is fun," I agreed but hesitated. "Well, the shucking is more work than fun, but the dancing afterward is the best part." I gave her a mischievous grin. "Unless, of course, you find the red ear of corn."

"Red ear? Why is that?"

"Well, whoever finds the red ear gets to claim a kiss from whomever they want."

Her face blushed slightly. "Really?"

"Yes." I nudged her with my elbow. "Who would you pick, Alice, to give you a kiss?"

She put her hand over her mouth and giggled. "Why, Bess, that's easy. I'd pick your brother Roy."

I drew back. Roy was my sibling and I never thought of him as anything else. It came as a bit of a surprise that a girl liked the way he looked. I glanced at him, in the middle of a group of boys, pushing and shoving at one another good naturedly. Roy threw back his head and laughed and I thought of Papa doing the same thing in the exact same way. With parents with dark eyes and hair, we all shared the same traits but Roy had gotten the best from both Mama and Papa.

When I turned back to Alice, she had a concerned look on her face. "You don't mind, do you?"

I studied her blond hair and blue eyes. What a beautiful contrast they would make to one another. "I think you're perfect for Roy, Alice. That makes me very happy."

She linked her arm through mine. "Let's go pick out a spot for the corn shucking, Bess. And keep your fingers crossed one of us gets the red ear." She gave me a teasing glance. "I told you, now you tell me. Who would you pick?"

I searched the room, telling myself I wasn't looking for Fletcher Elliott, knowing I was. "I'm not sure. Maybe I'll meet a stranger here tonight, Alice, a man who will sweep me off my feet." Giggling, we joined the women and men gathered around the stacked corn.

At Mr. Dunlap's invitation, we began to shuck the corn, Roy and his friends competing with one another to see who could do the most the fastest. Alice gazed at him from time to time, the ear of corn frozen in her hands, a wistful look on her face. Well, she was sixteen and I supposed most young women's thoughts turned to marriage at about that age. Would she take Roy back to Knoxville with her if they married? That seemed such a distance for him to be away from us. But Alice was a sweet and merry girl, and I thought she would be a good match for my brother.

I looked around for my younger siblings. Loney sat with her friends, playing with Jack, who gurgled and cooed at them. Thee, like Roy, was amidst a group of children his age, playing with one of Mr. Dunlap's dogs, who liked to chase the ball they devised out of corn shucks and bring it back to them. Papa remained outside and I imagined he was conducting business while drinking. That seemed to be his favorite past-time of late. I smiled when I spied Miss Cordy walking down the length of the tables laden with food, stopping at times to pinch a bite of this or that and feed it to Little Bit, prancing along beside her.

I caught sight of Fletcher Elliott from time to time, sitting with other male employees of Mr. Dunlap, busily shucking the corn. At times, I felt someone watching me, and when I raised my head, caught him staring at me, his gaze earnest and unreadable. Each time our gazes met, he would lower his eyes to his task. You're such a coward, I mentally said to him, wishing he could read my mind.

I froze when I saw the red kernels of corn peaking out between the corn husks. I dropped it in my lap, unsure what to do. I could throw it back in the pile for someone else to find or give it to Alice. I raised my eyes and my gaze met Fletcher Elliott's. No, I thought, I'll keep it.

I shucked the husks off the ear of corn and stood, waving it in the air. Alice clapped her hands with glee and the men and women cheered.

Mr. Dunlap approached me, wiping perspiration off his face with his sleeve. "Well, Bess," he declared, rocking back on his heels. "Looks like you're the belle of the ball. Who are you going to pick to give you a kiss tonight, little lady?"

I hesitated, apprehensive about such a bold gesture. Would Fletcher run away if I named him? Would he refuse? How would he react?

"Well, little missy, who's it going to be?"

I looked around the room, saw Papa standing nearby, a small smile on his face. I drew myself up and said, "I choose Mr. Fletcher Elliott."

Alice giggled and men clapped and some women nodded their heads with approval. Roy frowned at me and Papa turned on his heel and went back outside. I turned toward Fletcher, red-faced at the attention he was getting.

"Fletcher Elliott, come on over here and give this pretty girl a kiss," Mr. Dunlap boomed.

Fletcher rose to his feet, dropping the corn cob he held in his hand. The men around him pushed him forward and he stumbled but quickly righted himself. At first he seemed to approach with great reluctance and I regretted naming him. I didn't want to be embarrassed if he chose to bolt. His eyes met mine and he must have read the challenge in them. He straightened his shoulders and strode toward me, our gazes locked. When he reached me, I saw a glimmer of amusement in his eyes and this relaxed me somewhat. I smiled at him and was relieved when he reciprocated. He tilted his head toward me and gave me a fast peck on the cheek before turning around and rejoining his friends, receiving teasing remarks about his quick kiss.

The group went back to shucking corn. I noted people eyeing Fletcher and me. Wondering, I'm sure, if there was anything between us.

The shucking finished, the men made a fast chore of gathering up the husks, which would be used for fodder, and carrying the ears of corn to corn cribs Mr. Dunlap kept at the back of the barn. After the floor had been cleared, the musicians took to the stage and began to tune their instruments. I saw Doc Nanny join them, a fiddle tucked under his chin. He smiled at me and I waved at him, wishing I could go up and accompany him on the piano. Doc was the best musician in Madison County and it pleased me Mr. Dunlap let him play, unlike that sanctimonious Pastor Bishop.

Mr. Dunlap stepped on stage to call out the movements to the square dances. The music started and men and women immediately partnered and divided as the dance progressed. Alice and I stood to the side, watching them, and I nudged her when Roy walked toward us. So the attraction between them must be mutual, I thought. Alice blushed prettily and when he asked her to dance gave him a small curtsy. Roy grinned at me as he took her hand and I blew him a kiss. He was a good brother and I loved him so. I watched them dance, thinking they were the most beautiful couple there. What would it be like, I wondered, to love someone the way Mama and Papa had loved one another? To create our own world together, as man and wife, share adventures, secrets, family and home? I was already into what some considered spinster age. Would I be an independent woman, traveling the world, writing about my adventures, or teaching in an esteemed school in a big city somewhere? Or would my life be that of the single aunt or daughter who took care of everyone but herself? All the more reason for me to have my own career, I told myself.

I turned to go to the tables to help the older ladies with the food and ran into Fletcher Elliott's chest. I stepped back, flustered at the tingling that went through my body when mine touched his. "I'm sorry, I didn't see you." I moved to sidestep around him.

He cleared his throat as he reached out a hand but stopped short of touching my arm. "Um, I was wondering if you'd like to dance, Miss Bessie," he said, his eyes staring at something over the top of my head.

"Yes, of course."

He took my hand and led me onto the dance floor. We joined the others in a complicated square dance with lots of stomping and shouting. I was winded by the time it ended but laughing from fun. I looked around and Fletcher had disappeared. Where in the world could he have gone to? I decided he must be out back with the other men.

Mr. Dunlap's son Jason asked me for the next dance and I moved through the throng of people, smiling and laughing, having a good time, but always, always, searching the room for Fletcher. When the dance ended, he was once more by my side and, without a word to each other, we partnered, and it pleased me to see him smile and even laugh. Why was he such a solemn man? I knew his enigmatic nature was the attraction that drew me to him. A man I could not figure out who seemed mysterious and sad. I longed to make him smile, laugh, have a good time. More than that, I wanted to see those penetrating eyes sparkle with affection when he looked at me.

During a break, we walked over to the apple cider kegs to get refreshment. As we stood together, an awkward silence ensued between us. By this time, I decided this would begin or end tonight. I could not stand the thought of going through my life pining for someone who in all probability didn't like me very much.

I turned to him and before I could stop myself, said, "Why have you been avoiding me, Mr. Elliott?"

He blinked, shifting his gaze this way and that, not looking at me.

"It's obvious you have. If I've done something to displease you, I'd like to know about it. If you don't like me, that's certainly your choice, but it would help me to know the reasons for your actions."

He finally looked at me and his eyes darkened. With anger or desire? I would never know. "No, Miss Bessie, it's not that I don't like you. I do. I certainly do. Especially after what happened at the sawmill that day with the dog." He grinned. "I like your gumption." He closed his mouth with a click and looked away.

"Well? What is it, then?" I said, impatience in my voice. I softened my tone. "Like I asked you before, would you please look at me when you speak to me?"

He raised his eyes to mine and it took several tries before he finally spoke. "I don't have anything to offer such a woman as yourself, Miss Bessie. I'm as poor as the day is long. And I don't—well, I don't have the education you do. You should be with a properly educated man, a man who can give you everything you want in your life."

I stepped back. "Do you realize, Mr. Elliott, that's the most you've said to me the entire time I've known you?"

He didn't respond.

I sighed. "Don't you think it's my decision who I want to be with, not yours or anyone else's?"

He took his time considering this. "Well, I reckon you're

right, Miss Bessie. But…"

"Oh, hush. If I decide I like you and want to be with you, it's my choice. And if you feel the same way, why, I see no need for us to keep dodging one another like we've been doing."

He blushed at this. "I do apologize for that. I just felt it was best for you."

"Well, it's not." I put my hands on hips. "So, Mr. Fletcher Elliott, what do you propose we do about this?"

Fletcher's eyes glinted with humor. "Well, I reckon, if you've a mind to, we commence to courting."

I smiled at him. "I've a mind to. And you can start by walking me home from church tomorrow."

He ducked his head toward me. "It'd be my honor, Miss Bessie."

We danced together the rest of the evening, as did Roy and Alice. I sensed an aura about them of great happiness with a future bright with hope and was glad for them. As for Fletcher and me, my perceptions were dampened. He seemed so standoffish at times while at others he seemed genuinely interested in me. It confused me and I didn't know if things would work out for us or not but hoped they would.

That night, on the way home, Roy, Thee, and Loney asleep in the bed of the wagon, Jack snuggled up tight in my arms as I rode beside Papa, he said in a low voice. "What made you choose that no-good Fletcher Elliott to give you the kiss, Bess?"

This shocked me. I had no idea Papa felt that way about Fletcher. "Why do you think he's no good, Papa?"

"Why, he's a transient. He ain't from around here, works at the sawmill for practically nothing. He can't provide for you, Bess, so what the hell were you thinking asking for a kiss from him and then dancing most of the dances with him?"

"Because I like him, Papa. I like him a lot."

Papa was silent for a long time. "Hell, Bessie, he's a damn Republican. You don't want to be messing around with a no-count Republican."

I laughed at that. "There's just something about him that

appeals to me. I'm sure you felt that way about Mama and she had to have felt the same way about you, seeing as how her family didn't want y'all to marry." I hesitated. "But you did marry, Papa."

"Bess, there's other, better men out there. That's all I'm saying. I want to see you settled with a good man, a good provider. I want my young'uns happy, that's all I want."

I leaned against him. "I love you, Papa. I want you happy, too."

Chapter Twenty

Fall 1900

He's so useless if he had a third hand he'd need another pocket to put it in.

Papa didn't mention Fletcher Elliott again after that, not even when he walked me home from church the next day. Of course, Papa wasn't in church with us that morning because he had something he needed to do in town and he wasn't at the house when we got there so it could have been that he just didn't know. I guess he figured he'd said his piece and I, being a good daughter, would take his words as gospel and forget all about the man I was pretty sure I would marry one day. I didn't say anything, either, which was probably for the best or who knows what kind of tension I would have stirred up. I didn't want to be at odds with Papa anymore and Fletcher Elliott was a subject sure to have us pecking at each other like a couple of broody hens.

Besides, Christmas was coming and I was determined to make it a happy one despite the fact that Mama was no longer with us. Christmas had always been Mama's favorite time of the year. From the traditional church services on Christmas Eve and Christmas morning through the Twelve Days of Christmas, all the way to Breaking Up Christmas on Old Christmas Eve, she had loved every minute of it. With her gone, I wanted this year to be one the children would remember with happiness instead of sadness. It would take careful planning and a lot of work, but I hoped I could carry on in her stead.

Jack and Thee kept me busy during the day while Roy

and Loney were at school, but as soon as they got home, I often turned the care of the little ones and house over to them. With the colder weather and the fact that the new chapel had been finished, I didn't walk every day. Instead, I usually ended up in the barn loft, working on my Christmas plans or writing in my journal or just daydreaming about Fletcher Elliott and what our life would be like if we did marry. Those thoughts of marriage entailed quite a bit of worry, too. If we married, would we never have anything, as Papa said? Or would Fletcher surprise Papa and turn out to be a man who provided me with everything I could ever want? I was pretty sure he'd make me happy whether he made a good living or not—money and material things just weren't that important to me—but I wanted him to prove Papa wrong. I hadn't been raised like some of the spoiled girls who visited the springs with their parents. I didn't really need much to make me happy but I knew it would please me if Papa approved of Fletcher and welcomed him into the family.

Some days, when the worries about Fletcher got to be too much, I would brave the cold and take a walk to try and clear my mind. And of course, all I'd think about on the walks was Fletcher. It was exasperating the way he filled my thoughts and wouldn't go away.

As I headed back home one day, I heard someone calling my name. I looked up to see one of the Bearing sisters standing on her front porch, waving at me, a smile on her face. I smiled back as I approached the gate, curious as to why she would hail me. The Bearings tended to stay to themselves and were not known as a sociable family. In fact, the only times they were seen about town were shopping and going to church. The three girls resembled one another so strongly everyone simply referred to them as the Bearing sisters, or when speaking to one of them directly, as "Sister." Tommy, their younger brother, was only a toddler when their parents died, so the sisters raised him. None of them chose to marry and they lived together in their small home, caring for their "man of the house," as they called their brother. They fussed over him and pampered him as if he were a prince. They would cluster around Tommy, seeing that his every need was met, reminding me of a flock of blackbirds swooping and dipping over an exposed seed bed.

I hadn't seen hide nor hair of any of the Bearings in weeks, not since an unfortunate incident occurred after which they must have deemed it a good idea to stay out of the town folks' eyes for awhile.

Seemed one night, Tommy ran back inside after a visit to the outhouse, shouting, "I seen me a haint! I seen me a haint!" He instructed his sisters to bring him his rifle and when he had it in hand bravely stood on their back porch in search of his ghost. When he saw a white vision appear from behind the outhouse, he shot at it and jumped back inside, slamming the door shut behind him. The next morning, Tommy and his sisters were shocked to see that his haint was nothing more than the neighbor's white mule, lying dead and frozen on the ground.

"Hello, Sister." I walked toward her, wondering if their neighbor, Mr. Morris, had forgiven Tommy yet.

"Oh, Bessie, it's so good to see you. Come in and visit for a bit, why don't you? It's been a coon's age since we've seen you and we were just this very day talking about you."

This set me back a bit, and I hesitated, wondering why in the world she had chosen to be so friendly to me all of a sudden. Nevertheless, I planted a smile on my face. "I'd love to."

Her hands twittered around her face like a butterfly. "Oh, lovely. I just made some hot coffee. It's awful cold for this time of year, ain't it?" she asked as she led me inside.

I agreed even though the weather for the last few days had been unseasonably mild.

The inside of the house was dim and tattered but warm and immaculate, nonetheless. Sister took my shawl, hung it on a hook by the door, and settled me in the front room with its large fireplace, over which hung a metal coffee pot. "We ain't got no woodstove," she apologized. The other sisters were gathered together on the sofa while I sat on the lone chair, watching as the coffee was poured, uncomfortable at the way the sisters stared at me, as if entomologists inspecting an unknown bug. I accepted the coffee and blew on it before taking a sip, trying not to let my lips pucker at the bitter taste. Did they not have sugar or milk, I wondered, to sweeten the drink, or a dash of salt to cut the harshness of the brew? I made a mental note to put together a basket for them filled with such things. I put the cup down, saying, "Delicious."

They smiled at one another. As we made small talk, I noticed the sisters giving each other covert glances, their gazes darting toward a door leading to what I assumed must be a bedroom. And when Tommy strode into the room to their delighted chattering, I knew at once what this was about. The sisters must have gotten it into their heads that I would make a good wife for Tommy. And Tommy must have agreed. He strutted around, dressed in a suit much too small for him. His knobby wrists hung below the jacket sleeves, his bony ankles stuck out beneath the hem of his pants. His shirt was snowy linen and his tie black and somber, to match the suit. A bright red scarf was wrapped around his neck.

"I think I'll go for a walk," he said.

The sisters looked horrified.

"Oh, no, Tommy, you can't go out there," the oldest sister said. "Why, you're liable to suck down that cold air and catch your death of pneumonia." The other sisters nodded their agreement.

Tommy glanced around and pretended to be startled at sight of me. A slow smile came over his face as he preened before me, seeming unaware that I was not as appreciative of his appearance as were his sisters.

He turned toward me, took one step forward and attempted to bow. Putting too much enthusiasm in the gesture, he overbalanced and stumbled, arms flailing in an attempt to stay upright. I lunged out of my chair and moved back away from him. The sisters made a synchronistic alarmed gasp as Tommy crashed into the chair in which I had been sitting. I turned my back and covered my mouth, trying to stifle the laughter burbling in my throat. Tommy twisted as he fell and landed on his back with a loud crash, floundering about like an overturned turtle. The sisters hovered around him, their hands reaching out to help him, checking to make sure he wasn't injured. I sidled around the room, looking for an escape, and spied a clear path to the door.

I raised my voice over the concerned chirpings of the sisters. "Really, I'm so sorry, but I must be going. Papa needs me at home. It was wonderful seeing all you Sisters and you, too, Tommy. Be well." I grabbed my shawl and rushed out the door, their frowning, disapproving faces following my hasty departure. I ran down the street and once out of sight leaned against a building and let my laughter fly loose. I laughed so hard, tears ran down my face. Once I had myself under control, I looked up, into the soulful eyes of Fletcher Elliott.

He pulled a bandanna from his back pocket and held it out to me. When I took it, he tipped his hat and asked, "You all right, Miss Bessie?"

"I'm fine, Mr. Elliott. I was just doing a little celebrating."

"Celebrating what?"

I wiped my cheeks and smiled at him. "The fact that I was lucky enough to escape the clutches of the Bearing sisters. I swan, they're determined to see me married off to their brother Tommy."

He frowned and I had a moment to wonder if such a handsome man as himself could be jealous of drab, scrawny Tommy Bearing. It was something to think about, but before I could take it too far, he said, "May I walk you home, Miss Bessie?"

I handed him back his bandanna. "I'd like that. Are you through working for the day?"

"Yes, ma'am, I am."

Well, he was talking, but like the Sunday he'd walked me home from church, I could see it would be up to me to carry the conversation. I took a deep breath. So be it. "Beautiful weather we're having, isn't it? Winter's coming on but I hate to see it. Fall is the best time of the year, don't you think?"

"I like spring myself and summer's real nice where I come from."

"And where's that?"

"Over to the other side of Asheville, the Broad River section of Buncombe County. My parents live in the town of Old Fort now. It's just over the county line in McDowell County."

"I've never been there. Is it a big town?"

"No, ma'am, about the size of Hot Springs, I'd say. It's a lot like here, mountains all around, but it gets a lot colder over there in the winter time. It's not protected by a valley like this place is."

"Do you want to go back to Old Fort to live?"

"I suppose I do, or in that general area anyway, maybe one of these days when I make enough money to buy some property. It's a pretty place and all my kinfolk are there. I miss them."

I considered it a plus that he thought so highly of his family but where would that leave me if we did marry someday? Would that mean I'd have to move away from my family and friends here in Hot Springs? I must have frowned at that thought because he asked, "Something the matter, Miss Bessie?"

"No, just thinking about how much you must miss your family."

We were nearing our front gate and I asked impetuously, "Is it true you're a Republican?"

"Why, I'm not much for politics, Miss Bessie, but I guess if I had to choose sides, I'd go with the Republicans. Why do you ask?"

I looked at the front gate and wondered if Papa was home yet and what he would do if I invited Fletcher Elliott, a maybe-Republican, to come in and have dinner with us.

"No reason. Someone happened to bring it up at the corn shucking the other night." I waved it away. "I was just making conversation. Thank you for walking me home."

"I'll see you to your front door, Miss Bessie, if it's all the same to you."

"All right." Surely Papa wasn't home yet, and if he was, maybe it would be good for him to see that his daughter had a mind of her own when it came to men.

Fletcher pushed open the gate and waited for me to walk through. He might be a Republican but his mama had certainly taught him manners. I walked up the steps to the front porch and turned to meet his eyes. "Thank you again. I enjoyed talking with you."

He took off his hat, dipped his head. "So did I. Good evening to you, Miss Bessie."

I let out a disappointed sigh. I had hoped he would remember his words at the corn shucking about courting, but apparently his good manners didn't outweigh his shyness. I searched for a way to bring up the subject myself and finally decided to let it go. It wouldn't be proper for the lady to ask the man. I set it aside to think about after he left. Hopefully, I'd come up with a way to remind him of his words.

"Well, good evening to you."

He surprised me when he just stood there.

"Is there something else I can do for you, Mr. Elliott?"

He cleared his throat before he looked up at me, and after I stood there for what seemed like an hour, he finally said, "Ah, Miss Bessie, would you care to go for a walk with me on Saturday afternoon?" His eyes dropped back to his feet as he wrung the rim of his hat in his hands. I admit, my lips twitched at his obvious discomfort but I waited patiently. My reward came a few seconds later when he looked back up at me. "There's a group of musicians staying at the Mountain Park Hotel and I hear they're going to give an outdoor performance in the little park there on Saturday if the weather holds."

I didn't know if it was by design or sheer luck but he'd hit upon the one thing guaranteed to ensure my agreement, music. I smiled. "I'd love to go with you."

"I'll, uh, I'll come by for you at about two o'clock. That be all right with you?"

I nodded just as the door flew open behind me. Papa stepped out on the porch and took my arm. "Bessie, Loney needs your help in the kitchen. We've got company for supper tonight."

"All right, Papa. I'll see you on Saturday, Mr. Elliott."

Papa's mouth tightened. He glared at me but didn't say

anything as he followed me in the house without bothering to speak to Fletcher. I started to say something to him about his ill manners but a movement in the front parlor distracted me.

Papa had brought home the town lawyer, Mr. Grady Collins. Tall, with narrow shoulders and a skinny build, everything about him seemed long and constricted, from his nose to his feet. His pale-blue eyes were small and too close together. His fine blond hair flew about his face like dandelion fluff off the stem. Above his lip rode a pitiful excuse for a moustache, so light it was almost invisible.

When he spoke his voice was high and reedy, and I wanted to cringe.

"Evening, Miss Bessie. Your father invited me to share dinner with you."

I almost snorted. Dinner with me implied it would just be the two of us and I knew Papa wouldn't stand for that—or would he? Lord knew, he wanted me to like this scrawny, pretentious man but that wasn't going to happen. I would be polite and sit down at the dining room table with my family and I'd listen to him go on and on about anything and everything, but I would not be sharing dinner with only him. He could get that idea out of his mind right now.

I looked at Papa but he wouldn't meet my eyes. Instead, he brushed past me into the parlor and offered Mr. Collins a drink then told me to go help Loney with supper. I decided right then and there that the lawyer needed to go and not come knocking on my door ever again.

I barely said anything during the meal but that didn't matter since I couldn't have gotten a word in edgewise. Grady Collins loved nothing more than the sound of his own voice. By the time supper was halfway through, I knew he was a cynical, critical man and I imagined being married to him would be akin to being in prison. He was, in my eyes, enough to make a preacher cuss with his narrow-minded, judgmental opinions. He talked nonstop, and before we'd even cleared the dinner plates to make way for dessert, I knew exactly what he wanted in a wife: a slave to cater to his every need and whim and agree with his every word. Being married to him would be worse even than being married to Tommy Bearing, if that was possible.

He was definitely not the man for me and I wondered why Papa couldn't see it. I forced myself to eat Loney's apple pie though it tasted like sweet glop and dried up bark to me. As I played with the last of it while everyone else finished, I considered what I could do to make Grady Collins leave and never come back.

Papa gave me the answer when he pushed back from the table, complimented Loney and me on the meal, and told Roy to help his sister with the dishes. I knew Roy wouldn't like being relegated to the kitchen and what he undoubtedly considered women's work, but he didn't protest. Like me, Roy wanted to get as far away from Mr. Collins as possible.

"Bessie, why don't you come in the parlor and play some music for our guest?" Papa said.

I smiled at him. "All right, Papa."

When we got to the parlor, I waited for Papa and the lawyer to sit down before seating myself at the piano. Without asking if they had a song preference, I started playing the bawdiest song I could think of, "Seven Drunken Nights."

A quick glance over my shoulder told me Mr. Collins didn't know the song. He tapped his foot and bobbed his head on his scrawny neck and seemed to be enjoying himself. I played another verse then decided I'd have to sing the actual words to get him out of there. I skipped the first three verses and went straight to the fourth and fifth, which in my opinion were a bit naughtier.

"When I come home the other night as drunk as I could be, I saw two boots beside the bed where my boots oughta be. Come here my little wifey, explain this thing to me, how come these boots beside the bed where my boots oughta be? You blind fool, you crazy fool, oh can't you even see, it's nothin' but a hound dog my granny sent to me. Well, I've traveled this world over, a thousand miles or more, but laces on a hound dog, I've never seen before."

Still no movement from behind me so I continued with the last verse, "When I come home the other night as drunk as I could be, I saw a head on the pillow where my head oughta be. Come here my little wifey, explain this thing to me, how come this head on the pillow where my head oughta be? You blind fool, you crazy fool, oh can't you even see, it's nothin' but a cabbage head my granny sent to me. Well, I've traveled this world over a thousand miles or more, but a moustache on a cabbage head—"

The front door slammed and I knew Mr. Collins had gotten my message. Papa waited until I sang the last words then came over to stand beside me. I smiled up at him. His moustache twitched but he didn't smile back.

"Did you ever wonder why that song's called "Seven Drunken Nights" but it only has five verses, Papa? What happened on the other two nights, I wonder?"

All he said was, "Damn, Bess," before he turned around and followed Mr. Collins out the door.

I'd upset him and I was sorry for that, but after two hours of listening to the lawyer go on and on about nothing that held any importance to me, I was more determined than ever to marry the man I chose, not some sissified man Papa thought would be the best provider.

Chapter Twenty-one

Winter 1900

Breaking up Christmas.

Just as I'd planned, Christmas that year was much better than the one before though I still missed Mama and the rest of the family did, too. It was an added ache to my heart not to have Elisi with me. I tried not to let it show but I'm sure Loney and Roy knew what brought the solemn look to my face every time I thought of her. In the spirit of the holiday, by Old Christmas Eve, I had made up my mind that it would be best for my brothers and sisters if I forgave Papa completely for everything that had transpired since Mama's death.

That was harder than I thought it would be but when he bounced Jack on his knee and made her giggle as Thee sat at his feet listening to him tell the legend about the animals praying at midnight, I thought I could actually do it.

"Ya' see, boy, midnight tonight is when the baby Jesus was first presented to the world. That was when the three Wise Men arrived at the stables where Mary and Joseph had taken shelter so Mary could have her baby. The Wise Men had traveled for miles, following the light of a single star, because they wanted to honor the birth of their Savior. When they showed up and offered the gifts they'd brought, all the animals in the stables woke up, adding their praise to that of the three Wise Men and the angels singing up above. And to this day, they say if you go out right at midnight and stand quietly, you can hear the animals praying, and some say if you can get a look at them, you'll see them kneeling, too. Don't know how true it is, but I've heard tell that the wild animals out in the woods and up on the mountains wake, stand up, and then lay back down on their other side."

I looked at Thee, his eyes wide and filled with love, and knew right then and there that not only could I forgive Papa, I had to for the sake of my family.

Loney, who loved Christmas almost as much as Mama had, sat in Mama's chair beside Papa with a nearly completed quilt top spread across her lap. She'd heard the story many times, but when Papa started telling it, she stopped sewing and listened as raptly as Thee. When the story was finished, she smiled and asked, "Have you ever seen the animals pray, Papa?"

"Can't rightly say I have, but I've heard tell of people who sneak out at midnight and have seen it. 'Course, there's folks who say it's bad luck to go looking for the signs of Old Christmas, that if you do, something bad will happen to you. I don't think that's so, though, since the people I talked to that claim to have seen and heard it all looked hearty to me."

"But if you just happen to be out and see a sign, then it's all right?"

"Sure it is but why would a person be out in the barn at midnight?"

Playing along, Loney said, "Maybe they were late getting home and had to put their horse in the stable before they could go to bed?"

Papa laughed. "Could be, Loney, but we're all safe at home, as most people are on a cold winter night, so I guess we'll stay right here and let the animals and alder bushes do what they do without us."

"The alder bushes?"

Papa winked at Thee. "Did I forget that part? Well, Loney, the animals aren't the only ones who honor the birth of the baby Jesus. The alder bushes do, too. Right at midnight on Old Christmas Eve, no matter how cold the night is or how much snow's on the ground, the alder bushes burst into bloom and some say they even sprout new branches. I've also heard it said that if you listen closely, you can hear the bees roar in the bee-gum, as if they wanted to swarm."

Thee stood up, leaned on Papa's knee and said, "Can we see the animals, Papa?"

"Maybe in a few more years, when you're old enough to stay up until midnight but not this year, boy. This year, I'd say you'll be fast asleep by the time midnight rolls around. Why, you already look like its long past your bedtime and here it's barely gone dark. It's a long time till midnight."

Thee's little face crumpled and Papa patted his head. "Tell you what, Thee, if you can keep your eyes open till then, I'll take you out to the barn myself and we'll see what we can see."

Clapping his hands, Thee jumped up and down. Jack chortled and did her best to slap her tiny hands together, too.

"But Papa, what if it is bad luck?" Loney asked.

"Pshaw, girl, I've talked to lots of people who say they've seen just such a thing and they were all living and breathing when they told me."

Loney picked up her needle and started working on the quilt top again. "Wouldn't that be a lovely thing to see, all the animals honoring Jesus like that?" She looked down at Thee and smiled. "I think it might be worth taking a chance on some bad luck, don't you, little man?"

Thee nodded and clapped his hands again. "Tell us some more, Papa."

"Why that's all I know to tell, boy. Maybe Bess knows more."

Thee ran over to me where I sat on the sofa. "Tell, Bessie, tell."

I smiled at him and ruffled his hair. "I'll tell you what else happens during the twelve days of Christmas, Thee, but it's about people, not about the animals."

He looked doubtful but sat down at my feet, prepared to listen.

"There are some things you shouldn't do, like lend anything to anybody during the twelve days of Christmas because if you do you'll never get it back." I pointed to the fireplace. "You see how the ashes are piling up in the hearth over there? That's because it's bad luck to clean them out during the twelve days. It's also bad luck to wash your bed sheets until Old Christmas is over." I leaned down and sniffed at Thee. "Good thing we only have one more day, else we wouldn't be able to stand the smell."

Thee giggled and dramatically sniffed the skirt of my dress, wrinkling his little nose.

"Tonight is Old Christmas Eve and at midnight people everywhere will be breaking up Christmas." His face crumpled again and I went on hurriedly, "That's not a bad thing. What it means is most people will drink sweet cider and burn a piece of cedar or pine in the fire as a way of saying farewell to the season.

"Do they have to break it because it's old?"

I smiled. "No, sweetie. You see, some people believe the twenty-fifth of December is the day when the baby Jesus was born and the sixth of January is when He was first presented to the three Wise Men and to the world. But a long time ago, most people believed the sixth was the day when He was truly born and that's when they celebrated so that day came to be known as Old Christmas. There are twelve days between the two dates, from December 25th, the 'new' Christmas, to January 6th, the 'old' Christmas, and that gives us the twelve days of Christmas. During those twelve days, people have what they call Breaking Up Christmas parties. Tonight's party is at Aunt Belle's house and there will be lots of sweet cider to drink and music for dancing." I leaned down. "And I'll tell you a secret if you promise not to tell. Promise?"

He nodded.

I bent down and whispered, "Aunt Belle is planning on having a small fire in the street outside her house right at midnight so that people can burn a piece of cedar or pine to officially Break Up Christmas. Don't tell Papa though, or he might have to arrest Aunt Belle."

Thee laughed and whispered back, "I won't. Can I go and see the fire?"

"If you do, how will you see the animals in the barn when they kneel down to pray?"

He frowned. Uncle Ned boarded his horse at the town

211

livery stables so Aunt Belle didn't have a barn or any animals he could spy on to see if they really did pray at midnight.

I took his chin in my hand and lifted it to give him a kiss. "Why don't you stay here with Papa and Loney, and if you can stay awake, Papa will take you out to see the animals. You can see a fire in the fireplace any old time and Roy and I will be sure to burn a piece of pine in Aunt Belle's fire to break up Christmas for you."

Roy came in from the barn, bringing the crisp smell of winter with him. "You about ready to go, Bessie? I've got the horses hitched up and they're champing at the bit."

I stood, lifting Thee with me. "You keep those eyes open tonight, Theodore Norton. I want to hear all about what you see tomorrow."

He put his arms around my neck and hugged me, whispering, "I will, Bessie," in my ear. I squeezed him before kissing his cheek and setting him down on the floor.

Walking over to Papa, I kissed Jack on the top of her head first then bent further in to kiss Papa's cheek. I turned to Loney who set her quilting aside and stood up.

"Have a good time, Bess." She stepped forward and kissed my cheek, which surprised me. Loney wasn't usually given to outward signs of affection.

I took her hand and squeezed it. "You sure you don't mind staying home with the babies? I can stay and you can go to the party if you want."

She smiled. "I don't mind a bit. You know how much I enjoy taking care of them. You and Roy have fun."

I hugged her goodbye. At the door, I turned and looked at my family and the strangest sensation washed over me, as if I stood far away, seeing them in a dream. I could feel their love for me, just as I could mine for them, but there was a distance there, a deep chasm keeping them from me.

Roy took my arm. "Come on, Bessie, I want me some of Aunt Belle's sweet cider. She makes the best in the land."

I started to tease him about what he really wanted, to see Alice again, but then it dawned on me that the reason I was so excited about going to the party was that I knew I'd see

Fletcher Elliott so kept my mouth shut and let him tug me out into the hall. "Good night, everyone," I called before Roy could get me out the front door.

"You sure are in a hurry just to drink some of Aunt Belle's sweet cider."

He winked at me as he helped me into the wagon and the sensation came back, that feeling of love tempered by distance. What did it mean? Surely I wasn't about to lose another member of my family. Hadn't I lost enough loved ones in the past few years?

I wished I could talk to Elisi about it but she was far away and Papa wouldn't be very happy with me if I asked him to take me to see her. He'd do it, but he wouldn't like it. Maybe I could talk Fletcher Elliott into taking me. Except then, I'd need to ask Loney or even Roy to go along with us. It wasn't proper for a young woman to go traipsing all over the countryside alone with a man.

Roy and I were both quiet on the way to Aunt Belle's house, thinking our own thoughts. Mine were all about Fletcher and the feeling I'd had twice tonight, and Roy's, no doubt, all about pretty little Alice.

It wasn't long before I heard the music from the party. Aunt Belle and Uncle Ned would have all the furniture moved to the side of her parlor and some of it undoubtedly rested on the front porch. The musicians, in order to make space for the dancers, would be standing in the open doorway which is why the music could be heard before we got to the house.

Most likely Aunt Belle was still in the kitchen putting the finishing touches on the food she'd cooked or arranging the dishes others had brought. Earlier that day, I'd sent Roy along with a huge baked ham and a sweet potato casserole so we wouldn't have to worry about carrying dishes with us tonight.

Roy sniffed the air. "Smell that? That's the smell of Christmas dying."

I slapped his arm. "No, it's not. It's the smell of good friends gathering to honor the end of the Christmas season. Christmas never dies. It just fades into the background until it's time for it to take center stage again."

"Guess you're right, Bess."

"Of course I am, and if you're smart, you'll do like Mr. Dickens said and keep it in your heart every day."

"Oh, don't go quoting your smarts to me, Bessie. I can read, too, you know."

"True, you can, but do you ever bother to?"

"Shucks, Bessie, as long as I keep up with what's happening in town, there's no need to read. Reading's for sissies, like that lawyer fellow Papa brought home for dinner the other night. Heck, if reading makes me as boring as him then I'll never read anything ever again."

I couldn't argue that point since I agreed with him, but still, not to read just seemed like heathen talking if you asked me. "It helps if you use the brain in your head instead of the one in your backside."

Roy laughed. "Oh, his brain's in the right place, but reading all the books in the world won't help him any 'cause his head's so full of himself there's no room for anything else."

I couldn't argue that point either so changed the subject. "Will Alice be here tonight or is she still in Tennessee with her family?"

"School starts up again on Monday and she was planning to get back today. Don't know if she made it, but I sure hope she did. I guess if she's not here tonight, I'll see her in church on Sunday." He nudged me. "Mr. Elliott gonna be here tonight?"

I was glad the darkness hid my blush and tried to act as if I didn't care a whit about Mr. Fletcher Elliott. "I have no idea if he's going to be here or not. For all I know, he's gone home to Old Fort to visit his family for the holidays."

Roy snorted. "Nope, I saw him at the sawmill the other day. He's here which means you won't have a second to yourself all night long. If he's not squiring you around the dance floor, he'll be standing somewhere nearby watching you."

I nudged him back. "You'll be doing the same thing if Alice is here."

"Yep, I will."

The rest of the short trip, I thought about Fletcher Elliott and the promises in his intense eyes the last time I'd seen him. I had a feeling tonight was going to be special in some way but wasn't sure if it was a premonition or just a general feeling of excitement for the party.

When we got to Aunt Belle's, Roy pulled the wagon around to the back of the house, set the brake then leaped to the ground. He came around to help me down and we walked arm in arm to the back porch. Before we got there, the door burst open, spilling light across the yard and silhouetting a man and a girl standing side by side.

My stomach fell as we got closer and I saw it was Fletcher and Alice. They looked so perfect together, like they were meant to be. With Alice's petite build, Fletcher seemed to tower over her, unlike me, who stood almost eye-level with him. Standing so close together it seemed as if they were connected, I couldn't help but think what a pretty couple they made.

But then Alice said, "Mr. Daniels," as she stepped forward and held out her hand, and the illusion of togetherness faded. I looked into Fletcher's eyes and his lips curved in the smile I'd come to know so well. He walked over and held out his hand to help me up the steps, and when I slipped my hand in his, the feeling I'd had earlier turned into a certainty. Tonight would be a night I would remember for the rest of my life.

And it was. Shy, reticent Fletcher Elliott gathered his courage and, as we threw small pieces of pine—I wouldn't let him burn a cedar branch because of what Elisi had told me about the meaning of the cedar tree to the Cherokee—into the fire, asked me if I would allow him the honor of walking me home. The formal way he said it, the grave look he gave me, I knew whatever he wanted to say must be quite serious. I glanced at Roy and Alice, holding their hands toward the fire for warmth, their faces reflecting the flames dancing wildly before them, heads tilted toward one another, seeming lost as if in their own world. Knowing Roy planned to give Alice a ride back to the mayor's place, I nodded my acceptance.

During the walk, I darted a glance at Fletcher. The moon

shone down with such brightness, I had no trouble discerning his troubled features. His usual somber mood had been replaced by restlessness, a nervous demeanor as if something worried him. And he had been remarkably quiet, even for Fletcher. I didn't think we'd actually had a conversation the entire night. He put his hand out and placed it on my arm in the middle of the bridge over Spring Creek. The water beneath us glided gently over the rocks, a soothing sound, belying the cruelty of that place, the shrill death knoll I imagined waited for another poor soul pulled into its harsh embrace.

I shook that sad thought off and gave him an inquisitive look.

He cleared his throat. "Miss Bessie, there's something I've been meaning to ask you."

"Can it wait until we get inside? It's awfully cold out here." I wrapped my shawl around me, longing for the comfort of home.

Fletcher took off his coat and draped it around my shoulders. "I'll just be a minute."

I grasped the lapels and pulled it closed, glad for its warmth but concerned for Fletcher, whose shirt didn't offer much of a barrier against the wind whipping around us.

He hesitated and I wondered if this was the end of our relationship. Had he decided to return to Old Fort? Had he found someone else?

After several false starts, he straightened his shoulders and said, "Miss Bessie...Bess, I reckon I've never known a woman like you." His lips lifted in a slight smile. "Why, when I see you, my whole world lights up. Sometimes it's so bright, I don't know if I can stand it."

I drew back, not expecting this.

"And I ... well, I reckon I'm asking you to marry me. That is, if you'll have me."

My eyes widened and I took another step back, bumping against the wooden rails of the bridge.

"I know your Papa doesn't think I'm the right man for you but I intend to prove him wrong." His mouth set in a stubborn line and I could see this meant a great deal to him. "I don't have much to offer right now but I promise, Bess, I'll be a good husband to you and will provide for you and do my best to see you never lack for anything."

My mind reeled. I couldn't seem to open my mouth to respond to him.

"And if you want to have your career as a teacher, why, you go on and do that, if it's important to you. I won't stand in your way." He stopped and met my gaze. His eyes shone with a desperation I'd never seen in him before. My heart went out to him. But my practical nature won out.

"And where do you plan to live? Surely not at that house where Mr. Dunlap's employees board?"

"I've been thinking about that, and if you've a mind to, I'd like to go back to Old Fort. We could live with my folks. They've got plenty of room for us, and we could stay there until we save enough money to buy us some land of our own. There's a place I've got my eye on, the Old Zachariah Solomon plantation, between Old Fort and Black Mountain. It's always been my dream to raise cattle and do some lumbering of my own and that'd be a right good place to do so."

He stared at me. "So, what do you say, Miss Bessie, will you have me as your man? I swear on my life I will do everything I can to make you happy."

Tears sprang to my eyes, and before I realized it, I said, "Of course, I'll marry you."

He grinned at me as he took off his hat and threw it in the air in a celebratory gesture. I smiled at him, happy to see the way my answer affected him.

"All right, then." Grabbing his hat before it blew over the bridge and into the water, he jammed it securely on his head and took my arm. "Let's get you home before we both freeze to death."

Chapter Twenty-two

Winter 1901

A sight for sore eyes.

I turned before the small mirror Loney held before me, studying the way my white graduation dress hung, hoping it would make do as a wedding gown. I wished Mama, who had been so talented with a needle, were here to sew me a wedding dress or I could have worn hers. But I was several inches taller than Mama and not blessed with her petite figure. Tears sprang to my eyes and I bit my lip, reaching out for her. Would she know? Would she be there?

My eyes met Loney's and she gave me an encouraging smile. "It's going to be all right, Bess. Papa will be there. You'll see."

But I doubted he would. Papa made it clear he was against my marrying Fletcher, and not because he was a Republican. Papa felt I could do better for myself than spending my life with a mountain man whose father held the irreverent reputation of being the best whiskey maker in the Broad River section of the state. When Fletcher told me he intended to ask Papa for my hand in marriage, I insisted I be present, hoping Papa would see how much I cared for him and give his consent. But Papa interrupted Fletcher before he got past the words, "Sir, I'd like to ask your permission," with a blunt, "I'll be damned," and stalked off. I followed Papa and tried to talk to him but all he would say was, "Damn, Bessie, you'll never amount to anything if you marry him." Fletcher caught up with us just in time to hear that. Of course, I got stubborn and told Papa I loved Fletcher and wanted to marry

218

him. Fletcher echoed my sentiments but Papa only shook his head and headed for the saloon and I hadn't seen much of him since.

When I apologized to Fletcher for Papa's remark, he surprised me by saying he understood why Papa thought that but he was committed to seeing to it that I never wanted for anything and intended to make me as happy as possible. This made me want to marry him even more. Of all the men I knew, he was the most masculine, not sissified like so many of the others I'd met, and hard work didn't bother him, as his muscular stature and hardy body proved. I blushed, thinking about this.

Miss Julia and her sister, Miss Amelia, offered to put together the wedding ceremony and a small reception for us if we would get married at the Dorland chapel and we agreed. As a traveling preacher, Pastor Linton was in Hot Springs only one week out of the month. Since he was in town, we had to get married a week before we planned to leave for Old Fort to stay with Fletcher's parents, Lafayette and Caroline Elliott. I wasn't happy about living my first week as a married woman at my childhood home but it couldn't be helped. We couldn't afford to stay at the hotel and Mr. Dunlap only allowed men at his boarding house. I wouldn't see much of Fletcher anyway since he planned to work at the sawmill that week in order to earn the money for our train tickets.

My stomach jittered. Truth be told, that wasn't the only thing I was worried about. I was apprehensive about meeting my in-laws when we got to Old Fort but Fletcher assured me they would accept me as one of their own. Miss Julia had written me a lovely letter of recommendation for the teaching position slated to open up in Black Mountain within the near future. An unexpected thrill swept through my body. An adventure lay before me: starting life with my husband, traveling to places I had never been before, realizing my dream as a teacher. But my excitement was overshadowed by my father's feelings. I wished more than anything for Papa's blessing.

I wasn't, however, willing to wait the rest of my life to get it.

Another disappointment: Elisi, along with my cousin Caroline and her family, would not be attending my wedding. They had gone to Georgia to visit some of Elisi's people and had not yet returned. I felt if anyone should be present, it should be Caroline. After all, she was the one who told me I'd marry Fletcher. I wanted her to be part of my bridal party, to celebrate the marriage with me. Instead, I had to make do with a long letter, telling her how much I loved her and would miss her, and acknowledging she had, indeed, been right. I penned another letter to Elisi, who should be there, sitting where Mama would be if she were alive. I sighed, wondering if their absence was somehow a sign to me that this wedding should not take place. Well, too late to worry about that now.

I took the mirror from Loney and patted at my hair, wishing I had a way to see how it looked from behind. Loney dashed out of the room and returned within moments, bearing a nosegay of dried wild flowers and herbs bursting with the muted colors of the rainbow. She must have picked and dried them last summer, thinking to put them in sachets but instead used them to create a wedding posy for me.

I put them to my nose and inhaled their faint scent. "Loney, you sweet angel."

Loney nodded, tears glistening in her eyes. "Here, sit down, Bess. I want to weave some of this ribbon through your hair."

I sat on the stool in front of the vanity, holding the mirror up, watching as Loney laced the delicate ribbon through my hair. I liked the contrast of the white, shiny strips against my black hair, one of my best features I had gotten from my mother. I studied my face, my dark eyes and brows, wide cheekbones; another good feature from Mama. Did Fletch find me pretty? Beautiful? He was a man of few words and not prone to compliments. What would it be like to be his wife? Would he have kind words for me or only voice his complaints?

Loney spoke, bringing me out of my musing. "We're going to miss you, Bess."

I leaned against her. "I'll miss y'all, too, Loney." I studied her, still more girl than woman, and felt guilty I was leaving her behind with so much responsibility. "I'm sorry the household will fall to you, Loney. I know it will be a burden."

She shook her head. "You know how much I like taking care of the house and the children, Bess. It won't be a problem at all."

Such a caring soul, our Loney. Would she have a family of her own one day, a husband and babies to care for? This brought me back to Fletcher, my husband at the end of this day. What would our life be like together? Would we get along or be one of those couples always at odds with one another?

Roy burst through the door. He stopped when he saw me and a slow smile spread across his handsome face. "Well, lawsy mercy, Bessie, don't you look awful pretty."

I rose from the stool and hugged him. Roy was the one I'd miss most of all other than Papa. "Thank you, Roy," I said, stepping back.

"I reckon we better get a move-on if you want to get hitched by five. I've got the wagon all ready to go."

As we walked toward the door, I said, "Is Papa out there, Roy?"

Roy hesitated and I did not miss the glance that passed between my brother and sister. "Uh, he got called away, Bessie. Told me to tell you he might not be able to make it."

I grabbed Thee's hand while Loney picked Jack up, settling her on her hip, and tried to hide the disappointment in my voice. "Well, if that happens, would you mind giving me away, Roy?"

Roy puffed up a little, a proud gesture. "Sure, Bess, I'd be honored."

I rode beside Roy on the bench seat and Loney, Thee and Jack sat behind us on slats Roy placed in the bed of the wagon. When we reached the new Dorland church, Miss Julia and Miss Amelia were waiting outside. Their eyes shone with happiness and I was thrilled they had encouraged me to be married at Dorland.

Roy helped me down and I hugged the Phillips. I looked around. "Is he here yet?"

The women exchanged knowing glances. Miss Amelia said, "We put him in the coat room. It's unlucky for a groom to see his bride before the wedding, you know."

Miss Julia studied my outfit and colorful bouquet. She tenderly tucked a trailing tendril of hair up. "Bessie, you're a beautiful bride. I'm so happy you're marrying inside our church."

"Me, too, Miss Julia."

She took my hand. "Are you ready?"

Fear shot through me and I tried not to let it show. Was I? These next moments would plot a course that would change my life forever. According to Papa, in a way not for the better. Was he right? Should I have thought more before saying yes to Fletcher's proposal? Was I doing the right thing? I almost wished Fletcher had followed the old mountain custom of showing up at my door with horses and a magistrate and stealing me away to get married.

Miss Amelia, sensing my uneasiness, whispered in my ear. "You don't have to do this, Bessie, if you're not sure. Everyone will understand."

I straightened my spine and gave a small laugh. "Just a case of the jitters, I guess. Yes, I'm ready."

Miss Julia looked around. "Where's your father? Isn't he coming?"

Roy cleared his throat. "He got called out, Miss Julia. He said if he wasn't here, to go ahead without him."

She looked at me. "Are you sure you want to do that, Bess? We can wait for him."

I shook my head. "Roy's going to give me away. When Papa gets called out, he can be gone for hours."

"Let's go inside, then," she said and led us up the steps to the open front door. When I caught site of the chapel inside, I gasped with surprise. Greenery was everywhere, standing out in bright contrast to the dark wood of the pews and pulpit. Candle flames danced in breezes created by moving bodies. The setting sun shone through the stained-glass windows, casting colorful rays across the room. The pews were filled with people, some from the town, most Dorland students.

Alice, who had been talking to Pastor Linton, spied me and rushed through the door, wearing a beautiful pale blue dress, holding two small bouquets of holly with bright red berries. She smiled at me as she handed one to Loney, my maid of honor.

She hugged me tight. "Why, Bess, you're the most beautiful bride I've ever seen. Thank you so much for asking me to stand with you. I'm so excited. I've never been part of a wedding party before."

Pastor Linton approached, his hands held out in front of him to take mine. With an encouraging smile, he asked, "Are you ready, young lady?"

"I reckon I am."

He patted my hand. "Fine. I'll get the groom situated up front." He looked at Loney and Alice. "When you hear the music, girls, you come in. Miss Bessie, when you hear the 'Bridal March', you and your brother enter." I found it strange he didn't ask where Papa was, but since he didn't know our family as well as Pastor Bishop, I supposed it might not be such an odd thing to him.

Miss Amelia and Miss Julia gave me final hugs before hurrying into the chapel, Miss Amelia carrying Jack and Miss Julia holding Thee's hand. Alice, Loney, Roy and I stood outside, waiting. Roy and Alice bent their heads toward one another and whispered in between loving gazes and smiles. Loney looked like she wanted to say something but I ignored her, afraid if she did, I'd change my mind and bolt, straight into Papa's arms. I couldn't do that, though. How would I ever prove him wrong and show him Fletcher Elliott was more of a man than Papa thought him if I did that?

The organ began playing and I kissed Alice and Loney on their cheeks.

Alice led off, followed by Loney. Roy and I waited for them to reach the front. He cleared his throat and opened his mouth. I interrupted before he could say anything.

"Promise me one thing, Roy."

"Um, what's that?"

"If I faint, you'll catch me before I hit the floor."

The music changed and he smiled as he held out his arm, elbow crooked. "Here we go, Bess."

I hesitated. "I love you dearly, Roy. I hope you know that. I'll miss you."

He glanced away uncomfortably. "I love you the same, Bess, and I'll miss you, too."

We stared at each other for a moment. He raised his eyebrows. With a sigh, I took my first step toward the rest of my life.

As we walked down the aisle, people rose from their seats and I smiled at them as we passed by. I was afraid to look at Fletcher, afraid for that searing gaze to lock onto mine. When I finally glanced toward the pulpit, I saw him standing with his boss, Mr. Dunlap, and one of his friends from the sawmill. Fletcher wore a black suit that fit him quite well with a sprig of holly in his lapel. When our eyes met, he surprised me by smiling. He looked happy. My heart soared thinking I was the reason why.

As I passed by, I smiled at Aunt Belle and Uncle Ned, sitting where Mama and Papa should be, Aunt Belle holding Jack in her lap and Thee sitting between her and Uncle Ned. Aunt Belle beamed at me, dabbing at her eyes with a handkerchief. She had surprised me by supporting this marriage. Since there wasn't time for a quilting bee, she collected the requisite 13 quilts from friends and gave them to me, along with her blessing. She helped decorate the church and had cooked most of the food that would be eaten at the reception. She and Uncle Ned presented us with a cherished wedding gift: spending our wedding night at the Mountain Park Hotel. I found myself wishing she and I had found a way to like each other long before now.

To this day, I could not tell you what our wedding vows were. Fletcher squeezed my hand reassuringly from time to time as I repeated the words after Pastor Linton. I was mortally afraid I would pass out in front of all those witnessing our marriage, and if not for his hand holding mine, I think I might have. When the pastor pronounced us husband and wife, Fletcher gave me a chaste kiss on the cheek and we walked down the aisle together, hand in hand. Miss Julia hustled us outside, surprising us with a photographer, there to take our wedding picture.

Miss Julia and Miss Amelia hosted a grand reception for us in the sewing room of the institute. Fletcher and I greeted all those who had come to our wedding, surprised at the small stack of gifts on a table by the door. Aunt Belle was in her prime, flitting about the room, socializing, making sure no one lacked for food or drink. Roy and Alice were inseparable, and it occurred to me they were a natural couple, complementing one another in every way. I could sense a happy future for them and was glad for that. As for my future with Fletcher, I had no feeling or intuition about what it might be. Would we be happy? Would we have children? I prayed for that, but always in the back of my mind a small voice whispered if I were doing this to prove Papa wrong, I was marrying for the wrong reason.

Every time someone new entered the room, I looked toward the door, hoping to see Papa walk in, a big smile on his face. I tried to push my disappointment to the back of my mind but wished more than anything he could be there for me. By eight o'clock, almost everyone had gone home. I kissed Roy and Loney goodbye, told them I'd see them tomorrow.

I hugged Miss Julia and Miss Amelia and set off with my new husband to the hotel. We walked down Bridge Street, holding hands, not saying much. Just before we went up the steps to the entrance and into our future, Fletcher stopped and faced me. He held my hands in his and said, in a solemn voice, "I mean to do right by you, Bessie. I'll try to be the best husband I can. I'll make sure you never want for anything. And I—I want to thank you for marrying me. You've made me a very happy man."

I leaned forward and brushed my lips against his. "You've made me very happy, too, Fletcher, and I promise to be the best wife I can," I said, as he led me up the stairs.

The next morning, I returned home and Fletcher went to the sawmill. He promised to visit me each night and assured me we would be leaving for Old Fort in a week. I opened the door to the kitchen and smiled at Roy and Loney, sitting at the table. Thee sat on the floor, playing with a small horse Papa had whittled out of wood. Jack sat at Loney's feet, trying to pull herself up on Loney's skirt.

"Where's Papa?" I asked, tying an apron around my dress.

"He's still out, Bess," Roy answered, not looking at me.

I sighed. Surely Papa wouldn't stay away the entire week. But as the days went by, we saw very little of him. I assumed he spent the night at the marshal's office. I longed to say something to him the few times he came home but didn't know where to begin. Although we were civil to one another in tone and manner, Papa never asked about the wedding or mentioned my leaving.

The night before we were to take the train, I folded my few things and tucked them into Mama's old valise. Earlier that day, Roy had taken my trunk to the railroad depot to be loaded on the train tomorrow morning. Loney watched as I packed, a sadness in her eyes that brought tears to mine every time I looked at her. Although she and Roy had been supportive about my marriage, they never indicated to me their feelings about Fletcher.

"Do you love him, Bessie?" she asked me.

"Yes. He's very different from me, but maybe that's what appeals to me about him, Loney."

"Do you think you'll be happy with him?"

"I hope so."

"You can stay here, you know."

"Oh, Loney, I'm twenty years old. I need to go."

"Papa doesn't like him."

"Yes, I think he's proved that." I looked at her. "Do you think he'll be at the train station to see me off tomorrow, Loney?"

She cut her eyes away. "I don't know, Bess. He hasn't said."

I turned my back, swiped at the tears. Leaving was hard enough, but to leave without saying goodbye to my father seemed too much.

The next morning, I rose early and made a hearty

breakfast for my brothers and sisters. At the table, our talk had a forced happiness to it, and I wished we could just skip this part. At eight, Fletcher knocked on the door and I stepped outside, my valise in hand. He took it from me, squeezing my hand when he did so. I turned back to Roy and Loney, hugged them hard, and told them I loved them. I kissed Thee and Jack, clinging to Loney's skirts, then quickly turned and walked away.

At the train station, I waited for Fletcher to pay for our tickets, my gaze traveling the yard, and onto the road. Would Papa come? Would he just let me leave without saying goodbye? Oh, could I stand it if he did?

Fletcher and I stood on the platform, waiting for the signal to board the train, people milling around us. I watched couples pass by, some holding hands and looking happy, others stilted and rigid with one another. I glanced at my husband, standing straight and somber, wondering which way we would go. Would we find happiness in our shared life or would we become one of those couples who rarely spoke and even more rarely showed affection?

The train whistle blew and Fletcher nudged me forward. I stepped toward the train and heard someone call my name. I looked back and there was Papa, standing on the platform, looking at me. I turned from Fletcher and started walking toward Papa but quickly broke into a run and flew into his arms.

"Oh, Papa, I'm so glad you came," I said into his neck.

"I couldn't stay away, Bess."

I burst into tears. "I love you, Papa, and I'm so sorry we've been at odds over this."

"I love you, too, Bess." He stepped back from me and gave me a stern look. "You're sure this is what you want?"

I straightened with resolve. "I'm married to him now. I reckon I'm committed to it."

He nodded. "I want you to know I love you dearly, Bess." His eyes moistened and he stopped for a moment, his mouth working. "I'll come see you when I can. I hope you'll come back and visit us when you get the chance."

"I will, Papa. I promise."

"You write me and let me know how you're doing. Let me know where you end up, if you get a teaching job like you want."

"I will, as soon as I know."

"You're my daughter and I want you to be happy, Bess. More than anything, I want you to be happy."

"I am, Papa. And I want you to be happy, too."

"You take care of yourself. And if he…" he nodded toward Fletcher, standing near the train watching us "…don't do right by you, you write me or get word to me and I'll come get you."

I smiled at him through my tears. "You're the best papa a girl could ever have."

He drew me in for another hug and then gently pushed me away. "Go to your husband, girl. I'll see you directly, I reckon."

I kissed him hard on the cheek. "I love you, Papa," I said as I walked away. He lifted his hand at me and I saw his eyes turn to Fletcher and harden. His mouth thinned and he nodded. I could read the message in his eyes and was sure my new husband could, too, "You take good care of my girl."

I stepped onto the train, Fletcher behind me, and turned to see if Papa had left but he remained on the platform, staring after me. I blew him a kiss and watched as he pretended to catch it and blow one back. The train started with a jerk and Fletcher nudged me to move inside, but I couldn't. This might be the last I would see of the beautiful little town in which I grew up and who knew how long it would be before I saw Papa and the rest of my family again. Tears sprang to my eyes and I didn't bother wiping them away, instead I reached my hand toward Papa, watching as he dwindled from sight. When I could see him no more, I fought an overwhelming urge to jump from the slow-moving train and run back to him.

I wanted to beg his forgiveness for my unrealistic expectations, for placing him on a pedestal of my own creation. Papa wasn't a god; he was simply a man trying to live his life to the best of his ability while doing everything he could to make his children's lives better.

Fletcher touched my arm then slid his hand down and

linked our fingers together. I turned and my gaze locked onto his intense eyes. I could see the worry there, but I could also see the possibilities—children, my own home, a teaching job, a life as the whistling woman I'd vowed long ago to become.

Elisi's words suddenly came to mind: *In the end, your heart will break but you're strong enough to deal with that, and when you look outside yourself to mend it, you will find the right person to help you.*

I looked up at my new husband and knew in my heart Fletcher Elliott was the person Elisi had been talking about.

He smiled. "Let's go find us a seat, Bess." Holding tight to his hand, I let him lead me inside to whatever the future might hold.

Books in the Appalachian Journey series:

Whistling Woman, Appalachian Journey Book 1

At the turn of the 20th century, Bessie Daniels grows up in the small town of Hot Springs in the mountains of Western North Carolina.

Moonfixer, Appalachian Journey Book 2

In the dawning years of the 20th century, Bessie Daniels leaves her home town of Hot Springs and travels over the mountains with her husband Fletcher Elliott to live in the Broad River Section of North Carolina.

Beloved Woman, Appalachian Journey Book 3

In the second decade of the 20th century, major world events resonate even on secluded Stone Mountain where Bessie Elliott lives with her husband Fletcher.

Wise Woman, Appalachian Journey Book 4

Traditionally, a Wise Woman is a woman who possesses knowledge, passed down through generations, of time-honored folk medicines. They deal with all kinds of illnesses and medical conditions, often using practical herbal remedies, drawing on plants and the rest of the natural environment, which they know well.

Acknowledgements

There are so many people who contributed to the creation of *Whistling Woman*; friends, family, and fellow authors. In particular we'd like to thank:

Our father, John Tillery, for all the wonderful stories he told us, as kids and adults, about his Aunt Bessie, Uncle Fletcher, Grandpapa John, the rest of the Daniels family, and the people they encountered while they lived in Hot Springs. It's hard to top a natural born storyteller, but we did our best to do justice to his skill on the stories we incorporated into the book.

Meghann French Parrilla for her truly awesome research and photography skills. We love you, Meghann!

Celia Miles for editing the manuscript and her many useful suggestions on how to improve upon what we'd written.

Our husbands, Steve French and Mike Hodges, for their love and support over the four long years it took to plot, research, and write this book. We don't say it enough but we are grateful to have you both in our lives.

The citizens of the town of Hot Springs for your kindness, generosity, and all-around interest in our project and for giving us that feeling of "coming home" whenever we visited your lovely town.

Deb Linton, librarian, Hot Springs Library, for helping us when we first started and for inviting us to a reunion of Dorland-Bell Institute. And to her husband, Pastor Gene Linton, for taking us on a tour of the beautiful Dorland-Bell Presbyterian Church chapel which plays an important part in *Whistling Woman*.

Also, the other librarians at the Hot Springs Library, Lisa Ledford and Winnie Broglin, for invaluable help regarding the town. And an extra thank you to Winnie for going above and beyond by taking her lunch break to run home and get us a copy of an article from the May 27, 2009 "News Record & Sentinel", about the historical houses and businesses in Hot Springs.

Keith Gentry, owner, Gentry Hardware, for helping us on our quest to find Sandy Gap cemetery.

Klaus Nelson, owner of Harvest Moon Gallery, Gifts & Music, for generously allowing us to wander around in the beautiful historical house that contains his business and home–we know it's not actually the house our great-grandfather built but it's enough like the one we heard about as kids that we felt we'd stumbled onto the set of our book.

Don and Melanie Prater for the use of your beautiful cabins while we worked on the edits.

In Marshall, North Carolina, the librarians at the Madison County Public Library for allowing us to look through the genealogy room and answering all our questions.

Marla Gouge, Administrative Assistant, Marshall, NC, Madison County, for searching for information on the original courthouse in Marshall.

David Hunter, author and friend, for answering our question about what it would feel like to stick your finger in a bullet hole.

Jackie Burgin Painter, author and cousin, for providing a plethora of information about the Dorland Institute in her book "The Season of Dorland Bell, History of an Appalachian Mission School" and historical facts about Hot Springs and the surrounding area in her book "An Appalachian Medley: Hot Springs and the Gentry Family, Volume 1".

The late John Parris, author, for his book "These Storied Mountains", from which we learned about trying fortunes and other western North Carolina folklore and beliefs.

Rick McDaniel, Citizen-Times Correspondent, for his article "Melungeon Mystery" in the September 2, 2007 "Asheville Citizens-Times".

We used several on-line and written resources for the history and legends of the Cherokee but would like to acknowledge three books: "Long-ago Stories of the Eastern Cherokee" by Lloyd Arneach, "Medicine of the Cherokee, The Way of Right Relationship" by J. T. Garrett and Michael Garrett, and "Trail of Tears, The Rise and Fall of the Cherokee Nation" by John Ehle.

The on-line sites we consulted in the massive amount of research on everything from how a body was prepared for burial in the late 1890's to the traditions and celebrations of

Old Christmas Eve were many and varied. We'd love to name them all but that would be a book in and of itself so we'll have to settle for saying a simple thank you–our gratitude is longer than our Favorites list. We do, however, wish to acknowledge four sites that proved invaluable to us: the Hot Springs, North Carolina home page, http://www.hotspringsnc.org/, for help with the history of the town, the Cherokee NC Eastern Band of Cherokee Indians in North Carolina site, http://www.cherokee-nc.com/, for help with the history and folklore of the Cherokee, the Melungeon home page, http://www.melungeons.com/, for help with the history of the Melungeon people, and the Online Etymology Dictionary, http://www.etymonline.com/, for help with language and word usage in the late 19th century. From these sites, we found most of the information we needed to write *Whistling Woman*.

The lyrics to "Seven Drunken Nights" may differ from the lyrics as you know them or have heard them. The words we used in the book are the ones we were taught by our father as kids. Thanks, Daddy!

And finally, like the stories the book is based on, we tried to stay as close to the actual history of this amazing area as possible. We did, however, take the liberty of changing some of it to help the flow of the story. While we did use the names of some of the actual people who passed through Great-aunt Bessie's life while she lived in Hot Springs, we took some liberties with them and may not have been true to their characters and personalities. Hopefully, we got more right than wrong, but any mistakes in the history or the people are solely our own.

About the Authors

CC Tillery is the pseudonym for two sisters, both authors who came together to write the story of their great-aunt Bessie in the *Appalachian Journey* series. Tillery is their maiden name and the C's stand for their first initials.

One C is Cyndi Tillery Hodges, a multi-published author who writes paranormal romance based on Cherokee legends under the pseudonym Caitlyn Hunter. To find out more about her work, visit http://caitlynhunter.com.

The other C is Christy Tillery French, a multi-published, award-winning author whose books cross several genres. To find out more about her work, visit her website at http://christytilleryfrench.webs.com.

For more information on the Appalachian Journey series, visit http://whistlingwoman.com or follow CC Tillery on Facebook at http://facebook.com/appalachianjourney.